CJ's Marines:

An after-action report on the Nudge engagement

By Ron Davis

Copyright © 2020 by Ron Davis.

This edition updated and published July 2020.

Published worldwide by FourNecklaces.com. All rights reserved. No part of this publication may be reproduced, distributed, or transmitted in any form or by any means, including photocopying, recording, or other electronic or mechanical methods, without the prior written permission of the publisher, except in the case of brief quotations embodied in critical reviews and certain other non-commercial uses permitted by copyright law.

***

Original and modified cover art by Ron Davis and CoverDesignStudio.com

ISBN 978-0-9899-3416-9

Dedication

This series of books titled CJ's Marines are dedicated to the U.S. Armed Forces' current and former members. Have no doubt about it. Your service no matter what it was, where it was or when it was contributed to our country's freedom. As one of you, I genuinely thank you for your service. And to the men I served within the Marine Corps in Vietnam may God bless you, and though we may have lost touch, you have never left my thoughts. Semper Fi my brothers.

Chapter 1

My name is Geraldo Rivera. Yeah, just like the famous guy and also just like him, my name wasn't Geraldo at birth but Gerald. You see, I live in Austin, Texas, and I want my name to sound as Hispanic as possible. Because there might arise an opportunity someday, to get some kind of advantage, say a government set aside or something. The government might require you to be a minority to get it, so I changed my name from Gerald to Geraldo. Not saying the famous guy did the same thing. Naah, I'm sure for him, he was genuinely getting in touch with his roots and never using the minority thing. Unlike say, Elizabeth Warren.

I don't know why I told you that. It doesn't matter at all and has nothing to do with what I am about to say to you. Maybe I said it so you can see I have this habit of interjecting things not strictly applicable to the story. So then if something is in this account and you say to yourself, Who the hell said that? Then you can figure it was Geraldo or Gerald, Jerry even. I don't care which name you use as long as there is no government grant on the line because if there is, then use Geraldo, and I'll answer with my Hispanic accent. OK senior?

I am paid to do this. I am a corporate archiver. This is called an after-action report, and CJ and his company, CJN, named with his initials, use after-action reports to learn how to do things better. CJ whom you don't know yet, but he's big in the story, is my boss and also my friend. He saved my life on more than one occasion in the Marines in Afghanistan. Afghanistan is a real dump if you haven't figured that out yet. And he saved my life again in Iraq, which is another dump. A dump, unless you are from Afghanistan or Iraq, and have always lived there. In that case, you think a dump like Iraq is an excellent place. Just like the folks living in shotgun shacks or trailer parks in Appalachia think Appalachia is Almost Heaven because of the John Denver song titled, 'West Virginia.' Who am I to tell them differently? If they knew the truth, they would head for Texas, and then I am in deep trouble. Especially with Gunny. Another guy in the story. A real character, but if you ever meet him in the flesh and he says some John Wayne movie quote? Just roll with it but not super enthusiastic because then he'll think you are also a super fan of The Duke and if he finds your knowledge lacking? He'll suspect you are a deceitful person, and he doesn't like deceitful people as you'll see once I quit blowing gas and get into the story proper.

I try to get everything straight and in order, but when you are dealing with people trying to remember what happened and when they, of course, color it to favor themselves. Well, separating truth from fiction can be daunting. The dead folks in the story? As a group, they were unanimous in having nothing to say. So, I had to think of what they might have been thinking. And some of these dead folks? Excuse me here for saying mean stuff about dead people, but they were dumb as a chicken. Did you know that chickens will drown if they look up when it is raining? No kidding. Don't believe me? Goggle it. See? I was lying to you, and you were dumb enough to almost believe me but smart enough to verify. OK. You passed. Your probably smart enough to follow what happens. Here we go. Remember when you see little kind of out of context things? That's Jerry being a wise ass. Geraldo would never do that, the famous one, or me.

The jogger, breathing hard, was paralleling the stream that Canyon Trail followed after having turned right a half mile back at the intersection of Little Fern Trail and Canyon Trail. Sweat streamed down his forehead, overflowing the capacity of his red, white, and Blue sweatband. He crooked his arm, bringing his wrist close to his face struggling to see the digital display of the lap timer bouncing to the rhythm of his feet impacting the ground. The task complicated by perspiration sneaking out of the sweatband and into his eyes whenever he tilted his head down and made more difficult by the flickering shadows of the twilight filtering through the trees. The trail climbed as the path went towards Tributary View, where the stream entered a pipe and crossed under the trail heading west while Canyon Trail continued North. The jogger was displeased, almost discouraged, with the lap timer's revelation. He deflected his mind from the throbbing in his legs, determined to increase his gait, precisely what his rebellious legs did not want to do. He knew he wasn't running enough, losing conditioning. He still had over two miles to go to the turnaround point and then retrace his steps back to the trail entrance. Altogether, a six-mile run rated as intermediate. So, rated because of the uphill slopes that featured logs planted perpendicular to the trail. He dreaded the logs thinking it was like running up a stair master. The sun, low on the horizon, was partially hidden behind a cloud, making the shadows long as he approached the bridge over the stream.

It was when the jogger turned with the bend of the path that he first saw the man-in-black. The man stood facing the jogger in the center of the trail, effectively blocking it a dozen or so yards before the bridge. The man was standing in the undulating shadows of the trees that grew along this stream's exposed area. The moving shadows played on his face, making recognition difficult. The man-in-black stood loose, his shoulders squared to the path, legs spread, shoulder-length apart, knees slightly bent, and weight balanced - a fighter's stance. The man-in-black, dark pants, and black shirt chose to blend into the shadows stood watching the jogger run towards him. He knew how to blend into the background, how to stand ready, and that the jogger would not see the threat.

The man-in-black knew the jogger quite well, although he had never spoken with him. He had learned about the jogger during long intimate conversations. Not spoken conversations, but the written kind, which can be much better than spoken words. Better because you need to search your mind for the words, the right phrases. Better because you can look over what you say and think about it and change it before you send it. Think about how she would feel after reading it. Get the tone just right. So much depended on keeping her wanting to write back. Keeping her thinking about the man-in-black and keep her sending those delicious photos.

She told him about how the jogger had changed over the years. About the same time as he started to ascend in the 'Yuppie – Puppy world,' as the man-in-black called it, how he began not to value a good woman. In his writings, he pointed that out to her often. She told him as her husband's career started to rise was when the wife-beating started.

The man-in-black told her that was because her husband saw his career as much more important than she was. Feed the fire. She said it was just a slap at first, followed by the jogger begging his wife for forgiveness and promises never to repeat the slapping. As the man-in-black told the wife in those long, written talks, they all said that, but don't mean it. And he was proven right as the slaps turned punches and then to kicks and whoopee away we go. She had enough, and so had the man-in-black. But he couldn't help her from prison. That is until a miracle happened. Probably an administrative screw-up. Maybe a general push to lower the prison population. Whatever. He didn't care except that now he was out. Now he was standing on the jogging path.

"Well, Yuppie – Puppy", whispered the man-in-black as he watched the jogger close the distance between them, "you done had your last piece of that wife fight stuff. Now you get some of my fight." The man-in-black found the joggers' wife-beating to be offensive, which was at least odd, considering that he was a wife-beater himself. But his wife, the bitch, deserved it, you see, and the jogger's wife, well.... she didn't.

The man-in-black didn't fit here to the joggers' first glance, and the first tingle of uneasiness came into his mind. The guy just didn't look right to be on a jogging trail. There was something about how he stood looking prepared. Expectant. Confident. As if he was waiting for the jogger, which unknown to the jogger, he was.

The jogger gave no serious thought to the twinge of oddness he felt at seeing the man and continued his unbroken gate down the path towards the darkly dressed stranger. The uphill climb running on those damn logs and lap timer's distressing display had precedent over warnings of danger to this educated jogger that had spent his life in the cocoon of acceptable behavior incubated in academia. That was too bad. It was a big mistake.

The jogger couldn't ever be faulted for this error in judgment since street-smart, at least the street-smart that educates about violence, had not been a part of his life. The jogger, instinctively feeling that the stranger in the middle of the path might not move, eased over to the left, expecting the man to move to the right. But, no, he continued to stand in the middle of the jogging trail, appearing to the jogger to be waiting for him to close the final dozen yards that separated them. It was hard for the jogger to see in the shadows, but the posture of the man-in-black and his facial expressions gave the jogger a feeling that he knew the man, or that the man knew him.

"How ya doin?" The jogger pushed out, keeping the words short to conserve breath. It was a courtesy not meant for a reply, said instead to get the guy to move, but he didn't move or reply. Except one corner of his mouth turned up in response to the jogger's words.

This is strange, though the jogger, one of the last thoughts he would ever have before the pain came. The jogger's uneasiness almost became fear. It was closer to irritation than genuine fear. However, if he had time to reflect on the situation, he would've thought fear was reasonable and probably the correct response to meeting a strange man.... in black.... during the evening.... blocking the path. The man-in-black didn't have fighting in mind. If he had thought about it, which he didn't, he would've been amused to think of this as a fight. To him, fighting someone meant they could win, and why would he give someone a chance to win? To the man-in-black, violence was a normal part of life. He had grown up learning to fight as part of his culture, part of his environment's survival requirements. He had learned it as a kid then became more proficient in his early teens when he added weapons of convenience such as bats and bottles. He had taken his Master's courses in the state prison system, graduating with honors. In his professional life as a psychologist, the jogger would've found analyzing such a person as the man-in-black academic and fascinating. Dissecting the man's exposed feelings, examining them for causes – discussing the reasons with his colleagues and his wife. The wife he was beating.

Having gotten no response from his greeting, the jogger altered his direction slightly and moved off the path to go around the man. The man-in-black's disabling punch came as a shock. The jogger hadn't been physically assaulted in his entire life. The blow was a well-aimed stiff punch to the abdomen, which caused a temporary paralysis to his diaphragm with the force of the punch magnified by the roll of quarters the man-in-black held in his fist. The blow expelled the air from the jogger's lungs, causing an explosion of stars in his eyes and sending him hard to the ground. The jogger's forward momentum, redirected by the punch, caused him to spin out, sending his legs flailing as he plunged headfirst on his back down the stream bank. The jogger slid all the way down the bank to the stream and now lay on his back, fighting the forces that had frozen his diaphragm. Trying to allow breath back into his lungs. Terrified that he might never breathe again. He looked like a human fish that have been swatted out of the stream by one of the native brown bears that had prowled the banks of the stream in search of an easy meal in the not so distant past. The man-in-black and brown bears having much in common, both being experienced predators.

The man-in-black followed the sliding body down the slope to the stream. He crouched down near the jogger's head to talk to him. "Didn't see that one coming, did you?" He paused. Grinning. Watching the jogger's eyes darting to his face then to the stream bank, no doubt hoping for help. But no help was coming today. "Rebecca can't hit like that can she?"

The jogger heard his wife's name, which added more confusion to his pain as he felt his throat begin to reopen, letting the air reenter frozen lungs and hope arise in his mind. Hope springs eternal, even false hope. His well-trained mind flew across possibilities searching for a key to unlock this puzzle. What to say, when he could talk, what to do?

"That was just a taste," said the man-in-black, "ready for the main meal?" He flipped open the straight razor and waved it in the jogger's face. The jogger stared at the flashing blade that caught the last rays of the setting sun. The jogger struggled to push himself down and away from that shimmering cold steel blade. The man-in-black would've liked to have made the jogger suffer more so that the payback for his beating Rebecca was more personal, more fun, more boogie-time. But Rebecca had a soft spot in her, and she just wanted it done and done quickly. So, he had to satisfy himself with that disabling blow and the memory of that horrified look on the jogger's face as he straddled the joggers body and used his knees to pin the jogger's arms to his sides. He grabbed the jogger's hair, bent back his head to fully expose the throat, then drug the razor across pushing down deep on the neck catching some of the blood spray on his shirt and face. Before the blood flow ceased, the jogger sweatband turned crimson with his blood. His body lay with his head near the exposed stream. His torso lay up the stream-bank so that his blood flowed down the bank to mix with the stream. The man-in-black used the creek water to splash the jogger's blood from his face. Might see somebody on the way off the trail, on his way to Rebecca's house. Nothing could be done about the blood on his shirt, but red blood and black shirts blend.

The police radio network in Austin TX was monitored waiting for the body's discovery, waiting to see if it worked. If the man-in-black had done his job. Just observe the police radio calls just like some Gypsy news reporter. The release plan dictated that the second operation must wait for the first to be announced. The system didn't have any concept of waiting. It just ran other routines and a recursive loop monitoring the police radio calls. Its electronic version of waiting. It would never run out of patience. It didn't have that human weakness.

Chapter 2

The young woman was preparing for her morning run down Little Fern Trail and up Canyon Trail and back. There was no loop on River Place nature trail; you had to turn around either at the end or partway. She prepared by going through her routine of stretches and twists loosening up her muscles. Her dog, a smallish English Setter, sat watching the warm-up routine anxiously waiting to go on the daily run. She usually ran with the dog, keeping it on a short leash so that the dog didn't try to pull off into the brush, breaking the jog's rhythm. This morning she had a different leash, one that, with the push of a button, allowed the dog to go where it wanted while pulling the leash out from a spring-loaded reel. Not the kind of behavior you would typically want when jogging but precisely the action the young woman needed for this morning's jog. As she stood straight arms extended high and bending backward at her waist, she watched across the parking lot. Waiting for him to arrive and park his bicycle.

She had been watching him for several weeks. He ran with a backpack that she believed was heavy by the way it sat on his shoulders. She estimated his weight at around 200 pounds thinking that muscles weigh more than fat. She thought he was just over 6 feet or so, certainly not under 6 feet and maybe as tall as 6 feet 2. He wore his hair short, unusually short on the sides, dark brown or perhaps black. He dressed like a military guy. He had a strong face with a short beard the kind that was in style but, she thought, he wore such a beard not because of it being in style, but because the look fit him. Over the last several weeks, when he would catch and then pass her, he would say good morning, and she would say good morning, as they ran together for a short time side by side, but that had been the extent of it.

She liked how he looked, and she was hoping that he was not married, nor involved with anyone. She thought if he is married, it's a dead deal no matter what. But if he is just involved well, if only involved, he could get uninvolved. How terrible is that, she thought. Thinking he could get uninvolved, though it made her smile. She ran through her list of what she and her friends called her assets. She was physically fit, early thirties, medium tall, and worked hard to stay under 120 pounds. And very attractive if you like the fit blond look and who doesn't, she thought. But her best asset, so her friends told her, was that she was hilarious. She felt hilarious is not going to do me any good unless I can get a chance to talk to him. Enter the plan with her dog and the leash that extends.

She had planned this out. Get the leash, wait for him to finish his stretches, start his run, then off she goes running, getting ahead of him, waiting for him to catch up with her and begin to pass. When he was close, and she could hear him start to move, she would push the button and let the dog run out, making sure that she stayed on one side of the path and the dog pulled the leash across the way, hopefully interfering with him so that they had a conversation. Then, at least in her mind, she would rein the dog in and apologize, and that would be the icebreaker. She thought if that doesn't work next week, I'm gonna fall down and twist my ankle right in front of him like a Victorian novel. Yep that'll do it, she thought, but hopefully, we will let the dog leash trick do the work.

She saw him enter the parking lot, get off and chain up his bike, spend some time stretching, unstrap the backpack from the back of the bike, put it on, and start a slow jog towards Little Fern Trails entrance. She slowed her stretching, stood sideways to his approach so she could watch him without being obvious, let him get halfway across the parking lot, turned and took off down the trail moving to the side of the trail, and let the dog have the middle waiting to hear the man's footfalls behind her.

She wanted him to know she was in good shape, so she kept ahead of him with him slowly gaining ground. He was getting closer as she swung right onto Canyon Trail and closed on the section where the trail rose near the bridge. She had to time this right, but darn if she didn't hit the release too soon as he was still too far behind her to be blocked by the long leash. Her dog didn't cooperate either. Instead of just moving off to the side and blocking the path, he began aggressively barking and pulling, trying to go down the slope to the stream, pulling so hard that it jerked her to a stop, which surprised her because he was not a big dog.

Backpack man reached her and stopped and asked her what was wrong. She replied she didn't know and that the dog had never acted like this, but whatever it was, the dog aggressively wanted to go down the bank towards the stream. The man, CJ Niedzwiecki, called CJ by everyone, told her to shorten the leash commenting that he never saw her use one of those let-em-run kinds of leashes before and that they might not be a great choice for jogging. Wonderful start girl, she thought, he's got me pegged as a moron. CJ reached down and petted the dog, looked up at her, great eyes, she thought and said he would go down and take a look to see what was bothering the dog.

She thought to herself, say something witty, stupid, or explain what did he call it? The let-em-run leash. Here's your big chance. I have got to come up with something to say and it has to be funny. I'll never get this chance again.

Before CJ started down through the brush, he paused and looked at the weeds. The woman jogger noticed and asked if something was wrong and told him he didn't need to go down. Probably a small animal or something had got hold of the dog's attention, she said, wondering why she hadn't said that in such a way to make him laugh. I should have said, probably a zombie passed this way earlier and needed a drink at the stream. Maybe it's not too late. I could say it now? But he was already moving, the moment was lost.

He carefully moved forward, making sure not to walk in what appeared to him to be the slide path. He hadn't gone far before seeing the body of a man lying on its back with his head towards the stream and not moving. CJ increased his pace on the chance that the person was injured and not dead though even at this distance, he looked dead to CJ He reached the bottom of the bank and stood to look at the body. CJ was sure he was looking at a dead man having much experience seeing the deceased from his time in combat in the Marines. He knew he could not go close to the body because this was an apparent murder, and he did not want to disrupt the crime scene. His eyes played over the bank, where the body lay then over the body cataloging what he saw. He yelled to the girl to call the police and tell them a body was lying on the path.

CJN concentrated on the footprints around the body because they would tell the tale. He knew the police would be using forensic information, but the knowledge that CJN used was not forensic but gained during his summers spent with his father's best friend, Taza Naiche, Taza's family and clan. The summers were usually spent on the Fort Apache reservation with the White Mountain tribe of the Western Apaches but sometimes on the Navajo reservation. Taza had relatives with both Apache and Navajo.

The young woman called down to him, asking him if he was all right, and he answered that he was fine and would stand near the body and wait for the police to make sure nothing would disrupt the body. She heard what he said and started to have second thoughts about whether or not she wanted to have a relationship with someone that would just stand near a dead body and whose tone of voice sounded completely unperturbed about finding a body on a hiking trail in Austin TX.

CJN yelled to the woman to go back to the trailhead so that she could direct the police to the spot when the police arrived. She pulled in her dog and sprinted back towards the trails intersection. As she ran back towards the parking lot, she saw that the police standing at the intersection of Little Fern and Canyon trail. She waved to them to come her way, and they jogged towards her. She reversed her run, slowing on the return, turning her head to watch the trailing cops, so she didn't out distance them. She stopped at the point where C.J had descended and pointed down the bank. When the officers arrived, panting with exertion, they let their eyes follow the direction of the girl's pointing arm. They could barely make out CJN At the bottom of the slope in the underbrush. One officer stayed at the top with the woman while the other descended, staying off the slide path just as CJ had. As soon as the officer got to the body, he radioed in telling the dispatcher that he needed a supervisor and also the medical examiner telling dispatch that the body was dead. However, he knew it would take a medical examiner to do a pronouncement. He asked CJN if he had touched the body and received a negative response, he told CJ to go back up the trail and wait saying the responding detectives would have some questions for him. Before CJN left the officer, he said to him that the man whose body they have found was Dr. Richert.

"You knew him?" asked the cop.

"I did," said CJN

"OK, please wait at the top of the trail. The detectives are going to have more questions for you."

As CJN turned to head up the slope back to the trail, the cop got back on his radio and called dispatch, telling them to tell the supervisor that the person who had discovered the body also identified the deceased. He further told dispatch to tell the detectives that the body had its throat cut and cut really deep as he thought he could see the spinal cord.

At the top of the bank, where the slide path started, CJ stood with the other officer who was on his radio talking to his partner and to the approaching emergency vehicles. The young woman was there with her dog now on a decidedly shortened leash. CJ stepped a few feet away, wanting privacy to make a cell phone call. He placed a call to Lawrence Cunningham chairman of the board of Cunningham Industries, the father-in-law of Dr. Richert, who lay slain along the stream. CJ and his security company acted as consultants to Cunningham Industries. CJ thought it would be better for Mr. Cunningham to hear about his son-in-law from someone he knew rather than from a stranger from the police department. As soon as the phone was answered, he identified himself to the receptionist and told her to put him through to Lawrence Cunningham immediately. She protested, and CJ switched to his command voice and told her in no uncertain terms that Mr. Cunningham would want this call no matter what he was doing.

"CJN What is so important to pull me out of a meeting?" said Lawrence Cunningham as he picked up the phone.

"Sir," and CJ paused for a second, "I need you to brace yourself for some terrible news," CJ said the words slowly dragging them out, making sure that they were heard and understood.

"What is it?" said Lawrence Cunningham at the seriousness of CJ's voice. He leaned forward in the chair, pulling the phone closer to his body, preparing to hear hard words.

"Your son-in-law Dr. Richert."

"Yes, what about him?"

"He is dead and has probably been murdered. His body is on the jogging trail on the Panther Creek Nature trial. The Canyon trail where the stream is exposed. He is lying by the stream, and he had his throat slit." CJN just laid it out there as he felt that was the best way. Whether it was or was not, it was his way. There was silence on the phone as CJ knew there would be.

"How do you know this? Who told you that it was murder? How can you be sure it is my son-in-law?" The questions poured out coming from a mind that was now in a scramble. CJ waited for the questions to stop before responding and did not respond in the order the questions came but instead told the man what he needed to know.

"I was the one that found the body after having been alerted by a dog. That your son-in-law is dead, there is no doubt. That it was a murder will be up to the police to make the final decision, but I am confident that it was. I made that determination by examining the condition of the body and the footprints near the body. The man that assaulted him did not just attack but instead crouched down to talk to him."

This statement by CJ caused Mr. Cunningham to experience a jolt of fear pass over his body. "Are you sure?" He said.

"Sure? Well, as sure as you can be when observing these things. But sure, enough to tell you my suspicions."

"Does my daughter know yet?"

"I haven't told her. The first call I made was to you. Frankly, I don't even have your daughter's phone number. You probably should be the one that calls her or go and see her."

"I want to tell her. I am up in Roundrock at Dell's headquarters. I'll leave immediately, but it's a good 45-minute drive with the damn construction on I35. Can you go there? She lives in Hyde Park in one of the townhouses."

"No, Sir, I cannot. I need to stay and talk to the police. You could send your in-house security people, or I could call my father, who lives on 45th, which is close to Hyde Park. Would you like me to do that?"

"Your father? Would he be able to handle the situation? I just want him to make sure she is OK and not scare her; I just want him to wait for me to get there. Could he do that?"

"Sir, believe me, my father could handle any situation that he ran into. Once he arrives, your daughter will be completely safe. And I will tell him what happened and that he should not reveal anything to your daughter but wait for you to tell her."

As soon as CJ hung up from the call to Lawrence Cunningham, he dialed his dad, known by the nickname Gunny, from his career in the Marine Corps and called as such by everybody, including his son. He told his dad what happened in very few words and that Mr. Cunningham had requested that Gunny go and babysit the daughter making sure she was safe and that Gunny should not reveal anything but wait for Mr. Cunningham.

"Well, there we go just like an officer. You call the enlisted scum to do you a favor and can't just ask for the favor but got to lay out exactly what you want. As if I am too stupid not to know it," said Gunny.

"Hit the Scotch last night, Gunny?" said CJ knowing that would fire him up even more.

"Never you mind about what I did last night, sonny-boy. Are you going to talk forever on this phone, or do you want me to take care of this woman?" As he said this, he was already moving quickly around his place to get out the door. He placed an S&W

40 caliber automatic into a belly holster in the small of his back. CJ gave him the address, and they confirmed that was about a 10-minute drive which Gunny would make in under seven.

As Gunny pulled out of the driveway, CJ continued to wait for the detective to question him. He stood patiently with and the young woman jogger and the cop who was still on his radio.

"I don't know that I'll ever feel safe to run down this path again." said the woman jogger to CJ, who turned his head to look at her.

"We'll get yourself a real dog," said CJ looking down at the woman's dog.

"What do you mean, a real dog? "She said, irritated, giving a slight frown and stretching her neck up to try to get more even with his height. CJ stopped looking at the dog and turned to look at her. He wondered if she wanted information on how to be safe, and if not, what was it she was asking?

He continued "like a shepherd or a large breed, something that will intimidate somebody. That thing you have, what is it an English Setter? That wouldn't intimidate a big squirrel. You might as well be jogging with a cat."

She was quiet for a moment, looking up at him, feeling the anger rise in her. "I love this dog," she said as she bent over to pet it, "and he has been a loyal friend, and you are kind of a jerk." To hell with him, she thought. Bet he isn't married and not involved because what woman would want such a jerk?

Oh no, thought CJ stumbling over his words, "Ma'am, I meant no offense I'm sure it's a wonderful animal. I thought you were asking how you could feel safe again jogging, and I was trying to give you some advice."

She stayed quiet, crouching, and petting her dog. Thinking, well, he apologized, and he spoke to me respectfully, maybe it's OK? Wait. He called me ma'am. Does he think I'm old? She glanced up at CJ He looks military, she thought, and they say ma'am all the time. She let it go, turned her head up to look at him, and though she had the advantage, so why not press it? "You owe me lunch for saying bad things about my dog."

Bang right out in the open. Call me, ma'am, will you? Insult my dog, she thought.

CJ felt relieved and attracted. Wow, what a babe, he thought. His mind flashed back to watching her run in front of him and how each time he would slow his pace to enjoy the view. He could never say publicly that is why he slowed his pace to anyone except maybe his workout buddies in the locker room where male talk was still engaged in because such talk was frowned on in this age of PC censorship though it is as much a part of human behavior as yawning.

"OK, that works for me, and again I'm sure it's a nice dog, but you could make a muzzle for that thing out of tissue paper." Sorry, he said it as soon as he did.

"Will you leave my dog alone?"

She had him on the ropes. She could play this. Act a little offended and let him become conciliatory. She knew there was a body lying not far from them. Still, she had not seen it just heard about it, so she wasn't distraught. Just nervous. If this worked out, it would make a hell of a story to tell her friends how she met her new boyfriend, of sweaty T-Shirt and big hard muscle fame, which is the way she would like to think about CJ. Boyfriend and sweaty big hard muscles. Eat your heart out, girls. She wondered when would be a good time to ask if he was involved and, if so precisely how she would do that. She decided no, not so fast, but to keep things going, she said, "so are you going to keep jogging on this trail after this?"

"Of course. Why wouldn't I?" shrugging and moving the backpack up and down. The response again amazing her with his nonchalant tone after finding a dead man.

"Why don't you take the backpack off? I am sure they will keep us here for a while, don't you think?" She said as she knowingly reached up to pull the tie holding her ponytail. She shook her head, flashing blond hair across her face. Give him an eyeful of my blond tresses, that always works, she thought. Then gathering her hair behind her head, she retied her ponytail. She extended her hand, "Briana Kempler."

CJ took the offered hand, "CJ Niedzwiecki. Call me CJ"

"OK, CJ," said Briana raising her eyebrows and giving a little smile. "So here is where we are. One CJ, you will not say anymore mean things about my dog like comparing her to a cat and two you owe me a lunch." CJ nodded.

"What does the CJ stand for?" Briana asked, smiling, showing her perfect snow-white teeth and thank-you daddy for that.

"The first initial of my first and middle names."

"Ahh yeah, I kind of figured that. And those names are what?"

"They are C. and J."

"OK, private subject." she said, "That's OK. I can deal with that."

She decided that she had pushed enough and would wait to see what developed. Briana wondered if this was an excellent time to bring up the when and where of the owed lunch, or she hoped that he would bring it up first. But the idea of a bigger dog did sound like a good one. And that would surely get him to talk to her again, and if not, it's back to the Victorian ankle routine.

While they talked, the area had become congested with more police, paramedics, forensic teams, and the medical examiner. Finally, Detective Dawson, who had been down examining, the body climbed back up the bank and went over to question CJ

"Sir, are you the one that discovered the body?"

"Well, the dog discovered the body; that is, he was making a fuss trying to get down the bank, and I came along and went down to investigate."

Dawson was experienced and had already been informed by the responding officer that the man, CJ, who had discovered the body, also knew the deceased identity. The person who found a body and knew the person was uncommon except in the tried and true domestic violence murders that were all too common on the downside but on the upside quickly cleared, which looked good on the stats that his Lieutenant obsessed over.

"I understand that you knew the deceased is that correct, sir?"

"I knew him in a professional capacity. My company does work for Cunningham Industries, and Dr. Richert, the deceased, worked there also."

"Do you ever jog with him?" said Dawson.

"I have seen him running on occasion, but he is an evening runner, and I am a morning runner, but sometimes either I would be running in the evening, or he would be running in the morning, and we would see each other. However, I run faster than he did."

Faster than a locomotive, though Briana, who could hear the conversation. Dawson noticed that the woman could hear, so he moved away, motioning with a wave of his hand to CJ to come with him. Once out of earshot, he continued.

"Uh-huh. We are going to need to talk to you further," said Dawson. Dawson asked if all of the personal particulars had been collected and received confirmation from the other officer.

CJ interrupted, saying, "Yes, I've given him everything. But there is something further. I would like to tell you."

Dawson stood still and went completely alert, waiting, quiet, listening. Maybe a confession? Weirder shit has happened, Dawson thought. "And what is that, sir?"

"I am confident, not positive, but confident that the man who assaulted Dr. Richert had a conversation with him either soliciting information that he did not receive or disliking what he heard."

"How would you know that?"

"If you examine the foot patterns around the body, you will see where the man had stood with his feet shoulder length apart and then had crouched down. If you're just going to kill someone to slit their throat, you probably won't do that. You just lean over and cut. But this guy, and I'm assuming it's a guy, because of the body weight, and you know the bodyweight by how deep the indentation was, he crouched down."

Dawson thought that CJ might be a nut job or watched that damn CSI show on T.V where budgets are unlimited for forensics. The show makes life miserable for the cops because the public thinks that if a bicycle gets boosted out of a garage that the cops should do a full DNA analysis of the garage and maybe examine all footage of traffic cams for twelve hours before and after the boost. What the hell it's technically possible to solve the theft. Yea and in America, only 60 percent of murders are solved, and that number is lower if you consider the murdered by relative factor. CSI? Bullshit. You want murderers caught? How about a TV program called Be-A-Rat. Why don't people inform on murderers? Even murderers have friends, and rats can get killed.

Dawson asked, "You see a lot of dead bodies? Ones with their throat cut? "

"More than my share. Over a decade in the Marine Corp. Force Recon."

That made sense to Dawson, who waited, but CJ said nothing more, so Dawson prompted him, "How would you know he crouched down?"

"I'll show you," said CJ, "follow along with me. Stand with your feet shoulder-width apart. Crouch down slowly, bending your knees to where your butt almost touches the ground. Pay attention to the soles of your feet; notice how they have turned out? That's because your body needs to balance the weight. So, to balance the weight the outside of your feet need to press outward."

CJ stood saying to the detective as he also rose, "Carefully step away from where you were crouching down and look at the impressions your feet made." Dawson examined the impressions that his feet had made while crouching.

"See it?" asked CJ

"I think so," said Dawson bending over and staring at the place he had crouched.

"You'll see it better in a minute," said CJ "For comparison bend straight over bending your knees enough to get the neck in range of your blade."

"Stand up and step back and compare the two impressions, crouching down compared to bending over."

Dawson's eyes went from one-foot impression to the other. "I'll be dammed," he said. "Where would you learn such a thing?"

"I learned to track and read signs during the summers with the Apache."

Dawson was processing this and a little amazed at what he just heard, he said. "Apache like Geronimo?"

"Kind of yes, as Geronimo was Apache but more like the Apache Mickey Free," said CJ

"Who? Never heard of anybody named Mickey Free. Was he Apache? What kind of Apache name is Mickey Free?"

"A historical person," said CJ, "He was kidnapped when he was about 12 by a Comanche that was raiding the ranch Mickey Free lived on and sold as a slave to the Apaches who eventually adopted him into the tribe. He worked as an Indian scout for the U.S. Army and had superb tracking skills and, as such, was the only man that Geronimo ever feared."

Dawson stood slightly nodding his head, thinking he might run this crouching vs. bending theory by the forensic people or maybe a sport's medicine doc? Maybe not. He would hate to have to try to explain to some judge that he used Apache tracking methods to assist in locating the murderer.

"OK, but we will need to talk to you again and go through all of this." Dawson turned to the woman who was still waiting, "and Miss, we will need to talk to you again to verify what you have told us. Don't be worried there's nothing wrong. I have been doing this a long time, and when people have an opportunity to calm down and think, they often can come up with details that they didn't realize at the time."

Chapter 3

The Richert home was in the Hyde Park neighborhood of Austin TX with tree-lined streets and where some dwellings built at the turn of the 20th century were still-standing. The Richert lived in a two-story 2,200 square feet refurbished and renovated townhouse, which they had bought for about 800 large, a steal in downtown Austin.

Before the historic district renovation program, townhouses were called row-houses. When the developer's marketing team saw the proposed selling prices, upwards of a cool three-quarter of a million, they knew that the name row-house had to go out into the dumpster with the hot water radiators and town-home had to come in with the central air conditioning. No matter how much you love whales, you don't want to be mistaken for the hoi polloi.

The town-homes, previously row-homes in their former unenlightened lives, were in pairs, with each side a mirror image of its partner, distinguished by exterior architectural details. According to the town-home sales brochure, the details, such as house numbers done in an ornate period script named Brush Script Cursive, gave each home its uniqueness. Not mentioned in the advertisement was that the particulars repeated every twelve households because being too unique, eliminated construction efficiency, and that would quickly push the homes over a million. At least with the custom every twelfth house repeating details, you had a chance of figuring out which town-home was yours. Especially on the nights when you swam home from restaurant row a couple of blocks away on Guadalupe street, having filled your bilge with too many Margaritas to make reading the house numbers in that damn period script, possible.

Each pair of Siamese twin town-homes was separated from the town-home clan by small strips running between the couples. Each separating strip was split neatly in half by an 8-foot redwood privacy fence. Even in families of well-bred, three-quarter of a million, Siamese twin homes, there might be someone who thought a champagne flute was a brownish instrument in the local high school band. You see, all those high-tech companies that had taken over Austin hired anybody with computer wizardry skills, and never you mind if they didn't know who Martha Stewart is.

The dividing strips billowed out at the rear of the houses allowed a small area or garden terrace in marketing terms. There might be room to fit a swing set in the yard if you could locate a swing that could go perpendicular. Most of the owners just had the developers add a wooded patio to the area and a small jungle, oops I mean, a little rain forest of hanging plants. Squeeze in a lawn chair or two, add a solar-powered BBQ grill, solar-powered so as not to disturb the patio rain forest, and you have country living in the city.

Dravin Mells, state Department of correction inmate number J342336, convicted felon, two-time loser, overall thug, a.k.a. the man-in-black, in case that description appears too judgmental, add this: accomplished correspondent and trusted confidant, had slipped into the backyard right after he saw the coast was clear. The lock on the fence presented no problem for a professional all-around bad guy. But even so, Rebecca had said she would leave a key under the front bush, the one that was second from the right. If she had, he sure couldn't find it, but no matter. Dravin realized that if anyone happened to see him rooting in the bush looking for the key like a rabbit at a lettuce buffet, it might raise suspicion, even in the renovated, tolerant and enlightened land of urban rediscovery. Instead, he casually worked the lock on the fence, giving the impression to any pain-in-the-ass neighbors that might happen to be watching that he had a key.

Once in the side yard, he went to the back and tried to open the rear window to gain access to hide out in the house and wait for Rebecca. They had agreed that the cops would never look there since there was zero to tie Rebecca to the crime with their planned airtight alibi, which made her home just the perfect place to lie low. All he had to date from Rebecca was her words and a few photos, such as the one she had sent him to identify her husband, and where he could be found jogging, and a few more revealing pictures of herself, none of which gave a perfect view of her face with her being a little modest. Draven could ease that out of her. Yes, sir. Draven had big plans in the old townhouse tonight.

But Draven's Rebecca had slipped up again, just like with the key out front that was not under the shrub. The window over the kitchen sink was locked, as where all the windows. Draven sat down on the deck and pondered his next move. He couldn't pick the window locks. He would have to break them, and without something to cushion the sound, some meddler might hear breaking glass. Rebecca was due home anytime from the alibi laying trip. Draven rubbed the latest prison tattoo he gotten just before the remarkable and surprising parole came through. The tattoo was an interlocking R for Rebecca and D for Draven. The prison tattoo artist was able to reform the old A into an R. The A stood for his ex, the bitch that deserved the beatings. Just when Draven was about to take a chance and bust the window, he heard the garage door start-up and the purr of a Beemer pulling into the garage. Draven thought of those pictures semi-naughty Rebecca had sent and licked his lips.

Draven, hearing the car engine shut down, wondered how he should surprise her. Rebecca would think he was waiting for her in the house per plan, but not per plan was the locked windows. Draven slipped off of the back porch and stood in the shadow of the fence. He still wore black, but not the same black shirt and pants as last night, as he thought that might have that bit of a downdraft effect on Rebecca's ardor. Cloths stained with the blood of a former loved one were not a usual ingredient in aphrodisiacs. Everybody in this family always meets me for the first time in the shadows, he thought.

Rebecca emerged from the detached garage and strode across the cobbled footpath towards the back door, her backless heels clicking on the cobblestones. Just as she inserted the key, clever Draven, always one who liked surprises, jumped from the shadows into the patio's full sunlight and sang out, "Hey baby, come to Papa."

Rebecca, who was so startled from Draven's Super Bowl halftime entrance she simultaneously dropped her package and involuntarily sent a blast of air out of her lungs, resulting in a scream that bested the Wilhelm scream, the most famous two-second sound bite in all of film. Loud screams can have strange and different effects on different people. There were three people affected by this one.

First up was Rebecca. After flushing her lungs of air from the scream, she inhaled with enough force to draw all the secondhand vaping smoke from the patios on the restaurant row down on Guadalupe into her lungs, preparing for round two of her Titanic foghorn imitation.

Next up, Draven, at the number two spot, who was so accustomed to violence than when a surprise weapon confronted him, he would only give a slight smile, but when confronted by this, the mother of all screams, he leaped backward against the privacy fence causing it to crack one of its cross members.

Finally, the third person was Gunny, who had parked out front as Rebecca pulled into the garage, got out of his car, and walked past this town house's twins side fence when the scream erupted. Gunny, in his younger years, would have been over that fence and into the yard like an Olympic high jumper before the scream stopped shaking the family of town-house twins. But after many years of experience, loud noises no longer sent Gunny up and over, they sent him down and under, which was where he was currently. He was pressed tightly against the fence, waiting for the first incoming rounds to hit or the bullets to fly, or some indication as to what the hell that had been.

Things were getting a little weird here for Draven. First off, there had been the bush with no key and no rabbits I might add, then the locked window, then yodeling Rebecca. And Rebecca just didn't look quite right. Not exactly like her pictures. He couldn't put his finger on it, but something was wrong. What the, he thought, as he reached for his trusty razor, is this some other broad? Am I at the wrong house? Still, whoever this broad was, she looked good, and if he could shut her up, there was still the distinct possibility of some hot times in the old house tonight.

The site of the razor in Draven's hand caused more involuntary action from Rebecca. Her vocal cords discovered the beauty of silence while the old splinter muscles just said to hell with this and retreated from all restraint, causing a visible stain on her five hundred fifty, sale price that is, Ralf Lauren Mid-rise Skinny Jeans. She pressed herself against the door, still holding onto the keys in the lock and trembling, unable to get enough control over her hand to turn the key in the lock.

Draven was pretty sure he was at the wrong house. This broad was close, but maybe no match for the photo. Rebecca would have recognized him because he had sent her a link to an Internet site with a picture of him. The finding of the link, with the excellent photo, took some searching because of all of the law-enforcement mug shots of him, which he did not want to send to her. Dravin thought he looked like some kind of criminal in those mug shots as the cops used cheap-ass cameras and not letting you arrange your hair or nothing. Add all of that together, and he has some work to do here. Damn, he thought, all that planning and I am going get screwed by house numbers that Stephen Hawking couldn't read. Still, if this chick was not Rebecca, she could be tonight's mystery date.

Gunny paused a few seconds against the fence and the cover of the ground until he confirmed that standing up would not result in his body being shredded by flying metal from mortar rounds or pierced by bullets. He jumped up, looked at the fence's height, and gave up thoughts of a Batman leap. He tried the latch, but Draven had relocked it after entering. Gunny took a measured step back from the wooden gate, put his weight on one leg, curled the other up bent at the knee, tightly held against his body. He delivered a kick to the gate with his $325.00 Lowa Camino GTX heavy-duty hiking boots purchased at his favorite store in the world Recognition Equipment Incorporated, REI. The ad copy for the REI boots stated that they were designed for those who were part pack animal. Gunny loved that line. He bought not one but two pairs because, as Gunny used to preach to the young Marines he trained, one is none and two is one, meaning always have a backup plan. The lock surrendered, the gate blew inward, and dropped half off its hinges with pieces scattered on the ground. Gunny grabbed one of the splintered boards and ran full charge into the side yard towards the screams source.

Draven, who had started across the patio, easily dangling the razor at his side, just in case it was the wrong house and this wasn't Rebecca of naughty-photo fame, heard the gates implosion and thought cops. He turned to see to his delight that it was not a cop but just some old guy.

Gunny stopped and took in the whole scene. He saw a guy dressed all in black with a razor. Flattened against the back door of the house was a woman he assumed was Rebecca Richert. She was frozen in place and trembling, with an unsightly stain on the front of her skinny jeans. The guy with the razor looking relieved when he saw no gun. Gunny considered pulling the automatic out holstered in the small of his back. He hesitated, thinking that he would wait and see how this played out.

"Hey, old guy," said Draven as he turned from facing the woman to meet Gunny "what are you the neighborhood watch? Bet you didn't sign up for what's gonna happen to you now. Got you a board? What you think old guy? Which is going to win here? Razor or board?" Rodney started to slowly close the distance between himself and Gunny as he continued to talk trash.

"Did you hear about the guy down by the creek? That was my last tango. And guess what? As I live and breathe, your next on my dance card." Draven eased toward Gunny, closing the distance across the patio, talking to Gunny, wanting to distract him, to hold them in place.

"Maybe you're thinking this is a fair fight old guy? Well my very favorite book is called the No Fair Fight Guide to Victory. Ever hear of it?"

To Draven, it appeared that his trash-talking monologue had the effect he was hoping for. Gunny stood still waiting for Draven to get within striking distance. Draven snapped his hand to lay open the straight razor away from his knuckles allowing his hand to form a solid backing for the blade. When he was close enough, Draven slashed from right to left, not going for a kill just yet, going for a flesh wound. Such an injury would be enough to enlist terror and surprise as his ally, if he needed an ally, against an old man.

The surprise was Draven's because somehow, the old guy had gotten lucky enough to bring up the board. The blade from the razor plunged into the board driven with the force of Draven's swing, and then, damn luck, the old guy had twisted the board and pulled the razor rate out of Draven's hand.

Then to, Draven's delight, luck moved over to his side, because the old guy screwed up and dropped the board. Draven smiled because his prison fighting skills would make short order of this dude, who is old enough to be his father, big son-of-a-bitch that he was.

Draven stepped into the fight and saw the old guy twist his stance sideways to the left, putting all of his weight on one foot. A hell of a mistake, because that set him off balance, a real goof in a fight. Gunny, who practiced standing on one leg every day during his warm-up exercises, again raised the leg, bent the knee, and kicked with his 3-pound Lowa Camino hiking boots so that the shoe's outer flat edge hit the guy just below the knee. If locked fence gates could talk, they would have mentioned to Draven to watch out for that one-legged kick, especially as knees aren't half as strong as locked gates, but, sorry Dravin, this is not the land of talking fence gates but is the land of busted knees. Draven's knee bent backward beyond the 15° required to cause severe hyper-extension of the joint. With severe hyper-extension, all kinds of things to go wrong, not the least of which is unbelievable, disabling pain. Gunny, always one to not leave a job half done, continued his body's forward motion. Except he altered the kicks direction so that the boot scraped down the front of the leg causing hairline cracks in the fibula bone finally, the force of the kick ended at the top of Draven's foot. Ended but not finished, as Gunny's final stomping motion broke the talus bone on the top of Draven's foot and cracked several others.

Draven didn't care much about the broken foot. The knee kick had caused him to collapse into a puddle of pain, reeling from the bone breaks. All thoughts of the big night with Rebecca. Of taking care of a nosy interfering old man. Of party time in general flushed from his brain. Replaced by a continuous stream of oh-my-gods and oh-fucks, which erupted from his mouth like water from a fire hydrant.

Gunny watched him for a few seconds, then when the screams started to slow down, he looked over at Rebecca Richert and said, "have you called the cops yet?"

She shook her head no but started immediately to fumble for her phone. Gunny knelled next to Draven, who was regaining his senses.

"I need to ask you a few things before the cops get here.

"Fuck you," was Draven's reply. "I know my rights. You got lucky with the board you old bastard." Draven said the words between clenched teeth as he got his hands around the pain of the broken bones.

"No," said Gunny "you're not understanding me we are in a hurry here. The police are on their way. I have some questions and you want to answer them."

"Hey old man. I ain't got nothing to say except get me an ambulance. I am in no talking mood here. My leg hurts like hell. Get me an ambulance. And get it now." Dravin went back to moaning.

Gunny gave a small nod and said, "Well this reminds me of a scene in True Grit, John Wayne, who plays Rooster Cogburn, and by the way he won an Academy award for that role. Anyway, he's questioning this outlaw that he shot a few minutes before. Can you envision it? OK, so the outlaw in the movie is whining about the pain, just like you are here. The outlaw says, 'man this hurts like hell.' and John Wayne, you know, playing Rooster, replies are you ready? You gotta see this in your mind because here's the good part. John Wayne leans over and says to him 'I bet it do Sonny boy'."

"John Wayne?" asked Draven, "fuck John Wayne. I need a doctor damn you".

"Did you just say fuck John Wayne? I don't like that. I don't like that at all. OK so that's how you want play it? Good with me, no more Mr. Nice Guy."

Gunny could hear the approaching siren closing the distance between them, and he saw his questioning window start to close. Gunny held his index finger up in front of Draven's face and wagged it left to right. "You see this finger? How would you like me to take this finger and start squishing it into your knee their Sonny boy? You, that bad mouths John Wayne." Not getting any response from Draven, Gunny formed an O with his index finger and thumb and flicked his finger into Draven's broken knee. Draven screamed and screamed and screamed.

Gunny wagged the finger in Draven's face again and said, "Couple of questions? Ready? And be fast with the answers. First off you killed this woman's husband, didn't you?"

"Yes," hissed Draven, never taking his eyes off Gunny's index finger.

"I heard you call the woman by her name of Rebecca. Do you know her?"

"Of course, I know over. She's my girlfriend."

That threw him. Gunny moved his gaze from Draven's face up to Rebecca, standing trembling at the door. He didn't think she had heard what Draven said. He said to her, "the cops are almost here ma'am. They're going to want to talk to you. You might want to go in and change." She dropped her gaze down and noticed the stain on the front of her jeans shook her head a trembling yes turned the key in the lock and went inside.

When the cops pulled up, they came into the side yard and immediately called for backup. They had placed Gunny up against the fence and removed the handgun in the small of his back, telling him that it was for everybody's protection. Gunny wondering how he was supposed to feel protected when they just removed his handgun. They called for an ambulance for Draven, who they had handcuffed despite his knee. They asked Gunny what happened, and he told them step-by-step. When he got to the part about the questions he had asked Draven, he said to them that Draven had confessed to the murder of Dr. Richert, but Gunny hesitated, and the cops noted the hesitation.

"Sir there something you're not telling us."

Gunny thought about it. Decided, he could not hold back what might be critical evidence. So, he told them what Draven had said, including the part about Rebecca Richert and Draven being boyfriend girlfriend. While Gunny was talking with the first police officer, the second, a woman, had entered the home and found Rebecca Richert in changing. The officer got a radio call from her partner, telling her what Gunny had just told him. She waited with Mrs. Richert as she finished dressing.

The ambulance arrived and whisked Draven away to the hospital. Gunny explained to the officers what had caused him to be here, saying that he got a call from his son asking him to come by. He further explained that his son CJ was a consultant for Cunningham Industries and that the owner of Cunningham Industries or that is the chairman of the board, whatever, corporate structures not interesting Gunny, was the father of Rebecca Richert and the father-in-law of the dead man.

After talking between the officers and over the radio with their supervisors, they decided to return the gun to Gunny and allow him to go back home, telling him that they would need to explore this more.

Gunny went back to his pickup and drove home, still fuming about that horse's ass bad-mouthing John Wayne. Maybe I didn't put enough force into that kick, he thought.

Chapter 4

Dawson had had a bad night. The cops responded yesterday afternoon to Rebecca Richert stuttering summons. They found Dravin Mells with the shattered leg, lying on the back patio of the Richert home. Mrs. Richert was in the home changing when the police arrived, and a man who went by the name of Gunny was waiting for them. The paramedics arrived, examined the injured man, and placed them into the ambulance for transport to the hospital.

After the ambulances warping retreat, the Austin city cops who had been the first on the scene summoned their superiors. Their superiors placed a call to the County Sheriff Department to discuss jurisdiction. The murder of Dr. Richert may have been out of the city and into the county. The Austin city cops and the Travis County Sheriff discussed current events, including the new overpaid and untested University of Texas football coach, the opening of a new Hooters restaurant, catch the redhead on the lunch shift boys, and oh yeah, a murder. The murder and the incident at Rebecca Richert home were probably linked, so maybe the Austin cops had jurisdiction, not that they wanted it, but neither did the Travis County Sheriff. After that, it was back to the coach's pay package and the waitresses' distinguishing merits at the new Hooters.

One might think that Dawson would be pleased by the rapid apprehension of Dravin Mells. When he was trying to rise to the enlightened level that his new hard-bodied coed girlfriend talked about, he was. But as he was tired and the Buddha wasn't looking, Dawson tumbled from Nirvana and was really pissed that a civilian had made the bust.

Dawson had summoned Gunny to come to a meeting at his office to obtain a complete statement on happenings. He had nothing but babbling from the Richert woman and Dravin Mells before both had been sedated last evening. The responding cops had filed a report that old Mr. Prime Suspect, a.k.a. Dravin Mells had made some reference to John Wayne before being chained to the stretcher and sent to the hospital. As the detective waited in his office for Gunny to show up for the meeting, the Lieutenant, Doran Dahlby, Dawson's boss, walked in. Bad nights have a habit of bleeding into bad days.

"We got national news coverage on this, and you let a civilian beat you to the home of the victim?" The Lieutenant gave no good morning, how ya doing, what's up, how they hanging? He just got Dawson caught in his high beams and steered right at him. The Lieutenant had well-tuned political senses and ambition beyond the police department, and all the detective bureau members knew it. Sensational cases, depending on how they were handled, could provide a push-up or push out. Dawson saw no upside to answering the Lieutenant's questioning attack, but he knew such an attack would be forthcoming. He had thought it through in the wee hours of the morning how he should respond and was prepared with a diversion which he felt had real merit. "Lieutenant, I have Dravin Mells rap sheet here and it reads like the lyrics from a Gangster rap song. The larger question here is who the hell would have let him out on parole?"

The Lieutenant put his hand on the desk and leaned forward to look at the computer screen to read the rap sheet. "Holy smoke, even the Governor of California would not have let this guy out in an off-election year," seizing on Dawson's bait and realizing that this file had a stronger smell than an employee of The Tiger King. "Anything from the labs yet?"

"Just preliminaries. Blood type matching, but no DNA yet. He's our boy though. We have the murder weapon, the straight razor he used. The question is why? Why did he do it and as I said the bigger question is why did he get parole? The parole thing is going come back and bite somebody Lieutenant."

"Two things, no make it three," said the Lieutenant "First and foremost, I want this tied up so tight that even O. J's "Dream Team lawyers couldn't get him off. Second, you screwed up, allowing a civilian to go over to the Richert house. I expect you to come up with a good reason to feed the press for that and third, no speculative motive stuff. I want an answer to the whys, including why he got parole. "

Dawson shook his head in agreement with the Lieutenant, pleased to hear that his screw-up had moved down to the number two position in the Lieutenant's list. He kept the chum coming. "Right, Lieutenant. There is more to this than what we see in front of us. That guy Gunny, he seems to be a bit of a character. Anyway, he told our boys when they there that the perp claimed Mrs. Richert was his girlfriend so that they were in a boyfriend girlfriend relationship."

'The civilian is Gunny? Gunny Niedzwiecki?" asked the Lieutenant.

Dawson fanned through the paperwork on his desk without responding, still reading the reports.

"Yeah, Gunny Niedzwiecki. Same last name as the guy that found the body. The Apache channeler", said Dawson, then cringed, hoping the Lieutenant didn't hear the Apache remark.

"Dawson, I know Gunny," said the Lieutenant "for a number of years he was the Chief of Police at Austin Community College. He is retired now, a double dipper, retired Marine and retired from the college system. He was a sharp guy and tough. He was a Recon Marine then transferred to the M.P.'s as I remember. He knew somebody in administration at Austin Community which is how he joined that force. I met him at different seminars and joint training sessions. As a matter fact before your time he helped to train our people in self-defense. He's damn good at it and I can't remember in what discipline, but he is some kind of a black belt martial artist. That John Wayne thing you mentioned? I remember he had this oddity of quoting John Wayne. But still a good guy, good cop and likable guy so treat him like that." The Lieutenant waited while Dawson chewed his intellectual cud.

"So, he used to be Chief of Police on the campus? I always see those college cops as more a security force than real cops."

"Yeah sometimes. But some of them are pretty good at investigations but still I'm glad we don't have to send our officers out to respond to every pantie raid or beer party or whatever that happens on that campus."

"Another thing Lieutenant. The man that discovered the body? CJ Is what he goes by. And the guy Gunny? That's his dad. From what I can figure out so far CJ owns some kind of security firm named CJN and Lawrence Cunningham of Cunningham Industries is a client so this CJ called Cunningham and broke the news to the father. Then the father asked CJN if he could go by and check on the daughter, that is Mrs. Richert but he couldn't because we had him at the scene so he called his dad and asked his dad to go over." Dawson paused, wondering if he should share the Apache thing with the Lieutenant. He decided to push on, "This guy, CJ, had examined the footprints around the body and I might add he did a good job because he did not disturb them. Anyway, he claims by examining the footprints that he could tell that the perp had talked to the victim before finishing him off. I asked him how he would know such a thing and he told me that he had lived as a child with the Apache."

"I didn't know Gunny's son. Not sure I even knew he had one. You said he is an Apache?" Asked the Lieutenant.

"No, he said he lived with them that is with the family of his father's best friend. He even gave me the name of the tribe. The White Mountain Apache's. And he also said he spent time on the Navajo reservation. He claimed he learned all this, how to read signs, tracking, that kind of stuff from his summers with the Native Americans." Dawson gave a slight smile and was really proud of himself for saying Native Americans to the Lieutenant's politically sensitive nose rather than Red-Men or Injuns or Tonto.

"So, on the weird off-chance that CJ is correct about the perp talking to the victim. And this claim that the perp is putting out about being boyfriend girlfriend with Mrs. Richert," he paused, thinking, "add in this out-of-left-field parole and I just feel there's a lot more to this case that we've got right now."

"Do you think the Richert woman was actually involved with the perp?" Asked the Lieutenant then immediately dismissed it on the grounds of not being believable. "OK we do have to look at that but that has got to be a some made up story. How could Mells, scumbag, career criminal, locked in the big house until some moron, bleeding heart, all-we-need-is-love pinko, checks the wrong box on the form be screwing with Rebecca Richert. Wife of a famous shrink and granddaughter of Lawrence Cunningham? That sounds about as likely as Dwayne Johnson The Rock winning a quilting contest."

Dawson minimally noted the Lieutenant was saying 'scumbag, career criminal, locked in the big house etc. etc. pinko checks the wrong box on the form.' Now, that sounds like the guy I knew back when he was just a Sergeant of Detectives. Before he tried to shake his old image and move to the Left for a run at Austin Political office.

"Right, Lieutenant, that's where my mind was about 2 o'clock this morning. But look at it again. Why the hell would he kill Dr. Richert but wait until the next afternoon to go to his house? He'd know that once the body was discovered that we be sending a car there. If he wanted to rob the place he would've went there immediately not the next afternoon. During the canvas, we came across a neighbor that said she thought she saw some guy looking in the front bushes of the Richert home late in the morning. All right we both know that people hide keys and that he might be looking for a key so he could get in easily and rob the place but he would not look in the damn bushes. If he was there to rob the place he might maybe give a quick look under the mat or over the door-jamb for a hidden key, right?"

The Lieutenant turned around to look out the window behind Dawson's desk, leaning back on the corner while letting Dawson's logic filter through his brain. While he was looking out the window, he failed to notice Dawson's partner Lisa MacMaster arriving.

"Hey Lieutenant, hey partner," said Lisa MacMaster raising one eyebrow to Dawson and wagging her chin up towards the Lieutenant. Without turning his gaze from out the window, the Lieutenant raised one hand to acknowledge Dawson's partner's arrival.

"There's more holes in this than Bonnie and Clyde's last car," said the Lieutenant, contemplating the window's view, allowing a strategy to hatch itself. "Play it this way. Because Gunny is a retired police chief, even one at a Junior College, make sure you emphasize that and work that into the press release and avoid the issue that he beat us over to the Richert house. Write it up and send it over to Public Relations. Have them do the on-going investigation thing." The Lieutenant turned to look at Lisa MacMaster, Dawson's partner, and said one word, "vacation?"

Lisa MacMaster was Hispanic despite the surname, which was a relic from a short marriage. She ended up falling out of love as soon as she found out that her then husband had fallen into bed with another woman. But she like the name, so she kept it after kicking his ass, literally, out of her house. She stood five feet six, was in her mid-thirties, and had been an Austin police officer for twelve years the last four in Homicide and having partnered with Dawson the entire four years in homicide.

Lisa had high cheekbones and full lips and tended to pile her jet black, thick hair on top of her head. She dressed exceedingly well, especially for a police officer, liking to wear designer pants suits, which looked great on her fit body. Somebody should post a picture of her with a note saying this is what you are supposed to look like if you wear pants suits. She had developed the technique of looking like she was always pissed when questioning criminals, giving them the impression that she might at any moment, for any reason, leap over the table and beat the shit out of them. She wasn't always pissed off, but she was ready to jump over the table and beat the shit out of them at any moment. She disliked bad guys.

Lisa said, "Yeah boss, Dawson called me this morning and told me what was happening. I wasn't really doing anything anyway. So, I thought it would be good if you got the brains of the team in here."

Dawson shook his head, and the Lieutenant chuckled. "You're right about that Lisa. And this is a bit of a strange one. So, Dawson what's your next move?"

"We are going out to the Richert placed to interview Mrs. Richert. We'll see where we go from there."

"We'll get along little doggies," said the Lieutenant "I am referring only to Dawson, Lisa, never, would the word dog have anything near an association with you."

This time Lisa chuckled. "Sir, senior commanders were obliged to take the gender-neutral language training, also weren't they?"

"OK Lisa you win. The remark applies to both of you. Happy?"

"Equality," said Lisa as they headed out the door., "sometimes it is not all that it is cracked up to be."

Lawrence Cunningham, looking disheveled in jeans and a wrinkled green pullover shirt, greeted the detectives at the door. He brought them into the living room where his daughter, Rebecca Richert, was sitting on a couch. He asked the detectives if they would like some refreshment. Both detectives declined and took seats opposite Mrs. Richert. Her father sat down close to her, their legs touching on the couch.

"I assume this is not going to take long," said Mr. Cunningham, looking stern, used to being in charge "my daughter has just been through two terrible shocks. The murder of her husband and then the very man that murdered him coming here to her house no doubt with the intent to murder her also." Saying this to push the detectives in the direction he wanted them to go. Away from any alleged involvement of his daughter with the murderer, which had somehow got back to him.

"Yes, sir and let us start by saying how deeply sorry we are for the loss that both of you have suffered." said Lisa

McAllister. Dawson and Lisa had agreed on the way over that she would take the lead talking to Mrs. Richert. The woman to woman connection maybe.

"We have a just a few questions," which wasn't exactly right. They would have only a few questions unless they didn't like the answers or felt they were getting the Texas two-step. In that case, they would have more questions and ask the same ones in different form, looking for story changes or omissions.

" Some things that we need to clear up you understand. This is just procedural. We do this in any case." said Lisa to put Mrs. Richert at ease while not mentioning that procedural could easily mean the procedure to file charges.

"What I am going to tell you Mrs. Richert will be upsetting. You need to think through what I say and give me a candid and total answer. OK?" Her being a witness so far and not a suspect, so they didn't have to Mirandize her. Rebecca Richert nodded her assent.

Lisa started questioning with what she assumed would be an easy one for Mrs. Richert to put her at ease. "Your husband didn't come home last night. Didn't that concern you?"

"No, because he often sleeps at work, my dad's company that is. He sleeps on the couch in his office if he is working late or if he is just tired and wants to nap."

"Did he call you yesterday?"

"Yes. He said he was going for a run, grabbing a bite and going back to work."

Lisa switched gears. "The man that was captured in your side yard that allegedly murdered your husband said some things which we need to check out. His name is Dravin Mills." said Lisa while removing a photograph of Mills from an envelope she had with her. She placed the picture on the coffee table between them then turned it around so that the face could be seen clearly and asked Mrs. Richert "look carefully at this picture. Have you ever seen this man before in any way at any time?"

Rebecca stared at the picture, slightly recoiling back onto the sofa. "This is the man that was in my side yard? The man that the other guy, I think you call him Gunny, disarmed? Is this the man that killed my husband?"

"Again Mrs. Richert look at the picture as I said before. Do you know this man? Have you ever seen this man? Think deeply in any way at any time have you seen this man?"

"No never," the words rushed out, even the thought that she might know the man who murdered her husband was repugnant.

"Do you use email? Any of the social networking sites? Or anything like that?" Asked Lisa.

"Of course, I use email and I use any number of the social networking sites including Facebook," she paused, trying to think what other sites she used then continued "sometimes twitter, sometimes LinkedIn and I can't think of any others."

"Mrs. Richert I have to ask this because of what the alleged murderer has told us. OK? We are not accusing you of anything. We must get all the facts straight. You want that, right?" Lisa had changed her posture, now leaning across the coffee table, staring directly at Mrs. Richert's face. Looking for a tell.

This is where Lisa really shined as a detective. She concentrated not only on the words that were coming but also on facial gestures. Whether the person Lisa was questioning hands moved, if their feet shuffled, how they held their body, everything. She looked for signs of incongruity searching to see if the person she was questioning was being deceitful. The detectives had a nickname for Lisa calling her the human lie detector. Lisa wore that nickname with pride.

At this point in the questioning, Dawson did his part of the plan that he and Lisa had set up on the drive over. Dawson asked Lawrence Cunningham to come with him to the side yard to look over where the assault had occurred and where Gunny had disarmed the perp. Dawson didn't really need to do this, but he didn't want Cunningham in the same room when Lisa dropped the next bomb on her.

"What is the question?" Asked Mrs. Richert as her father, and the detective went through the patio door to the side yard.

"Have you ever been on any of the dating applications? Such as Tinder or others?" said Lisa, staring, watching, and seeing nothing. Lisa was not full proof. There is no such thing as a human lie detector, and even lie detector machines just give indications. They look for deceitful patterns by measuring things such as blood pressure and perspiration. That is what Lisa did, but she watched for gestures, facial tics, eye shifts, and put them together. If she felt she was being deceived, she would loop back and ask the question in another form, then back again and hit again, then again. As long as the other person was talking, there was a good chance that Lisa could get them to open up. Lisa needed to get a feeling that what Mills had said was true or not.

"A dating app? I am married. Or at least I was," and she began to quietly cry. "The answer to your question is no, never. How could you think such a thing?"

"I didn't say that I thought such a thing Mrs. Richert, what I am doing is clearing out the debris of lies around the case so that we can get to the truth, OK? " Mrs. Richert nodded her ascent.

Lisa continued, "again in pursuit of clearing out falsehoods, not yours, but falsehoods around the case, may we have your permission to access your phone records and your messaging records and to take any personal computers that you have with us back to the office so that we can have them forensically examined?"

"I don't understand. My husband is murdered. And you're looking to see what I have been up to?"

"Ma'am it's just procedure. We have to do this. I would like you to voluntarily release them. If not, I will have to go for a warrant and we don't want that do you?" If Rebecca Richert denied them the permission, Lisa was prepared to wait right there while Dawson went and got said warrant. Mrs. Richert was well within her legal rights to say no and demand a warrant, but if she did, then she would move off the witness list onto the suspect list.

"No, no of course not. Yes, sure take them take anything you want. I think I've had enough of this for right now. Is that OK?"

"Yes of course ma'am. I'll go get my partner and will let you be here in peace with your father. Again, our deepest condolences."

The detectives gathered up the phone a laptop and an iPad, gave Mrs. Richert a receipt, and said goodbye to Mrs. Richert and Lawrence Cunningham. After the detectives had left, Lawrence Cunningham quizzed his daughter on what the female detective had asked while he had been outside with detective Dawson. She told him, and it greatly concerned him.

"I'm going to call CJ and tell him about this and get some advice. This doesn't feel right at all to me. I'm also wondering if we need to get you a lawyer?" As soon as he had said that he regretted it. Worried about the effect the question had on his daughter.

The detectives pulled the car out of the driveway and drove around the corner over a couple of blocks to Guadalupe then pulled into one of the parking lots on restaurant row. They sat in silence, Dawson letting Lisa think about the interview and specifically about how Mrs. Richert had answered.

"I didn't like her hair," said Lisa.

"Her hair?" Dawson waited for an answer. He had learned that hurrying Lisa when she was formulating an opinion was ineffective. She needed to think things through before she spoke. Dawson struggled with this behavior as he was more spontaneous and quick but knew that waiting for Lisa to be ready was the smart move. He literally bit down on the tip of his tongue to keep quiet.

"Yes, her hair. I didn't pick up any deceptive signals. You know after you ask a key question you have to wait and observe for five seconds. It's those five seconds where the signals come from." She paused. Dawson waited for her to continue as it was her habit to be both talking to him and talking to herself as she formulated her final opinion.

"Yes, I didn't pick up anything in those five seconds. Five seconds is the limit because it is only for about five seconds that you can both listen and observe with the observing being much more important than the listening to the answer. After that you have to listen to hear what they are saying else you can't respond because you're out of the moment. You'd have to ask them to repeat. Anyway, I didn't pick up anything that seemed deceptive."

"But the hair?" Asked Dawson. "What about the hair?"

"Well look at mine Dawson. How does it look?"

"It looks fine Lisa I don't know what you're getting at."

"Yes, it looks fine. It looks OK. It looks normal. It looks like I spent the usual amount of time on it right?"

"Oh, I see where you are going. Her hair looked perfect, didn't it?"

"Yes, it did. Not a strand out of place. Her husband was murdered yesterday and the murderer was waiting outside of her home when she got home. That would be tragic and terrifying. That would dominate your thinking. It would certainly overrun your normal concern for your appearance. She knew she was going to talk to us so I can understand her combing her hair but it just looked perfect and I didn't like that. It was odd. But other than that, I picked up nothing and she just might be one of those people that always has to look her best."

"So really, we've got nothing," said Dawson.

"Yup that's correct, but not feeling really good about this yet. Thinking we need to ask more questions. When can we go to the hospital to talk to the perp?"

"They operated yesterday, he was awake this morning, let's roll." said Dawson.

Chapter 5

Dawson and Lisa were denied permission to interview Mells by the attending physician until the next morning. The next day they arrived early only to have to wait until Mells was fed, they assumed burped, and his bandages checked. His chart was discussed by the surgeon with his following flock of young, eager future docs. The flock examined the wounds with interest as the dressings were changed and stole glances at the chains attached between Mells uninjured leg and the bed. The chain was there to prevent him from making a daring escape the flock assumed. Mells sure as hell could not escape daring or otherwise. Mells would never run again but instead would use a cane and walk with a pronounced limp. Once he was back in prison, his former exalted status of super bad-ass would be reduced to "hey gimp, get me a cup of coffee." Wonder if he ever watched John Wayne movies on prison TV?

No, the chain was there because Mells would be charged with murder sometime that day, and the procedure called for him to be secured. Finally, as the flock of young docs spread their white coats and flapped out of the room, Lisa and Dawson entered.

The two detectives sat in hospital chairs on each side of the bed, so they could ping-pong Mells' head with questions. Hammer his emotions, trip him up. They sat looking at Draven Mells, the perp, the man-in-black, who got his ass kicked and was now recovering. Lisa had taken the lead in questioning with Mrs. Richert, and here it would be Dawson that took the lead.

"Wow man you have a lot of tubes going into you. The docs told me they had to give you a new knee. My brother got a new knee. Let's see what you got going on here." Dawson pushed himself upright in his chair and pointing at the different tubes and devices attached to Dravin. He named them, "well you have an intravenous line known as IV, a catheter and we know where that goes in don't we? I see they got a drainage tube in for the swelling they're running an ice machine to reduce your inflammation, at least I think that's what it does or maybe it makes margaritas huh?" With that, Dawson turned to face his partner and gave her a wink. "And you've got one of the CPM machines which will slowly move your new knee so that it doesn't lock up on you."

"Really got your ass kicked didn't you Dravin?" said Lisa

"What you talking about? That old fool just got lucky. Him using a board. Then me going to take it easy on the old guy and get kicked in the knee. Another lucky shot".

Ping. "Did you know he had a gun Draven?" said Dawson.

"He didn't have any gun."

Pong. "Yeah, he had a 40 S&W in the belly band behind his back. He said he looked at you and could tell right away what a pussy you are." said Lisa.

Ping, "That old man Draven? His name is Gunny. And he is old enough to be your father dude." said Dawson "Gunny said as soon as he got into that side yard that he could smell there was more pussy in that yard than just Rebecca Richert."

Draven's head was snapping left and right as the questions kept coming at him, and his temper was coming up. Precisely the intention of Lisa and Dawson. They kept hitting him with verbal lefts and rights, throwing him off guard.

"I'm going to get me a lawyer and sue that old bastard," said Draven.

"Draven, my man, you got bigger problems then a busted knee dude. We are here to get your side of the story. Now I don't want you to think that we actually need your side of the story." said Dawson

Lisa piped in, "Naah we are just here as a courtesy Draven. You know when we are investigating a crime we look for three things. Motive first, second means and third opportunity. Well you certainly had the opportunity because your

DNA is going to put you at the murder scene Draven so check that one off the list and the means? Back to the DNA back to that razor. Yup, we got that one checked off also. Finally, the motive, which we don't know and that could be, you're thinking, a hole in our case, right? But you see Draven, the jury is going to look at you and see the typical scumbag. They're not going to worry much about motive. We don't need the motive at this point. When we need the motive is trying to discover who did the crime but after we know who did the crime the motive just becomes a curiosity. "

"Here in this situation, for you Draven, the motive may be your friend." causing Draven's head to snap back to Dawson. "The motive could stand between you getting a life sentence or getting juiced in about 10 or 15 years, after all of your appeals are exhausted. Stand between you being in the general population or being in isolation. And you never know Draven, things change. Maybe we get some governor like AOC in another 10 years or so and she would declare general amnesty even for you."

Lisa said, "Why Dravin during the civil war they let any prisoner out of jail, even murderers. Both the North and the South did it. Just so long as they would agree to put on a uniform. That could happen Dravin. You in the Army instead of jail then after the war free and clear. I mean it's been done before. And we are never ending fighting those terrorists Dravin."

Ball over to Dawson, who said, "you probably had a traumatic childhood or something right? "

"But if you're dead nothing good happens Draven so we are willing to sit here and listen to your story." It worked. Dravin was nodding his head.

"She set the whole thing up. She used me. She manipulated me. I am a victim here." said Draven.

"Hold on Draven I'm going to have Lisa read to you your Miranda rights OK? Now you know after that she will have you sign the Miranda statement. You been through this before. Remember you are entitled to have an attorney present and in this case, it would be a public defender. And I can tell you right now that what the public defender would say to you is to just keep quiet. And you can go that route."

Lisa said, "I kind of like that route Dawson. Maybe that is the way he should go? Because if he goes that route in about 10 years, long around my retirement time, I can get down to the big house in Huntsville and attend his execution which I would really enjoy. What do you think? Ever been to an execution Dravin? Big party all night long outside the prison. Like a UT-Oklahoma tail gate party. And then at the appointed time? Everybody starts singing," Lisa pointed to Dawson, and together they sang," Boom, boom, boom. Another one bites, Another one bites, Another one bites the dust."

"That is true Lisa. But maybe Draven isn't fully responsible for this. There is an off chance that the Richert woman pushed him into it maybe he is a little bit of a victim here." saying this for the benefit of Draven Mells, working his psyche.

"Go ahead Lisa give him his Miranda rights," which she did then had him sign the Miranda statement.

"Do you still want to talk to us Draven or should we allow Lisa to schedule her retirement party to coincide with your execution?"

"Yes, I want to talk to you and I am a victim you got that right that needs to come out in court. Maybe I can get away with time served, huh?" Clearly showing what a dumb ass he was.

"Draven the details are very important here." said Dawson

Lisa followed with "the details are going to make the difference between us believing your statement and a jury believing what you say and you getting who knows what instead of an injection. But you're starting from pretty far down. Right now, your credibility is on a level with Harvey Winestein." She let that sink in then followed with, "We have to compare what you say with what Mrs. Richard says. Going to take a lot of convincing Draven. So, answer our questions in all of the detail that you can OK?"

"Were going to go to the very beginning Draven. How do you allege that you first met Mrs. Richert? And we are going to record everything you say OK?" said Dawson placing a voice recorder on the stand next to the bed.

"It was on Facebook. She reached out to me with a friend request. I had never heard of her and I have no idea of how she found me. She was always evasive when I asked those kinds of things."

Lisa asked, "you are friends on Facebook? We have her computer Draven and access to all of her accounts so we will be able to find that, understand?"

"Yes, that will be good. We didn't stay on Facebook for long though she had me install a messaging app on my phone,"

Dawson asked, "where did you get the phone Draven?"

"She gave it to me."

"So, you met her?" Asked Lisa

"No, we never met physically. She sent me the phone. It is the phone you have taken from me. An iPhone, a brand-new one. Buying that kind of phone told me she had some money. And I like that."

"She sent it to you where Draven?" Asked Dawson

"To the halfway house where I was staying after I got my parole. I did' t know how to use it but I went to the iPhone store and they helped me to register it and explained everything about it. "

Lisa made a note to trace the origins of Draven's iPhone to see where it came from

"Let's explore that Draven," said Lisa.

"In detail, how did you first meet her?" said Dawson.

Draven spent the better part of the next hour answering questions from Dawson and Lisa and giving the details of his relationship with Rebecca Richert.

The interview concluded Deputy Dawson and Lisa walked out of the hospital towards her car. "Is that true about that Civil War murderers getting out of prison?" asked Dawson.

"How would I know? "said Lisa.

Dawson chuckled, "that was terrific, really got him going, took me aback to."

"Yeah just came up with that on the fly. And you joined right in. Very cool."

"We should take our act to the Jimmy Kimmel show, "said Lisa

"Naah, two cops? His audience would burn the place down, "said Dawson.

As they got into the car, Dawson noted that Lisa had stopped laughing about the Civil War ruse and was deep in thought. He waited for her to speak.

"For a man like Draven that has spent his life lying I picked up no sign of deceit at all," said Lisa. "He believed what he was telling us was the truth as far as I could tell."

Dawson responded with, "we have his phone and we have access to that computer that he was using at the halfway house where he claims that he met Mrs. Richert the first time."

"Yes, and that is what bothers me. Even an idiot like Draven would know how fast we could catch him in a lie having his electronics. And then there is still the hair. That just won't go away Dawson."

Dawson slowly sucked in his breath, thinking about what Lisa had just said. "You're getting me a little worried here Lisa."

"You know Dawson I feel like instead of closing out this case we've just started to open it up. Maybe we'll get back and find out we were wrong that Draven is dumber than a CNN anchor. And that there is nothing on his phone or at the halfway house computer to give credence to what he told us."

Now it was Dawson's turn to hesitate before speaking. "Lisa this is starting to look like" he wavered before finishing, "like a mystery. And I hate mysteries. "

"Me too Dawson." said Lisa, pausing, planning, and continuing, "I guess we need to go report in and tell the LT what we have found. See what he says."

"Let's hold off that until tomorrow morning. Think it over. But I do want to get the phone and computer into the Austin P.D. Technicenter. See what they say. Should be pretty easy for them with having the passwords. With the lab report we can give a more complete picture to the boss. Agree?"

"I do," said Lisa.

"By the time we run to the Technicenter and do the drop it will be on to Six. Oscars on Weberville Road opens at six. Beer thirty?" asked Dawson.

"Soon as we drop off the stuff at the lab and goose their asses," replied Lisa. And I came in off of vacation to provide you the benefit of a superior mind, so the first couple are on you."

Dawson nodded, wondering why beers with his partner sounded better than going home to his new hard-bodied girlfriend. Getting enlightened was hard work. To him, it felt more like getting beat up.

Austin PD Headquarters is on 8th street near downtown. It is a modern structure with one brown five-story concrete wall tilted at an angle away from the main entrance. Apparently, the purpose of this wall is to place multistory posters on the wall with public service announcements such as one with a picture of a young officer, and the slogan Tickets may hurt, but crashes kill. Click-It-Or-Ticket. Yeah, I know, but they are trying and hell they got almost a half-billion budget, and something has to cover that god awful brown wall. Then again, if they rented a cherry picker and hired some of those terrific graffiti artists, it would be more in Austin's spirit. Don't know, Austin?

I grew up here. By the way, I am a fifth-generation Texan whose ancestors helped get food into the Alamo in San Antonio before Santa Anna surrounded it. My folks tell me that Austin, real Austin, died with the Armadillo World Headquarters, a cheap nightclub, that allowed dope-smoking. It was a real hippie hangout where most patrons sat on the floor, rocked to country music, and got stoned. It closed around 1980 and was replaced by a 13-story high rise. The transition from dope-smoking, beer-chugging, carpet sitting, Rock & Rollers to people in business casual working in high rises tells you all you need to know about Austin both then and right now. Austin is also distinctly liberal right here in the heart of Texas. Weird huh? Which, for your further enunciation or maybe the word is edification, it's one of those I think, means learn new stuff. Lost my train of thought. Oh, yea, I reread this, and the weird part is that the unofficial Austin city motto is Keep Austin Weird. I am making my contribution.

Back to the after-action report, boys and girls.

Lisa and Dawson shared a cubicle in the homicide department at police headquarters. The homicide department is identified by a dark gray sign hung prominently at the entrance with the word HOMICIDE in bold, large font, in case anyone thought that they might be where traffic tickets were paid. Between them was a divider that came up to just below shoulder height. Lisa had the advantage of having a series of windows on her left, but the view was only parking lots, so it wasn't much of an edge. The department detectives all operated in pairs, and each pair sat side by side like Lisa and Dawson. Each pair of partners was separated from the other pairs by a cubicle wall that arose to above head height when seated but allowed them to stand up and be seen by other detectives. On Dawson's right was a small aisle that allowed the detectives to move between the paired cubicles and hold an impromptu meeting. The short connecting passageway had an opening that allowed passage to the main corridor. Then out to the elevators or at the end of the hallway, they could enter the Lieutenant's office.

Lisa drove her own car to the hospital that morning, beating Dawson to the office with him stopping for breakfast tacos. She grabbed a cup of coffee, black no sugar then fired up her computer. Displayed was the completed lab analysis of the computers and phones for Mrs. Richert and Draven Mills. She had read the reports not once but twice, the second time more slowly, looking for something to explain what she was reading. She was intent on her task when Dawson surprised her. He heavily plopped down, leaned over the divider, and said, "what cha doin Lisa?" with the remains of breakfast tacos showing on the corner of his mouth.

She pivoted her head, gestured to the corner of her mouth, which Dawson took to mean he had some taco remains on it. As he used the flat of his hand to clean the taco off, then lick it into his mouth off his palm, she said, "Just finished reading the reports from forensics partner."

"And?" said Dawson.

"Well, everything Draven said would be on his computer and on his cell phone is there."

"The suspense is killing me Lisa," said Dawson

"There is absolutely nothing on Mrs. Richert computer or phone to match the records on Mells."

"Well she could have deleted the files from her computer," said Dawson, "but she could not have deleted them from her phone as the phone carrier keeps all the texts. We can subpoena that."

"Yeah she could have deleted the emails files etc. from the computer but the forensic people see no sign of her having done that and they electronically tore her hard drive apart. There is software called shredders which will completely erase the contents of the file but even those are not foolproof and they leave kind of a digital fingerprint so you will know if they were used. And they weren't, so say the geeks. "

Lisa sat with her head half turned towards Dawson, still glancing back at her computer screen where the reports were still open. "You know how Mells said that the Richert woman didn't look like he expected? Well the pictures that were supposed to be of her on his cell phone were of a woman that bears a close resemblance to Mrs. Richert but I don't think it was her." said Lisa.

"So, you're saying what?" said Dawson.

"I don't know what I'm saying Dawson. Let's go chew this over with the Lieutenant. See if he can give us some Yoda kind of guidance".

Lisa and Dawson were in the Lieutenant's office seated in chairs across the desk from the Lieutenant, who was leaning back in his chair his arms above his head, fingers interlaced perched on top of the little bit of hair that the Lieutenant still had.

The Lieutenant had been briefed by the Lisa and Dawson and said, "What we need to do here is to clear Mrs. Richert. That is if she should be cleared. Where are we at on getting copies of her texts from her cell phone provider?"

"They know it's a murder investigation Lieutenant and they promised to expedite. Maybe later this morning." said Dawson.

The Lieutenant considered how he wanted his detectives to proceed what Lisa called 'giving Yoda advice.' Both Lisa and Dawson had respect for the Lieutenant and his years doing just what they were doing now. He said, "I'm thinking after we get the files from the cell phone provider and if there are no texts on Mrs. Richert's phone that confirm the perp's story." He paused, pursing his lips, making a kissing sound then continued. " Well then, we still need to take the pictures that where on Mells phone, do some print outs and take them over and show them to the Richert woman and see if she has any explanation."

"And while you guys are waiting for the texts from her cell phone provider I want you to check back and see how this guy ever got paroled in the first place. When the press checks that out somebody's asses will be on the line. Don't let it be ours."

"God don't let it be that Richert woman was involved in this," mused the Lieutenant saying it out loud but really just thinking.

"Boss I think we should go back to the hospital and see what Dravin says when we tell them there was nothing on the Richert woman computer or phone. Get his reaction. And another thing I am curious about. Dravin said that the Richert woman gave him the cell phone. I think we need to try to find out where that phone was originally purchased. It is after all an Apple iPhone."

"Set you back like a thousand bucks. And those guys track everything." said Lisa laying out for the Lieutenant actions that she saw as necessary for the case.

"Apple might cooperate," said Dawson, "they are kind of nutso on the privacy thing."

"Well we are not trying to crack the password, we have the password, we just want to know where it was bought. So, I think they will help us there." said Lisa.

"OK so we have a plan of action," said Lieutenant Dahlby taking his hands off the top of his head leaning forward in his chair and giving his instructions. "To review, first, you're going to the hospital to confront the perp. Second, you're taking the pictures over to the Richert woman and see what she says but you're not going to do that until you have the text messages from the cell phone provider. Third you're going to find out what happened with this parole and fourth see where and by who the cell phone was purchased."

Lisa had written down each of the commands from the Lieutenant, making a to-do list. Both Lisa and Dawson shook their head yes, stood up, walked out the door, and back to their cubicles.

Yoda had spoken.

Elizabeth Ponti, CJ's Personal Assistant, was sitting at her desk. From it, she had a sweeping view of the office. She surveyed her domain while drinking her morning coffee, taken with cream, no sugar. Not that she didn't want sugar. Every time she went for a refill, she looked at the little sugar packets at the coffee urn. Resist, she thought. My waist and ass sure don't need the calories. In her mid-fifties, Elizabeth was a widow for almost ten years in good but not excellent physical condition. She wore her blond hair, dyed blond to get rid of the gray; short parted on the left with a slight upturned wave at the end. The haircut exposed the lower half of her ears and often sported diamond stud earrings, not zirconium, but real diamonds. She dressed sensibly. Casual but feminine tops, maybe a light sweater. Today the sweater was a dark off yellow and black pants. Black pants always hide a few pounds; so, goes the thinking.

She liked CJ and felt motherly protection towards him. And CJ's dad Gunny and she had started to see each other as she would say. This consisted of getting together, usually at one of their homes, eating dinner, maybe some wine, and watching a British detective show on BritBox. Gunny didn't press to watch John Wayne. In the past, he had learned that women would tolerate The Duke's movies even like them sometimes, but a steady diet of them could sour a relationship. They had advanced to the kissing goodnight stage. Gunny's wife, CJ's mom, had died unexpectedly in 1982 from an automobile accident when CJ was eight years old.

Elizabeth's phone twirled, signaling a call had been received at reception for CJ the boss. Only a select few got to call CJ's direct line, which was changed regularly to assure a limited set of people had it. The receptionist, having gotten Elizabeth on the line, told her she had a woman on the phone that said she was calling CJ to confirm their lunch date.

Elizabeth was puzzled. She personally handled CJ's schedule, and there was nothing on today's schedule for any lunch. She was used to salesman calling and using all kinds of dodges to get past her to talk to CJ. The salesman didn't bother her. She knew it was their job to try to get to the decision-maker to make a sale. But this was a new one. She decided to take the call.

"Elizabeth Ponti," she said, answering the call.

"Hi Elizabeth," using the name Elizabeth like she knew her, "this is Briana Kemper. I want to talk to CJ about our lunch. Is he available?"

"Good morning Ms. Ponti," using Ms. instead of the Briana to establish that this was a no-nonsense allowed kind of place. "I am CJ's Administrative Assistant and I have nothing on the schedule about any lunch with you." Saying it politely but not friendly seeing what would be said next.

"Could you please tell him that his jogging buddy is calling. The one that he says runs with a cat on a leash. And I am calling to see about getting that lunch that he owes me." said Briana, not deterred by Elizabeth's attitude. After all, she was owed. A promise is a promise and no weaseling.

"Please hold a minute and let me check. I'll be right back to you".

Instead of buzzing CJ, she got up from her desk and walked over to his office, where the door was open as it usually was. She peeked in saw CJ looking at one of the two computer monitors and sat in front of him on his desk. She tapped lightly on the door frame. CJ pivoted from the computer monitors that he was looking at to face Elizabeth. He dropped his chin down and raised his eyebrows, indicating he wanted to know what she wanted.

"CJ, I have a woman on the phone that says she is calling about lunch. There is no lunch on your schedule unless you scheduled it without telling me," a tone of slight disapproval in her voice because she was in charge of the schedule. If he was going to do things outside of the plan, he needed to tell her, or else how could she do her job?

Elizabeth continued, "she said she is your jogging buddy and that she runs with a cat on a leash?"

A smile spread across CJ's face, and he told Elizabeth, please put her through.

CJ waited for Elizabeth to start heading back to her desk, then he picked up the phone, punched the button that was blinking, and said, "I thought you would be out dog shopping today."

Briana replied, "I thought we agreed that you were going to lay off of my dog, remember?"

"Yes, we did, but after you told Elizabeth that you were the lady that jogs with a cat I just kind of ran with it. Or I guess I should say jogged with it?"

Briana smiled to herself. He was playing with her. Joking along. This was good, she thought. "So, can I cash in my lunch chip today? The one you issued on the jogging trail after insulting my dog."

CJ glanced at his schedule on the computer that he had pulled up as soon as he got Briana on the phone. He was pretty open all the way until mid-afternoon, and the things that he had on his schedule, he thought he could get Elizabeth to just shuffle those around some. He said, "yes I would like that. When and where?"

"Before we do the when and where I need to ask you a question."

"OK," said CJ slightly taken back. Waited for the question, really wondering what it would be.

"You're not married, right? And you don't have a live-in girlfriend, also right?" Briana was just not going to start this if it had nowhere to go. She didn't need a free lunch. And she didn't need to start liking a man that was not available. That never went anywhere good. So, she knew, and all her girlfriends knew.

"Correct both times. No wife. No live-in. And you? CJ thought she was good to get this out of the way, and he would follow suit. Might not go anywhere. Might not even like each other. But if he or that is he and she did like each other, then better to know up front that it had someplace to go.

"No, I don't have a wife or a live-in girlfriend," she said toying with him. "Oh, you meant husband or boyfriend, didn't you?"

"No," said CJ "you got it right no wife or girlfriend," playing it back.

This is fun, she thought. I like this guy already. "Back to the When and Where. Where is your office?"

"I'm North of Austin in the 300 block of Grace".

"That's near Panther Creek Nature trail, isn't it?" she asked, trying to place Grace street in her mind.

"It is." said CJ

"You like to eat outside?" she asked.

"Very much. You OK with Panther Park after us finding?" CJ didn't finish the sentence thinking she would fill in the rest, which she did.

"Good with me. I didn't actually see the body just heard about it. As I said then I am not going to let that stop me from using the park. There's no benches that I know of so I'll being a blanket we can sit on and you can go to a sandwich or even a salad place and grab lunch. Plan?"

"Plan. 11:30 or so?" said CJ

"Yes. Whoever arrives first just text the other to let them know. By the way that number you gave me when we were standing around with the cops? It just rang to your office."

"Yeah, I know. Next time enter 7663 as soon as it answers and it will skip everybody and go to me."

"How about a text? How does that work?" she asked.

"Same thing but prepend 7663."

"Whoa," she said, "Prepend. We have a vocabulary, do we?" happy, teasing again, hopeful.

"No. It was in the instruction booklet that came with the system. I had to write it a hundred times on the chalk board." CJ teasing back, enjoying it, wanting to stay on the call.

"Sounds like your administrative assistant made you stay after class. See ya CJ"

"Hold on," he said. "What kind of sandwich or salad?"

"Surprise me." She said and disconnected.

Both CJ and Briana had small smiles on their faces after hanging up.

Chapter 6

Lisa took the job of finding the scoop on the iPhone. According to a Goggle search, she might see when it was purchased by going to an Apple site called CheckCoverage then entering the iPhone's serial number. How do you find the serial number, she wondered? Another Google search said it was in the settings under the General tab, and there it was. She went back to the CheckCoverage page and entered the serial number, then the little Captcha thing with the scrambled numbers and letters, which prevented robots from using the site, it was claimed, but also prevented many people from a, shall we say, pleasant user experience?

The result was no such phone exists. Lisa rechecked the serial number and saw that the letter O she had entered was actually a zero. She should have known because it had a tilted horizontal crossbar never mind that in the 12 digits serial number, there were only two numbers. She sighed, shaking her head and entered the serial number again. Success! She now knew that the phone had a valid purchase date. What that date might be was not revealed. What the hell, she thought all of that to get to a big green check mark on a web page.

The Web search said to go to the Apple Store, and another thread said to find an Apple Genius, which she thought was anybody that could enter the mile-long serial number the first time. The web page said an Apple Genius could give the information about when it was purchased and trough what chain like Best Buy or something. She didn't know any Apple Geniuses. Hell, she didn't know any Apple Semi-Smarts either. She looked up the Apple store in Austin, and there were two of them. She picked the one in Barton Creek Mall at the intersection of Loop 1 and Mopac expressway. She checked the store hours, then stood up, told Dawson what she was up to, and headed for the Mall.

At Barton Creek mall, she parked at Nordstrom, might as well see if anything was on sale, mixing just a touch of pleasure with business. She went straight through Nordstrom, straight down the sizable typical mall aisle with bright displays on mannequins on the left and right and to the Apple Store. Goggle had told her what Apple calls a Genius is called either a tech or sales support at other electronic stores. But if you are going to pay Apple prices and get almost forced into buying an upgrade every few, what seemed like days, you should be entitled to support not from any old basement-dwelling geek but from a Genius. Steve Jobs gave an afterlife thumbs up.

The store was busy and had a little sign-in pad. Lisa could have badged them, but that might scare them and get a genius to ask a supervisor what to do. Genius in tech areas are often mentally challenged in other non-technical areas. Lisa didn't want the supervisor. She wanted an Apple Genius that she had created a mental (liberals, please close your eyes and skip to the next paragraph else prepare to be shocked), profile for. Late twenties or so, not fit, fleshy, maybe going bald, and male. She saw several candidates but damn if the girl who read her name out of the queue didn't fit. Lisa, being a trained investigator, maneuvered on the spot. She waved her off, telling her she needed to answer an email and that she should take the next customer in line after Lisa. Smart move. Up came the genius that still lived in his parent's basement.

They walked back to his computer monitor and workstation, and he asked how he could be of assistance. Lisa took out Draven Mell's iPhone, placed it on the table between her and the genius, and left her hand on the phone. She then invaded the basement-genius personal space by leaning in, looking him in the eye, tilting her head and flashing a great smile. The Internet search said that the genius would be able to tell you the purchase channel if he opened a repair ticket. Still smiling, Lisa said the phone would not seem to stay connected to WI-FI, that the battery seems to drain fast, and the screen freezes. She got all of these complaints from an Internet search. She thought that putting three together would inevitably result in a service ticket getting opened.

The basement-genius said he would see what was going on. He needed to get some information from the phone, reached for it, putting his hand on Lisa's, who said that she was sorry and removed her hand. Invade the personal space, smile, tilt head, open eyes wide, force a minor physical touch. She had him. He blushed and opened the ticket. While he connected the phone to his computer, she said it had been a gift and wondered where it was bought. He read the monitor and told her it was purchased at Amazon. That's all she needed. Her attitude changed, telling him she needed to come back as her husband had finished teaching the Muay Thai kick-boxing Master class and was waiting to meet her. She needed to go now. She unplugged the iPhone and was out of the store heading back to her car with the slow down as she walked back through Nordstrom. Darn, no sales. But she thought she had given basement-genius something to think about. She knew what basement-genius would be up to in the basement that night.

Back at the office, she got onto her computer. Dawson was not there having left a note saying he would talk to a contact about the parole that Dravin should never have received. Lisa found that Amazon responded only to a subpoena sent to Corporation Service Company MC-CSC1, 300 Deschutes Way SW Suite 208 Tumwater, WA 98501 Attn: Legal Department – Subpoena. Hmm, she thought. Must get a bunch of them. She wrote out the request form giving her reasons and went to find a judge. This signing was pretty easy, and she was back within an hour with the subpoena and had a service in Tumwater, WA, serve it on Amazon.

Nothing more she could do until Amazon responded.

She checked, and the cell phone provider had sent all the text messages from the Richard's women's phone. They were just as empty of anything related to Draven Mells as her computer had been. So much for any theory of her having deleted things. She didn't want to confront Mells without Dawson. Still, she could go see Mrs. Richert and confront her with the pictures. Lisa was sure they were of someone other than Mrs. Richert, but some things you need to do, even knowing it was a waste of time. Or else some sharpie defense lawyer might use it against you to put a killer back on the street as long as either the killer's check cleared or it would enhance the lawyer's reputation so he could land a big rich scumbag client like Bernie Madoff.

Briana had arrived first, found a spot that was partially in the shade of a mature Mexican white oak tree, and spread out the checkered blanket that she kept in the trunk of her car. She had picked a spot that allowed her to watch the cars pull in and park though so far hers and one other were the only ones there. Briana watched as something big, black and boxy with massive, deeply treaded tires crunched across the blacktop. It had enormous headlights, and she assumed what were additional LED lights on the roof just over the windshield and an exterior black iron piping on the front that curved over the headlights and onto the hood. It demanded a parking spot and stopped. She half expected Chewbacca to get out, but no, it was CJ. She waved at him, he waved back, turned back and reached into the vehicle and brought out a bag containing, she assumed their lunch.

He walked up, smiling dressed in a black polo shirt, jeans and hiking boots, and wearing a baseball cap, not turned backward. Thank god, she thought. "Nice spot," he said, settling down across from her, looking at her and taking everything about her. She wore a light blue short-sleeved chiffon top with a bow tie built into it so that when tied, it gave more of an air of professionalism. She wore jeans, not the expensive skinny jeans that Rebecca Richert wore but skinny jeans non-the less that she had bought for under two hundred bucks. She hadn't tied the bow tie attached to the blouse. It dangled down in front, and she hadn't tucked the shirt into her skinny jeans so that it extended over the jeans. She looked from CJ back to the thing he drove and said, "What the hell is that thing you drive?"

CJ broadened his smile, raised one shoulder slightly in a semi shrug. He replied that it was a 1997 Hummer H1, the original Hummer, with a few extras he had added like the LED light bars. She asked if he drove that thing around town, and he nodded yes.

"Well it fits you to a Tee and I just love it." She said. "I drive a Cooper Mini. Can we swap sometime?" said with a slight grin. She tilted her head down and raised her eyebrows, waiting for the answer. CJ gave a small laugh and said, "Pretty tempting. Is the Mini a convertible?" That's laugh number one, she thought.

"No, but it has a white double racing stripe."

"Oh man, it just gets more and more tempting."

He asked where she was from, and she told him Chicago. He followed with what had brought her to Austin? She said to him that she took a U.T. course in advanced graphic design last year and found she just loved Austin. She thought about it for several months, decided why not, looked around for a job, found one, an easy thing in Austin, said smiling, and moved here just a couple of months ago.

"OK now your turn," she said

He told her that he had spent fourteen years in the Marines and decided to get out and go into the security business. His dad had moved to Austin after he retired from the Corp to take a job at Austin Community College as their Chief of Police. He was helped to get that Chief of Police job by a man that his dad had served with in the Marines. So, with the family connection, he had visited Austin over the years, liked it, saw that it had excellent growth potential and many high-tech companies. Those companies would be good candidates for his security company.

"What kind of security, like guards and stuff?" she asked.

"Well, we do offer body guards on a contract basis but these are all highly skilled special ops people. Almost always they are used when an executive is going to an area that may be dangerous or has a reputation for kidnapping and extortion."

"Really? What else does your company do?" said, leaning towards him, intrigued.

"Penetration testing."

Oh my god, she thought, is he hinting? The thought caused her to visibly blush and her nipples to become erect. She saw he noticed the blush and that his eyes moved to her erect nipples that showed trough her light fabric bra, which allowed them to push out against the blouse. His eyes immediately returned to her face, but having noticed his dropped eyes, her blush deepened.

"Penetration testing," he continued, and she thought, oh man, maybe he didn't notice. Or maybe I wanted him to? He was still explaining, and she had missed part of it. "And includes not only the geek side of firewall and internal I.T. checks, but physical testing of security at facilities. You know, can we get in and out without being detected." He had noticed her discomfort and also her physical reactions. Both the blush and the nipples and intentionally looped his response so she would not have to explain that her mind had gone elsewhere.

"So, how do you feel about bats?" CJ asked her.

"Bats?" she said, giving a small shake to her shoulders and a bewildered look. "That has to be the strangest question I have ever had on a first date."

"So, this is a date, not just lunch?" he said, smiling, playing with her.

She tilted her head to the left, thinking, you want to play, huh? "Well you said you weren't married and have no live in so I thought, out of compassion, I would allow you the illusion of going on a date because I am sure you really struggle to find someone willing to go out with you."

"Oh, so true, and so nice of you," he said, dropping his head and shaking it side to side, thinking he was really getting to like her.

"Briana," he said, pausing while she locked eyes with him.

"Yes?"

"How do you feel about bats?"

"Are you telling me that is a serious question?" she said

"Indeed, it is," CJ said

"A subject that I have not spent much time on. Why do you ask?" Briana said.

"You haven't heard about the bat colony that lives under Congress bridge in downtown Austin?" CJ said.

"I have not."

CJ told her of the nightly bat flights out from under the Congress bridge. That they were only there part of the year then migrated returning the next year to Congress bridge. That there were over a hundred thousand in the colony, and it was a magnificent sight to watch them fly out. It would be right around dark this time of year, but it is better if you get there a little early as bats don't follow any exact schedule. He asked if she wanted to go.

"When? Tonight?" Briana asked.

Oh yeah, she thought, he wants to take me out. She said, "Sounds cool. I'll go. Do you want to meet there or pick me up?"

"I'll pick you up," CJ said.

"In the monster truck thing? Is that what you would be driving?" she said.

"Nothing else," he said.

"Oh, hell yes, " she said, grinning from ear to ear already running through her wardrobe. Her phone started beeping.

"That's my timer. I have to get back." Both of them stood up. He helped her fold the blanket and commented that they had forgotten to eat. She told him to save it for the Bat cave tonight and gave him her address. They set a time, and she impulsively, and a little out of character for her, pushed up on her toes and gave him a light kiss on the cheek.

They were two happy campers on their way back to work.

In the great state of Texas, the parole system works like this:

1.)The Parole Division of the Texas Department of Criminal Justice identifies offenders six months prior to their initial parole eligibility, and four months prior to subsequent review dates, and directs the case file to be pulled for review.

2.) Notice is sent to trial officials, victims, and victim family members.

3.) An Institutional Parole Officer (IPO) of the Texas Board of Pardons and Paroles interviews the offender and prepares a parole case summary for the Board.

4.) The offender's file is sent to the designated board office for review and vote by a Parole Panel.

5.) A panel consists of three voting members, and a majority of two votes is needed for a final decision.

6.) Voting is sequential, with one-panel member recording their vote and passing it to the next panel member.

7.) If the first two votes are the same, the vote is final.

8.) If the first two votes differ, the third-panel member reviews the case and breaks the tie.

9.) An interview with the offender is at the discretion of the Parole Panel member, as are interviews with individuals in support or protest of an offender's release to Parole.

10.) Parole Panel members must grant an interview to victims, as defined by statute, upon request.

11.) Offender is notified of the Parole Panel decision via correspondence.

12.) A denial will include the next review date.

13.) Approval may include special conditions.

Dawson knew this as he, like most detectives, usually requested that he be added to the notification list, number 2 above, for any of the scumbags he sent to the big house. In Texas, the Big House is Huntsville State Prison, where Lisa had told Mells that she could attend his execution party. Dawson put himself on the notification list so that he could pen a letter saying why they should not get parole though a couple of times he had wrote saying he thought a certain felon should get a parole. He kept that quiet around the office.

Dravin Mells had been sentenced to the maximum for second degree armed robbery, which in Texas is ten years and a $10,000 fine. The fine? Good luck with that one. But the ten years? On average, in Texas, you, well surely not you, but

Dravin, the scumbag criminal that beat an old woman with his gun for seventeen dollars, would serve 58% of the time. And that was a hell of a break because he should have been charged with first degree aggravated robbery. That will get you life until AOC becomes Governor of Texas. At that point, Texas will have had enough and try seceding again. Draven had served for 18 months. Something very wrong here as Dawson had told the Lieutenant in their first conversation on the matter.

Dawson called the Parole Board and got to the Institutional Parole Officer, number 3 in the above list for those of you that like detail and for the great majority of you that lost interest in the list and skipped it after number 2, 3 at best. Caught you, didn't I? Dawson asked the Parole Officer, Alfredo didn't-catch-the-last-name, to pull up Draven's file. Dawson and Alfredo did the chit chat dance while waiting for the computer to spit out the data, during which Alfredo asked what Mells had been up to. Dawson told him murder, and Alfredo expressed his shock and sadness that another inmate had not been rehabilitated by the system.

Alfredo said the file was up and give him a second to review it. A few minutes later, after Dawson had asked Alfredo if he was still there, Alfredo asked Dawson in a high tight voice to hold the line. Dawson held and held and held. Finally, the Parole Officer's supervisor came on the line.

"Detective you still there?" asked the supervisor.

"I am."

"Well what I am looking at here is the greatest cluster-fuck I have ever seen in my twenty-eight years with Parole. Actually, it is beyond that. We've released people early before but never like this."

Dawson listened to the supervisor and took notes making him go back to clarify points. When the supervisor finished talking about Dravin Mells' Parole, he requested that Dawson keep it confidential until an internal investigation could be run at Parole to see how this happened. Please, he implored Dawson, don't let the press get hold of this till we figure out what happened.

Dawson sat stiffly in his chair and reviewed his notes. He cupped his hands in front of his face and rested his chin on his thumbs. Mells phone and computer had the pictures and texts that he said would be there. Mrs. Richert phone and computer had none of them. Her computer hadn't been wiped, so said the techs. He saw that a response icon was flashing on his monitor, and he clicked on it. It was the cell phone company's response with the last six months' worth of text messages from the Richard's woman's phone. He spent the next forty-five minutes reading through them. Nothing. Usual stuff and many back and forth with her husband were mostly normal, but a few were loving. Man, and wife stuff. Dead end there for Mells.

As soon as Lisa got back, they would go to Mrs. Richert's house, show her the embarrassing pictures of a woman that looked like her, and quickly eliminate her. Then zip back here and bring the LT up to speed. But that would have to wait because the Lieutenant popped out of his office, pointed at Dawson saying, 'We have an active shooter at Sand Beach Park".

Chapter 7

Briana stepped out of the shower, having washed her hair and body, she now stood in front of the large mirror that was made partially opaque from the condensed steam hanging like a warm fog bank in the bathroom. Her hair, wrapped in a plush towel, was piled on top of her head, waiting for the blow dryer and comb to shape it. She was naked, looking at her body in the mirror, making judgments about herself. She had a flat abdomen with distinct indentations on the sides of her abdominal muscles. Her waist was small; hips flared out as did her upper torso accenting the tiny waist. She had a long neck, made to showoff jewelry her Mom had told her. Her eyes wandered over what the mirror revealed, stopping, and looking at her breasts. Her breasts were medium bra size 34C and had that perky quality where the nipples pointed slightly up. Once when she was in college, she saw the old movie Body Heat starring Kathleen Turner. In one of the scenes, Kathleen Turner exposed her breasts from the side, giving the audience a riveting view. While watching that movie, Briana realized that she had Kathleen Turner's breasts and that Kathleen Turner was considered extremely hot.

Briana wanted to keep bouncy breasts for as long as she could, so being a natural problem solver, she researched the subject. Unfortunately, there were varying and contradictory advice on how to keep your breasts perky. Most of the advice was common sense relating to staying healthy, don't smoke, don't drink to excess, exercise, the usual. It also said to buy a quality sports bra when you run, but don't worry if your breast bounce, so she did just that. Another article stated that too much lift in a bra would make the breast muscles lazy. When you took the bra off, lazy muscles mean saggy breasts, so she tried to not wear a bra whenever possible.

She needed to make some decisions as to what to wear. CJ would be picking her up in a little over an hour, she thought so she needed to get a move on. She picked out a green lacy bra and matching panties. Maybe a bit sexy for a date going to see bats flying out of the cave, but surely that would not be the night's end. The bat flight started at around 8 o'clock at night, and in Austin, that meant it would still be rather hot. She chose loose-fitting faded Blue jean shorts that were short but not really short and for the top a sleeveless green T-shirt that exposed her waist. She would wear flats and a pair of sunglasses that were large and had pronounced white rims. A really casual look for a really casual date. She dried her hair, did her makeup, then dressed in her shorts and a sleeveless top, looked in the mirror, and was pretty satisfied with the way she looked. She was never delighted with the way she looked, but this was OK, she thought.

CJ arrived on time and knocked on the door. He didn't sit in his truck and text her to tell her he had arrived, he didn't sit in his truck and blow the horn, no, he parked and came up to her apartment and knocked on the door. Polite. She liked that. Briana opened the door and checked him out. She liked that their outfits matched. He was in dark cargo shorts with a white Polo shirt with CJN displayed discreetly above the pocket, no flats, wearing hiking boots that looked really rugged. She pointed at the boots and said that they matched his truck. He smiled and said they were Lowa Camino G.T.X. Heavy-duty hiking boots that had been recommended by his dad. She asked him if he wanted to come in and have a drink first or if they should go, and he said they better get going to make sure they could get a spot.

She grabbed her Kate Spade Cameron Convertible crossbody purse, slung it over her shoulder, and headed out the door walking towards CJ's Hummer. CJ was directly behind her heading around to the passenger side just like she was. When they arrived, he used his key fob to unlock the truck. The truck didn't give one of the little tweets when it was unlocked like most vehicles do, but instead, it made a growl. CJ reached in front of her and opened the door for her. More polite, she thought and gave a little smile. CJ went around the truck and got in the driver's side.

"Your truck growls when unlocked?" Briana asked.

"Yeah, I saw it on line so I bought it and had it installed. I think it's cool and fits the Hummer."

"I think it is hilarious and man it does fit this truck. It is so cool." She said. "Does it make any other sounds?"

"Well when low on gas it makes a stomach rumbling sound." He said

"Really?" she said, pivoting her head towards him with an incredulous expression.

"Ahh, no, not really, but if you like that I can do another on line search and see."

She dropped her shoulders while still looking at him and pursed her lips and said, "While you are searching for that, can you find a belching sound when you finish filling it up?

"I could. How about a yawn when it is running long stretches of interstate?" he countered.

"My turn?" she asked. "If a check engine light comes on can it sniffle?"

The custom truck sound discussion lasted halfway to the Congress Avenue Bridge parking lot, pleasing them both with the other's humor. They filled the second half telling each other about where they went to college and where they had lived aside from Austin. Her list being short and dominated by Chicago, and his list being extensive. She was captivated by the summers on the Apache reservation. She told him she wanted to hear all of the details. And also about his time in the military. She said to him that she felt like Dorothy from Kansas compared to him. He asked if that was where she got the idea for her breed of dog, like Toto in the Wizard of Oz, teasing her. She pivoted in the seat, raised her arm, and gave him a shot in the arm. Both happy. Having fun. Hoping.

They were standing close to the middle of Congress bridge. The flight had not started yet, but the crowd was growing. It was still hot, and CJ had asked her if she would like ice cream or a Coke or something from the vendor trucks in the parking lot.

She told him sure that she wanted whatever he was going to get for himself. He asked her to hold their spot while he went down and got the Cokes.

While she was waiting, she was approached by a man that started to talk to her. Briana was used to getting hit on and knew how to handle it without being rude. The man asked her if she had ever seen the bat flight before and she told him no. He wondered if she had been there when all the cops were up at Sandy Creek Park just to the North of Congress bridge. She shook her head no and asked what happened. He told her that some lady had shot and killed one or two people then turned herself in according to the radio. Happened along about lunch today. He was surprised she hadn't heard. She told him she seldom listened to the news and worked out of her apartment on a project all afternoon.

Briana was standing leaning against the rail looking out over Lady Bird lake that Congress bridge crosses. The man was standing sideways facing her. Maybe a bit too close, but she let that go. The man saw CJ approaching them about 20 yards away carrying the sodas. He said to be Briana, "Look at this guy, a slightly smaller version of Dwayne the Rock Johnson." The man trying to be cleaver.

She said, "Maybe slightly smaller and maybe a little stronger."

The guy stopped looking at CJ and turned his head to look at Briana. A few seconds later, CJ stopped right next to them and handed Briana one of the sodas. He stuck out his hand and said to the man, "Do you two know each other?" CJ did not look upset. He looked confident. Good, she thought, protective of his date but not one of the nut job jealous types. She had dealt with those types before, and it was not fun. Truth be known, it was one of the motivations for her to leave Chicago.

The guy took CJ's hand and shook it, mumbled his name telling CJ that no, they didn't know each other he had just talked to her and he better be leaving now so he could rejoin his friends. CJ just looked at him with a slight smile and shook his head then said, "enjoy your night."

The crowd on the bridge continued to grow, now starting to push in on them. CJ put Briana in front on the rail and placed his arms on both sides of her standing behind her. She could not help but smile. He told her he thought the bats would fly soon. Leaning over her right shoulder, inhaling her intoxicating perfume, he asked if she would mind if the two children standing behind scooted up and stood in front of her. She told him that would be fine. CJ motioned to the kids to come in front. Then leaned over her again, catching more of the perfume, and asked if it would be all right if the Mom came up. CJ told her the Mom was shorter than she was and so she would still have a good view because you mainly look up at the flight. Still smiling, she turned to him and winked and said, "of course she can." Add compassionate to polite, she thought but was caught up in the view. The first of the bats started to emerge and soar into the air. The flight growing in numbers, flooding the sky, climbing up and away, looking like a fast-moving low hanging dark cloud against the late evening twilight. It took the one hundred thousand or so bats just over forty-five minutes to finish their exit to find their nightly meals.

They didn't talk at all during the emergence of the bats. When it had trailed off to almost nothing, Briana turned around to face CJ, looked up at him smiling, and said, "That was just terrific. So, what do we do next?"

He told her if she liked they could go to a restaurant and eat or if she wanted they could go to his place on the lake and take the boat out. She asked him if it was safe to take a boat out at night. He told her it was quite safe he was experienced, and he had spent a lot of time doing various activities in the dark. He also told her if she was uncomfortable going to his house, they surely didn't have to. They could go to eat or listen to music or something else if she had something else in mind.

CJ told her that he lived on the lake and that the boat was on the Marina at his lake house. She asked him if maybe she should go back to her house and pick up her car so she could drive herself home after the boat ride. He told her she could do that if she wanted, or he is happy to drive her home, or she could call Uber, whatever she wanted.

CJ lived on Lake Austin in a two-story 2300 square foot home in the Villas of Rough Hollow. He gave her the tour of the house, including the Blue-lit swimming pool that came off the outside patio deck with the Marina's view where CJ stored his boat. During the tour, Briana asked CJ, in a rather matter of fact manner, if he was rich as she guessed the home at over a million. She was close as it went for a cool million and a quarter. He told her he was not wealthy but was maybe closing in on it.

"Security business is good huh?" she asked.

"Have you read the headlines? You can hire a contract killer in Philadelphia for under five hundred bucks. Just pay the Benjamins, give the name, and bam."

They sat on the patio, sharing a bottle of Gary Farrell Hallberg Pinot Noir 2016 while and looking at the night sky. They had decided to drink wine and talk instead of going out on the lake. She told him she wanted to wear her new bikini when she went out on the lake to wait until they could go during the day. She assumed that he wanted another date. She sure was. She told him she liked his house, but frankly, it was not what she expected him to be living in. He told her he agreed and that it was a temporary thing. He said he had bought a lot on the lake and that he and Gunny, his dad, would do most of the construction themselves. That the construction would take a good bit of time, and he would have to be squeezing it into his schedule when he could so he had this place in the meantime, then he would resell it.

They finished the bottle, and he asked her, "You go for another?"

"I could but then the only option would be Uber don't you think?"

"Yes, I agree. I don't take any chances with that." He told her scoring more points adding responsible to the list of his attributes which now were in no particular order, good-looking, great physique, polite, intelligent, good sense of humor, playful, protective but not jealous, kind, compassionate and responsible. She didn't add rich. She didn't see that as a virtue. She was rich, family money, and she didn't think that gave her virtue. But she did add, after thinking about it, not rich to the list but an entrepreneur, a go-getter.

He stood and went to the kitchen. Briana said, 'Wait, I'll go with you. I want to see the selection."

He had a Magic Chef combination wine and can dual zone wine cooler that was about 35 inches high. They both crouched down in front of it with their knees touching to see the bottles and choose. Briana looked at the selection acutely aware of his closeness. She turned and looked at him, their faces only inches apart. He was staring at her face. He reached up and brushed a strand of hair out of her face. She put her hand on his shoulder and ran it lightly over his front deltoids. CJ moved his hand from her hair to the back of her neck and gently pulled her to him. They kissed, softly, closed mouth then standing together they continued to kiss, opening their mouths exploring, their breath becoming shallow. She pulled away, thought about it for an instant, then went back to him, placing her hands around his neck, pulling him down to her. She broke it off again with her face inches from his and said, "I don't think you showed me the bed room on the tour."

CJ asked, "Do you want to see it now?"

She didn't talk just nodded then was back on his lips, hungrier, more urgent as passion arose in them. She felt his arm go down around her below her rear to the back of her thighs. He raised her up, cradling her in his arms, still kissing. Raising her as if she had no weight at all. He carried her to the bed and laid her down, lying next to her. Each worked on the other's clothes wanting to get to it, burning, needing. The first time went fast them both needing to get some of the heat off. The next went slower and more satisfying. The third was the best yet. She heard him say to her at some point during their night in the bed that he thought she was marvelous. She discounted it, writing it off to passion, but deep in her mind, she hoped that it wasn't just the passion, that he was falling for her because she was falling for him.

The next morning CJ watched her get out of bed as the early dawn brightened the room. He feigned sleep and watched her through slitted eyes. She dressed, panties, shorts, and top but no bra. That she left on the floor. Then she went into the bathroom, came quickly out, and sat on the bed.

"CJ are you awake?" she asked.

"I am. I have been watching you." He said.

"You have? Oh, good grief I am a wreck and you were looking?"

"You look great baby," he said, calling her for the first-time baby.

"Do you have a spare tooth brush?"

"Yea they are under the sink. Help yourself. I'll start coffee, OK?" he said.

They sat across from each other, chatting, familiar, talking about the bats again, the house he wanted to build. She looked at the time and said she should call Uber as she needed to get home and get changed for work. He told her he would drop her off on his way in. He asked her if she was going to put her bra on before he took her home.

"You noticed huh?" she asked.

His eyes dropped to her breasts, causing her nipples to respond just like in the park. She told him her theory on going braless whenever she could to keep her breasts looking as they did now for as long as she could.

"Well it sure seems to work, the perky business." He said.

"Do you mind the bra less thing?" she asked.

"God no." He said, dropping his eyes to her breasts, causing the nipples to swell and ache. "How long do you have before we have to get out of here?" he asked her.

"A while yet," she said, understanding the real question. She looked at him, watching his face, his eyes. She reached down, crossing her arms in front of her, taking the sleeveless shirt by the sides, and pulled it up over her head, throwing it to the side. She pushed her chest out to show her breasts in all their beauty, thinking this is how Kathleen Turner did it in Body Heat. She said as he stared at her, "I even have PTO time coming. Any ideas?"

She took her PTO day, CJ called in and said that it was a boss off day. Elizabeth had to scramble appointments and was not happy. Unlike Elizabeth, Briana and C.J were delighted. They were also diligent about their responsibilities, remoting into the office several times.

Chapter 8

Weeks before Dr. Richert was murdered, Catherine Nervy had been identified as a high possibility candidate. Not the only candidate, by far, but one with a high possibility of compliance to requests. This had accomplished by first creating multiple groups on social media sites. Then populating these groups by creating multiple user accounts through the use of software commonly called bulk bots. What bulk bots do is to first create email addresses. The email accounts are monitored by the software. Then, with the email addresses, they create the user accounts on a social media site. Each user account was populated with pictures that were harvested from various sites on the Internet. Then through the use of these thousands of accounts, they cross populated each other. They send invitations to other false accounts and add them to their friend's list. This creates an entire interconnected group of nonexistent 'people' in a group and groups within groups. The software then does fake postings from the phony user accounts that look like actual people interacting. Acting like an enormous deep-sea fishing net trawling behind a boat catching real people in it. But these virtual fishing nets were designed to lure certain types of fish. Once in the net, those candidates were tested with ones that failed being ejected and ones that passed becoming more entangled in the web of falsehoods.

To make the identification of these accounts as false other computers were probed and when found vulnerable infected with a virus that went to sleep and would wake up on command and create several accounts. By affecting and using thousands of infected computers as hosts, each computer's unique IP address never appeared more than a few times, effectively masking false accounts.

The group that Catherine joined was an on-line support group for the surviving victims of childhood abuse, specifically sexual abuse. Many reputable groups exist to help people who have been victims of childhood abuse. Still, it was essential to find people who would join an on-line group. In-person meetings were not possible as there were no actual people except for Catherine and others like her. The activity, specifically the postings, in the messaging activity within the groups, were closely monitored. It was essential to have one of the false accounts begin messaging to the candidates such as Catherine. That would establish an individual relationship that was used to further screen the candidates and then start to push them into the desired direction. The whole ruse was accomplished by using artificial intelligence, which used an algorithm based on Bayesian inference. What this did was examine essential criteria. Such things as prescriptions the candidate was on, a history of therapy, a willingness to discuss the abuse, and, most importantly, a volatile personality that could be manipulated.

Catherine fit the bill. She had established an intimate relationship with another woman she knew as Martha. The latter was not a real person but part of the software responding to Catherine by way of the messaging application recommended by the social media platform. The same messaging app that Dravin Mells had been responding to when he thought he was communicating with Rebecca Richert. Martha had told Catherine that she used a wheelchair, a victim of sexual abuse, and physical trauma so severe that she could no longer walk. Martha told Catherine that she lived in South America and was aware of many other children being systematically abused by wealthy Americans. Martha complained to Catherine that if it was not for her physical impediments that she would do something to stop at least one of these abusers. But she could not, because of her situation, even though she had identified them.

Previously software Martha had begun to see if Catherine would comply with requests starting with small ones and escalating. At first, Catherine just made postings in the group. Then at Martha's request, she began writing letters to the police and others vehemently protesting their apparent apathy towards this problem. Martha would give Catherine a nudge and see what she would do then escalate the knowledge again, watching what would happen. Software Martha felt, it was not a feeling but the crossing of a probability threshold by the computer algorithm, that Catherine was now ready to be launched on command. If Catherine refused to do the final nudge, she was only one of five identified as first-tier candidates. If not Catherine, then one of the other four, and if not them, there was a second tier to choose from. Other real people were regularly swimming into the net. The algorithm said with these many candidates, they projected a 98% chance of compliance.

The not real Martha, the one that was just software, delivered the final push to Catherine. Martha, who claimed to live in a city in South America, said she had been contacted by children that she knew and found them all to be terrified because their services would be needed in the next couple of days. The most terrible of all, the American abuser, had booked a flight and booked them. The abuse would be life-changing. They had begged Martha to help them in any way they could, but she was wheelchair-bound and could do nothing, and the authorities ignored her because they had been paid off.

Catherine asked what she could do and said she would do anything to help these children to save them. Martha asked her how committed she was to save innocent lives from life scarring abuse? Catherine responded again, saying she would do anything. Catherine had been off of her prescription drugs for her depression and paranoia for some time at the suggestion of Martha, who told her these drugs were designed to keep her controlled so that she would never reveal in any detail what she had gone through. Catherine had believed her.

Software Martha give the final push as soon as the Austin Police radio network broadcast about a murder on the Canyon Creek trail and the Austin American Statesman named Dr.

Richert as the murder victim. The second operation was now in progress and being monitored.

Catherine Nervy sat on a bench at the entrance to Sand Beach park in downtown Austin near the traffic loop at the intersection of Electric Avenue and N. Lamar Blvd. Sand Beach park has scenic trails that run along the Colorado River, and its proximity to City Hall and to corporations with downtown Austin locations make it a popular park for picnic lunches and noon joggers. One such corporation within easy walking distance to the park was Cunningham Industries H.Q. It was also near The Marriott Hotel, where Catherine stayed the night before, expense be damned, as she would soon not need money. And near Austin Police Headquarters, which would shortly become a beehive of activity thanks to Catherin and was currently where Detective Dawson sat less than a mile from her as he worked on the Richert murder investigation.

She had a picture of the monster that was heading to South America in the next few days to torture and molest the children that the software Martha had told her about. She sat and watched. Waiting for the pervert who, Martha told her, left his office most days around noon for his jog around Sand Beach park, often accompanied by a woman. The woman that didn't matter to Catherine. She was a lawyer in contract law at Cunningham Industries and like the target in her early forties. On those days, they didn't jog; they checked into the same Marriott that had housed Catherine and burnt their calories in other ways. Both were married. Neither cared. They would have if they knew how deeply the reporters from The Austin American Statesman would look at their lives. How the affair would be leaked and damn the emotional damage to spouses and kids. The publics' right to know trumping innocent victims. Circulation of newspapers was tanking, don't you know?

The alleged child-abusing monster, Elon Chong Ph.D., sociologist, and his running mate ran around the traffic circle and towards Catherine. Catherine spotted Dr. Chong and stood up. Just like our old pal Dravin Mells stood directly in the middle of the running path. She pulled the big Smith & Wesson Bodyguard 38 from her handbag and, at a distance not over five feet, shot Dr. Chong in the heart. Then turned to the screaming lawyer now with blood splatter of her lover on her face. For good measure, she took a shot at her as the lawyer must have known what a monster she was associating with. It's not so easy to shoot a boomer like the big 38 if you haven't been diligent about practice which Catherine hadn't been. The shot missed the lawyer but not the thirteen-year-old boy who had skipped school and carried his skateboard across the park. Catherine was utterly insane now. Ignoring the child, she killed in Austin while trying to save the South American children. She stepped up to Dr. Chong, who was seeing a white light but still living and at the one-foot range shot him in the head.

The screaming and running of everyone that heard or saw the shooting was immediate. One woman ran onto Lamar Boulevard without looking, getting plowed by a Blood and Honey brand beer delivery truck. She died eight hours later at the hospital. Catherine would have been sorry to hear that, but was over the edge and would never again join us in the at least semi-sane world. An interesting aside, not at all pertinent to the story is that Catherine would be released 13 years later from the North Texas Hospital for the Criminally Insane, return to Providence, live on the streets and die from a drug overdose. Guess software, Martha was not so supportive after all.

After finishing off Chung and the subsequent collateral damage deaths of the boy and the fleeing woman, Catherine lay down her gun. She placed her hands into the blood-soaked chests of Dr. Chung. She ran the blood through her hair, went back for another soaking, and then onto her face. All the while loudly proclaiming the alleged sins of Dr. Chong that had been reported by software Martha. This action was recorded in detail by several adventuresome U.T. students on their cell phones and hit the Internet faster than cheap pizza through your intestines.

Patrol arrived, SWAT arrived, ambulances arrived, the Press arrived, Dawson arrived. After the snipers zeroed on Catherine's head, SWAT yelled for her to get down on the ground and keep away from the gun. Two SWAT officers in the modern-day equivalent of a knight's suit of armor approached her, kicked the gun from her side, and handcuffed her. Her being blood-covered from both the blood splatter recoil and her hand painting of herself, the cops had the paramedics check her over after checking Dr. Chung.

A discussion with the supervisors ensued about whether to bring her to Police Headquarters or to the hospital. Not sure if she was hurt or not, she was transported, under police guard, to the hospital where she was physically examined then cleaned up. The E.R. doc knew a crazy when he saw one and called for a psyche evaluation. The psyche evaluation result sent the tragic Catherine Nervy into the system and never into the hands of law enforcement as she was adjudged insane beginning her journey to her life's end on the streets near where she was born.

Things could not be going better for the software named Nudge that had created software Martha. It erased all the group's records that Catherine had been in moving the other real people in the group to other groups for possible future use. The algorithm had no routines that simulated a human High-Five. No celebration parties, no early Happy Hour just zeros and ones flying over circuits moving to do more mayhem that Nudge was designed to do with the help of Social Media, cell phone trackers, and false reports on Twitter, to name just one of the dozens of postings that found their way into the legitimate Press. The Press was in total speed competition to get a story out, right, wrong, verified, rumored, whatever. No time was available for fact-checking, that was so 1990s and beside the whole industry is circling the drain. Go, man, go. Might be a Pulitzer prize out there. Pulitzer quit fact checking long ago ask Janet Cooke and The Washington Post.

Chapter 9

Lisa and Dawson sat in Lieutenant Dalby's office. Dawson and Lisa had been at the scene of the shooting at Sand Beach.

"This is tied together L.T.," said Lisa looking at him as he sat leaned back in his chair hand under his chin scratching at the beginnings of whiskers. He didn't reply, so Dawson took the opening. "We need more help boss."

"Yeah, I know you do. I already taken to the Captain and he is pulling Surf and Turf off the streets and putting them in here for the duration." said Dahlby. "They are on the way from their homes."

Undercover drug officers Frisco Cantú and Odel Tillman had worked the streets of Austin for two years, each specializing in different, shall we say, market segments of the drug scene. Frisco specialized in the hipster scene netting college kids and some executives though the later and sometimes the former had high dollar lawyers that often could find a crack in the system, and if not get them off, then get the charge pleaded down. Frisco liked to look cool casual, sporting loose-fitting khakis and floral shirts worn outside the pants with any of an assortment of straw fedoras he owned always worn at a jaunty angle. He wore a short, well-trimmed black beard with black hair that he greased into a bun under his fedora and various necklaces and bracelets. He always wore Birkenstock's to round out the cool-as-hell image. Hence the moniker Surf.

His partner, Odel Tillman, was more of the workingman type, so he specialized in methamphetamines and fentanyl, and man was that business good. Odel looked like either a bouncer at a Country and Western bar or a Country Baptist preacher, the two having a strong resemblance in hairstyles and builds. He wore cheap western shirts with button fronts. Boot-Cut jeans also cheap. And three-thousand-dollar brown and blue Lucchese Drea Distressed Floral made-to-order boots. The boots sport spiraling interlaced hand-hammered dual-toned sunflowers. Every other day he swapped them with his other pair of Lucchese Drea Distressed Florals, those in the bright red and blue pattern. Deciding on a single floral design had been too much for Odel, so he bought them both. You would think this would have resulted in the bestowing of the sobriquet of Cowboy on Odel, but no the Lucchese boots so obviously displayed won, so it was Turf. Get it? Turf is another word for ground. Am I going to fast?

Surf and Turf liked being on the drug squad, but it was a dangerous business, the most vulnerable in police work. Both had been in officer-involved-shootings, and both were cleared. But both were family men, and their wives watched the news and worried that Surf and Turf might shoot some drug dealer who had a gun one day. The drug dealer's gun might be deemed to have been an insufficient match for the 15-round capacity Glock 22 that Surf and Turf carried. In today's alternate universe, don't forget that Austin leans farther and farther left, out gunning a drug dealer might get you fired. Or maybe go to the Big House with no chance of an early out, being cops and all. Back in the ancient past, the wives of cops used to worry about them getting shot or hurt. Not now.

Politicians are looking and wondering why the cops don't just wing the guy in the leg or maybe be like the Lone Ranger and shoot the gun out of the guy's hand. Such questions show what dumb asses that politicians are with zero experience in anything that counts, which makes them qualified to be politicians. Oh, there are a few good ones, even a few great ones that are patriots. Still, in an after-action report like this one, I am not allowed to mention former Navy SEAL Dan Crenshaw, so I won't. Commentary over it's back to the report, we go.

Lisa said, "Boss before we switch our main effort I think we should take a quick trip out to Mrs. Richert house and show her those pictures. Make sure that we are correct in that she is not the woman in them and that she never saw them before. Close that door."

Dawson pivoted in his chair to address Lisa, "The hair? You given up on the hair?"

"Yeah," she said. 'She is just one of those that are always perfectly coiffed, I think".

"If you think we need to get that done first go do it and get back here. I'll get Surf and Turf busy reading through the Richert case until you get back."

"L.T. we aren't going to get anything out of the Sand Creek Park shooter. I tried to talk to her before they paramedics took her to the hospital. She is gone man, deer in the headlights, or more of a deer that doesn't know what headlights are." said Dawson

The Lieutenant shook his head and said to neither detective in particular, "Jesus did you see the video of her? With her washing her face with blood and screaming about child abuse and the victim she executed going to South America on the hunt for kids?"

"Get out to the Richert woman, clear her if you can, get back here and start digging. Assign Surf and Turf to whatever you want. We have an assistant D.A. on call if we need any help with warrants or anything that comes up. I'll be right here with you trying to not breath down your neck and trying to keep the Captain, the Chief, the Mayor and probably the President from interfering with you."

Lisa and Dawson gathered up the copies of the photos, called and confirmed that Mrs. Richert was home and headed towards the garage. They ran into Surf and Turf coming in from parking, they had ridden together, and all four of them turned around and went back to the Detective squad room. Lisa and Dawson talked fast telling Surf and Turf where they were going, directing them to read the case notes on the Richert killings, that the two killings were related it was assumed and that if by chance they finished the case notes before they got back to start on tracing the shooter's movements and the gun.

Surf and Turf saw this as their big break. A chance to get off the drug squad and into the detective bureau's relative safety a job they had earned. No more, or at least much less, worries for their families about being shot of screwing up somewhere and getting sent to jail themselves. They read fast through the Richert file and got started on the shooter's movements and where the gun had come from.

The Richert woman reacted to the extremely embarrassing pictures in a surprising way. She pointed out that the woman in the photos had a small colorful butterfly on her left breast. Without prompting, Mrs. Richert pulled her shirt off and removed her bra, not asking to have only Lisa there, just doing it. She asked if either detective saw any butterfly. Both the detectives were taken back, which is hard to do, by the abruptness of the disrobing. As Mrs. Richert put her bra and blouse back on, she asked if they were satisfied, she was not involved and could now get on with her life. They told her yes, they were satisfied.

In the car heading back to the squad room with Lisa driving, Dawson said to her, "Man I never thought she would do something like that did you?"

"No," said Lisa, "I guess the perfect hair don't mean much huh?" Both detectives were surprised that with their experience and two cases that were going to the National press, that something could happen entirely out of the blue that would surprise them even if it had no effect on the cases except to clear one person of any suspicion.

The National press was on the way to Austin to cover this sensational murder. The Internet video had blasted through social media being reposted again and again. It seemed everybody in America knew what happened. This opened the doors for Surf and Turf, making it easy to get people anywhere to talk to them. Any call from the Austin PD galvanized the person receiving the request to think they would have something thrilling to tell around the dinner table that night or at the local bar.

When Lisa and Dawson walked in and asked if Surf and Turf had gotten anywhere, they were told that they had the shooter's movements and the gun all traced. Dawson asked them to hold it while he got the Lieutenant in on this. The Lieutenant convened a meeting, including the Captain in the larger office on the next floor up.

All present and ready except for Lisa. The Captain, The Lieutenant, Dawson, and Surf and Turf. Surf and Turf had discussed it and decided Surf was the best presenter even though Turf could pass for a preacher. Dawson announced that Lisa was checking on something and would be joining shortly.

Turf delivered the verbal report then handed out the written version which follows:

Catherine Nervy was a Rhode Island resident and had a long history of mental illness and a spotty employment history. On several occasions, she had come to the attention of Providence PD for domestic disturbances and mostly petty fights. Though one time, she had to be disarmed when threatening her brother with a knife. No charges were filed for that instance. Instead, she was placed under the care of a psychiatrist. She claimed a history of having been sexually abused as a child. Still, no corroborating evidence could be found and the length of time since the alleged incident led the investigating officers to close the case without prejudice. Closing without prejudice means that the case is still active. The statute of limitations for child abuse in Rhode Island is 35 years, so the case was marked for a fresh look every year around the anniversary of it being closed without prejudice. No subsequent evidence had ever been found.

The day after the Richert murder, she sold her car. The day may be important because of the assumed link between the murders. Her brother, the same one she had threatened with the knife previously, had given her the car the previous year. Telling her to take the car and never darken his door again because he was sorry for what had happened to her, but she was too crazy to be around his family. She sold the car, a 2002 Toyota Corolla in poor condition, to Broad Street Auto sales receiving cash as she agreed to a 5 percent reduction in the offered price from the car dealer for giving cash instead of a check. She then took Uber nine miles to T. F. Green Airport and bought a ticket on Southwest Airlines flight 1199 connecting to flight 385, departing Providence at 6:30 PM, and arriving at love Field Dallas at 10:50 PM. On arriving in Dallas, she got a room for the night at Dallas Love Field Inn on Empire Central Dr. The motel is close to Love Field. It was also close to her destination for tomorrow, the gun show to be held at Market Hall on Stemmons Freeway in Dallas, which was less than a 15-minute ride from her motel via Uber.

The next morning Catherine Nervy went to the Dallas Market Hall gun show arriving at the opening at 10 AM. The gun she used was purchased at the gun show.

There is no background check for an individual to buy a gun from another individual at a gun show in Texas. You just walk in and buy it. If Charles Manson, The Boston Bomber, The Sandy Hook killer, The Menendez brothers, O.J. Simpson, El Chapo Guzman, or a weak misguided and deranged tragic person like Catherine Nervy wants a gun, the requirement is money. That's it. If politicians were serious about slowing the use of firearms in America instead of using headline-grabbing lines like 'no high capacity magazines,' or 'no military style rifles' they could take steps to end this one thing, but you see that would not get the desired effect which is publicity, not gun control. The preceding paragraph is not a part of the after-action report per se. Instead, it is an editorial by Geraldo Rivera CJ's company archivist and a gun owner and backer of the Second Amendment. Did you forget that I am writing this?

The report continues: Catherine purchased a used Smith & Wesson M&P Bodyguard 38 Crimson Trace for a cool thousand dollars, overpaying for a handgun that sells for five hundred new, but what did she know and what did she care. The gun was initially purchased legally by a background-checked purchaser at Bass Pro shop in Dallas. Bought by a salesman named Floyd Swank, who traded it several months later when sales commissions were slow to his mechanic who resold it to his buddy that had the booth at the gun show. The gun booth guy remembered Catherine when shown her picture by the Dallas PD because she knew nothing about guns and because she was a little squirrely and high strung (dealer's exact words as reported to Dallas PD). Still, she had the all-important cash, so the deal was made. She asked the seller at the show what would be the best ammunition for 'personal protection.' He told her that his preference was the Hornady XTP. She asked where to get those, and he said Bass Pro or Cabela's or Academy, to name a few. She told him she was catching the bus to Austin and if they would have any of those near the bus station. He did a Goggle search and told her that Academy had a store on Brodie lane about 15 minutes via Uber from Downtown Austin.

Catherine left the gun show and took Uber to the Greyhound bus station at 205 S Lamar St, Dallas, TX 75202, which is less than three miles from Market Hall. She caught the 12:30 bus to Austin, paying $30.00 for the ticket.

The bus driver has no memory of her. In Austin, she took Uber to the Marriott downtown at 304 East Cesar Chevez. The clerk that checked her in remembered her because of what the clerk called a disheveled appearance and no luggage except for a large handbag. She had the clerk call a Taxi, not Uber for some reason, and went to the Academy store where she is on video purchasing the ammunition for the gun.

The next day she apparently walked from her hotel to Sand Beach park about mid-morning. So far, we have not been able to locate anyone who saw her there before the shooting. The Providence PD at our request obtained a search warrant for her computer and have sent it to us via overnight priority.

This information about Catherine was gleaned from interviewing Catherine's brother, the management of the car dealership in Providence that bought her car, Southwest airlines information on the flight she took, the motel in Dallas where she stayed, the motel in Austin where she stayed, the gun dealer in Dallas, and the Uber and taxi drivers plus the surveillance videos from the Academy store in Austin where she purchased the ammunition.

After the presentation, the Lieutenant thanked the detective and asked Dawson, who was still the lead, what he saw as the next steps. Dawson stood and walked to the front of the table to address the group.

"Well the good news is that we have two murderers and have both the murderers in custody. The bad news list is long. We have no idea of their motives. Mells had things on his computer that implemented Mrs. Richert but we have cleared her. How and who put that on Mells cell and computer? The Bureau of Parole has no answer for how Mells got the parole except a possibility that either they were hacked or it's an inside job which they are looking at but discounting."

Lisa slipped into the meeting and took a chair. Dawson continued after she was seated. "Back on Mells if the Richert women didn't tell Mells where an opportune place was to find her husband so that he could be murdered who did? Mells couldn't have just wandered around and found him. If he followed him to the Canyon Creek trail, he would have had to jog behind him, which doesn't make sense and doesn't match the crime scene. By the way, Mells is sticking with his story, and his Public Defender is right there with him.

On the shooting at Sand Beach. Catherine Nervy was shouting about the vic that he was a child abuser and on his way to South America to do it again. She yelled that he was a regular there."

At this point, Lisa held up her hand and waggled it so she could add to the narrative. "I was able to trace the passport usage of Elon Chong, the victim and he has no record of ever going to South America. I was able to access his financial records and he was until recently up to his eyeballs in debt. A Vegas regular like twice a month and more. Appears to have been a compulsive gambler and with that PhD and working for Cunningham he must have made mucho dinero. I said until recently because he has paid off all his outstanding debts."She let that get digested.

Dawson turned to Lieutenant Dahlby and said, "Well boss we have our murderers. She is off to the nut house and will never face trial and the only choice still to be made with Mells is what degree of murder to charge him with. We investigated Mrs. Richert and can show that. The Parole problem is not ours. I guess what I am looking for here is if we should pursue this motive thing more to plug some holes or just close it and go with what we got."

The Lieutenant punted, turning to the Captain and saying, "What do you think Captain?"

The Captain said, "God I hate mysteries," to which everybody nodded. He followed with, "Let me talk to the Chief and I'll get back to you. Meanwhile snoop around a little more."

"Should we go to Cunningham and talk to them?" asked Surf, breaking peeking order protocol.

"Wouldn't hurt. But just background information unless they say something that opens it up. OK? That's it." said the Captain

Chapter 10

CJ and Brian Anna had talked about taking another PTO day both half serious half kidding, and both decided they just couldn't do that. CJ was sitting in his office, having gotten in not so bright and not so early as Elizabeth noted. She stood in the open doorway to his office and tapped on the jamb. CJ looked up at her from reading paperwork on his desk and raised his chin, indicating she should talk.

Lawrence Cunningham is on the phone, and he wants to make an appointment to see you as soon as possible. He also wants you to bring Gunny. She said.

"Did he say what it was about? And why he wants me to bring Gunny?" said CJ

"He said he would tell you when you got there and he emphasized he wanted to do it as soon as possible. He's still on the phone waiting for the answer. As to why to bring Gunny Mr. Cunningham said that he had never met him and wanted to thank him personally for intervening to save his daughter".

"What do I have scheduled?" asked CJ

"A couple of meetings. Do you want me to put them off?"

"Yes," CJ sat thinking, and Elizabeth watched him knowing he hadn't finished talking yet. "Tell Mr. Cunningham we will have to call him back then called Gunny and see what time he can make it, OK?"

"Will do boss. And CJ?" said Elizabeth looking at him intently, "Are you OK? You seem not quite here today. Not a bad not here but still different. That is really unlike you. Something going on that I should know about?"

"No Mom," said CJ with a smile, "I feel good." He smiled and raised his eyebrows, widening his eyes. "I feel way past OK." Another pause, thinking, then, "Do you and Gunny think you might be free this evening for a company dinner? I have to check with someone first. Ask Gunny when you get him on the phone, OK?"

Elizabeth tilted her head to the side, looking at CJ, wondering what was going on. She told him she would do that and went to the phone, then turned and came back before she reached her desk and said, "CJ I bet Gunny is not home. He is probably still at Muay Thai practice. Maybe I should wait like fifteen minutes?" CJ raised one eyebrow looking at Elizabeth, thinking how well she knew Gunny's movements. He half shrugged his shoulders in ascent.

Fifteen minutes later, Elizabeth was tapping on his office door again. "Gunny said to give him forty-five minutes. He just got back from practice. He also said that he didn't need to be thanked but if you require his presence he was happy to go, you know, earn his paycheck and all. He said as for dinner tonight he is always up to spend your money. He wants to know if you want to go to Stubbs for ribs. He wants to know who all is going."

"I'll fill him in on the way. In the meantime, please bring me in the Cunningham file. I want to reread the report on the software penetration testing that we did for them. Somehow, I don't think this is about that test but it might be and I don't want to get caught by surprise. I really don't know what this is about."

While waiting for the file, CJ placed a call to Briana, which she answered on the second ring.

"Hi CJ," she said, having his caller I.D. pop up on her cell.

"Hey Bree"

"What cha doin?" he asked, shortening his words.

"Thinking that maybe we should have taken that second day of PTO time. Other than that, the usual stuff. You know, *Working In The Coal Mine*," said Briana singing the title verse to the old song.

"Are you free tonight for some dinner? Maybe a double date?" said CJ

"Yeah I'm free, who would be doubling with?"

"Well my dad, Gunny, you said you would like to meet him, remember?"

"I did indeed say that. And who would his date be? He has a girlfriend?"

"Well he does have a girlfriend though you're not allowed to use that term with either one of them because they are not admitting it. And you have already talked to her."

"I did?" said with a question in her voice. "You don't mean the dragon lady, do you? The one I had to fight my way through to get you to go to lunch. Even though you owed me a lunch. Which by the way you still do because if you remember we never ate the sandwiches that you brought to the park."

"Yes, that's right. Elizabeth and you'll like her. She was doing her job that's all. She is to protect me from solicitors so that I can do my job."

"Tell me how will I be introduced? You know like colleague, jogging buddy, acquaintance, cat lady?" she said.

"I was thinking," and he hesitated, which she noticed.

"Thinking what CJ?" he didn't say anything, so she continued, "Tell me."

"Well," and he paused again, then continued, "Girlfriend. I would say that you are my girlfriend. Would that be OK? Or maybe cat lady instead. That does have a ring to it. Should we go with that?"

Now it was her turn to pause. "So, is that what I am? Your girlfriend? And that would mean you are my boyfriend? Is that where we are?"

"I am good with that. Are you?" said CJ

"Yep, I am good with that also." said Briana

"One thing Bree there is a dress code."

"OK and what would that be CJ?"

"Well this would be a bra night." chuckling as he said it.

"Aww. Really? Is that a must?" with her giggling back.

"You think you are disappointed? I am flat-out distraught. But you know. Convention." They set the time with CJ smiling broadly as he hung up. When Briana hung up, she stood up in her office cubicle, held her hands in front of her, pumping her fists up and down and making small jumps. Her coworkers in the surrounding cubes saw the little dance and wondered what was going on. One happy lady.

CJ had used the time after he hung up to read the Cunningham file and saw nothing in it that was out of the normal. They had performed a software penetration test. Essentially a way of determining if there were any security openings to allow unauthorized access by anyone into the computer systems at Cunningham Industries. They had found nothing and gave Cunningham a glowing report.

While on the drive over to get his dad, he ran through the report in his mind one more time. Had they missed something? They used the absolute state-of-the-art techniques and software. If they missed something that there is something brand-new out there that no one in the industry knew about yet. In software security penetration, business competitors shared information regarding security threats. They advised software vendors of any security holes they might find during the testing to get patched.

Arriving at Gunny's house, he left the engine running and blew the horn, which in the Hummer, with its customized sound system, came out like an air raid siren. Gunny trotted out wearing his company shirt, blue jeans, and the obligatory hiking boots matching what CJ wore except that their company shirts were different colors. Sort of like the tough man's dress for success outfit.

"What is this? What is this?" Said Gunny as soon as he closed the door to the Hummer. Said fast, running the questions together and smiling ear to ear. "Elizabeth lit up the phone as soon as you left telling me that we were going to double date tonight with you and your. And this was a guess on Elizabeth's part after watching you, she said, you were actually whistling at times around the office? Tell me it ain't so, a new girlfriend?" Looking affectionately at his son. "And if that's true I would just say it is about damn time. It's been too long since your last girlfriend CJ. Not normal. All work and no play. You know what I mean."

"You'll meet her tonight dad. And yes, I am happy to say her and I talked about it and she is my girlfriend which makes me her boyfriend. We have known each other for quite a long time. Like three days."

"Damn that long? What are you waiting for? Where are my grandkids?"

Switching the subject, Gunny said, "That guy that was killed downtown Austin. The radio said he worked at Cunningham just like other guy. Is that right?"

"Yeah, that's true, I wonder if this meeting has anything to do with those deaths? We did some work for them, standard penetration testing, nothing showed up. I asked Mr. Cunningham what this meeting was about and he told me he'd rather talk to me first and then have me decide what we could do to help him. All kind of mysterious."

They arrived at the Cunningham headquarters and parked the Hummer in the visitor parking lot backing into the space and taking up two of them. The Hummer just couldn't fit in one. Nobody ever complained about the Hummer taking up two parking spots because people made certain assumptions about someone that would drive a monster like the Hummer.

CJ and Gunny took the elevators to the top floor where Lawrence Cunningham's office was. Security had called ahead and was told to send them up immediately. Security quickly created a badge for both Gunny and CJ had them sign in and got them on the elevator. When they got off the elevator, they were met by one of Lawrence Cunningham's assistants and not shown into his office but taken to the executive conference room. The room was starkly modern, brightly lit with white LED's. The white light contrasting to the polished black accent wall having built-in shelving that contained a screen for projections. The conference chairs were highly polished chrome with off white fabric, surrounding a solid onyx conference table that stood on white and black marble pedestals. One wall of the conference room was all windows. There was no projector on the table but was one roof-mounted. The center of the table was a Bose

Vireobar VB1 conferencing device with six beam-steering microphones and a 4K ultra-HD auto framing camera.

Gunny pointed at the conferencing device and asked CJ if he thought anyone would notice if he cut the cords and stuffed it down the front of his shirt. CJ just shook his head. The door opened and in walked Lawrence Cunningham looking worn out, his shirt and suit wrinkled, out of character for the man that CJ knew. His assistant was with him. Cunningham asked CJ and Gunny if they would like some coffee or water or anything. Both shook their heads no, and they all took a seat at the conference table with Cunningham framed against the windows and CJ and Gunny sitting across from him.

Cunningham said while reaching across the table, extending his hand to Gunny, "Sir, I owe you a debt of gratitude."

Gunny shook hands then held his arms up, extended, with his palms facing Cunningham. "Sir I was happy to help. Frankly it was fun." Cunningham nodded his head and still leaning forward, shook hands with CJ

The meeting ready to commence, Cunningham seemed to shrink into himself, and he said that he was going to ask some others to join the meeting. That CJ and Gunny would hear quite a story. He turned to face his assistant and nodded to her to have the others enter the meeting. There were three of them.

The three entered the room while the door was held by Cunningham's assistant, who left the room and closed the door behind her. There were two men and one woman. They took seats flanking Cunningham with their backs to the window. Cunningham did not introduce any of them, nor did they introduce their selves. They had folders with them that they laid on the conference table, and each popped open a small laptop. Both CJ and Gunny watched the interaction between Cunningham and these three. They did not seem to be deferential to Cunningham, which indicated they were probably not his employees. CJ determined that the two men were wearing off the rack suits, perhaps Brooks Brothers not the cheap ones but the upscale Brooks Brothers still costing under $1000 each. They all wore white shirts, including the woman, and the two men wore rep ties with one of them having a nautical crest pattern in it. CJ figured them for government employees probably G.S. 11, 12 or 13, which would put their salary at maybe 90,000. He knew if they were spooks that worked for the C.I.A., the pay was probably unnecessary because many spooks are independently wealthy and just in it for the thrills.

Cunningham spoke first, "CJ," he said, looking directly at CJ and then pivoting his head to look at Gunny; he continued, "Gunny we are going to tell you about a project that we have been working on here called Nudge."

The un-introduced woman spoke up, "we need both of you to acknowledge that what we are telling you is top-secret and you are bound under penalty of law to not reveal anything that you hear here. Do you understand?" Both Gunny and CJ said they understood. She then asked them if following the restrictions, they were willing for the meeting to continue, and they both also said yes. She produced a document and had Cunningham bring back in his assistant. The assistant was a Notary Public, and she brought her seal. The woman had CJ and Gunny sign the document in front of the assistant, who asked both of them to produce their driver's license. She examined the licenses and noted them in the notary book. She asked what the document was and was told by the woman to write just government documents, which she did, then she left and closed the door.

Cunningham spoke again after the notary had finished and told them that they needed to understand the project's background, how it was developed, and what it was intended to do.

Next nautical-tie-man was up. His eyes moved from CJ and Gunny down to his laptop screen. They assumed nautical-tie-man was reading his notes. He looked up and speaking to both CJ and Gunny said, "Please bear with me. Some background information will help. All humans have tribal tendencies because we are social animals and herd animals. We join all kinds of groups, religious groups, sports teams as either fans or participants, professional associations. We like to locate people with the same sexual proclivities, hobbies, alumni associations, beliefs, and shared experiences like veteran groups. The list is endless. We have always been that way, and we will always be, which means being tribal and herd animals is built into us.

Now the third team member spoke up. "Yes, and this herd instinct, this tribal membership at least in the first world and quickly following, I might add, the rest of the world is now dominated by the Internet. Meaning that is where more and more people find the tribe or herd that they identify with.

Let's bring another factor into this discussion. There are two examples I want to give you that have to do with the Internet and groups. The first is a company, a rather famous company because of their cash prizes named the Publisher's Clearinghouse. No doubt, you've seen the commercials where they gave away a lot of money sometimes during Super Bowl halftime. When ads like that were their primary focus, they used mailing lists for their solicitations. They used U.S. postal mail, to try to interest people in buying magazine subscriptions and also returning questionnaires. People didn't even know they were filling out a survey, which was the solicitations brilliance. Those questionnaires are gold because it takes an effort to return the questionnaire. You would have to go in, remove little stickers and put them in individual boxes, etc. All kinds of psychological tricks that bond you into Publishers Clearing House. This created human herds for Publishing Clearing House. The herds were then segmented into groups as to how long they had been returning the solicitations and what effort they put into moving the stickers around etc.

Today they've gone digital on the Internet but still pretty much use the same tactics that is they gather lists of people that will send back in envelopes with questionnaires and also people that will go on-line and click certain boxes. As long as these people are engaged, the Publisher's Clearinghouse can sell them something. They know that people who fill out questionnaires or move little stickers to receive a cash prize fit into a group. They also know that if they continue to engage these people, a certain amount of them will eventually buy something. It is a very profitable business.

The second company is Amazon. They do something similar. They have what is known as a recommendation engine which, when you buy something, puts a list of other things with small pictures of them, the images are essential, and it says something like people that purchased this purchased that. Seems like an easy thing. It is not. It is expensive and takes a lot of computing power, so is it worthwhile? Amazon reported a 29% sales increase using the recommendation engine."

Nautical tie-man took over, "Back to groups. Most groups are socially beneficial or at least harmless. But some groups are not, and it is those groups that we were interested in for Nudge. The 80/20 rule or the Pareto Distribution tells us that in any group of people, 20% of the group is responsible for 80% of the activity be in sales, income, fund raising whatever. If we were looking at a group such as Al Qaeda, we would need to find the 20% that control group. Members of destructive groups have psychological profiles that closely resemble addictive behavioral disorders. Knowing this, we can create a generic profile saying that we are looking for people with behaviors similar to addictive disorders.

If the goal is, as it was, to not locate a group with the characteristics that we need, but to create such a group, the solution has been handed to us. Social media is the most significant psychological experiment ever conducted, and no one knows how it will turn out. However, the preliminary conclusions are all bad. Social media encourages people to join groups because social media is financed by advertisements and advertisers.

Like Amazon, these advertisers want to get their message in front of someone that meets a particular set of characteristics. A buying profile or a joining profile whatever we were looking for. The social media platforms like to see dissent and arguing because that causes engagement and gets clicks. It stirs the emotions and keeps people on line either yelling at the other side or encouraging their like-minded friends. It is the opposite of reasonable dialog, the opposite of looking for a compromise, the opposite of trying to see other points of view. When you are emotionally charged as an individual or as a group, you make decisions based on your emotions' heat, not on your rational reason. You lose the ability to see the world as it is. Social media breaks down epistemology. The dangers of such widespread anger and its encouragement have no precedent in history."

CJ held up his hands, 'I get it. You create groups on social media, no doubt with fake profiles and pictures, then see who joins then fire them up. I assume they locate these groups through keyword searches?" he sat for a few seconds thinking, and nobody spoke, then he continued." And your cost is near zero once the software is written."

All three team members nodded. Gunny said, "After somebody is in the group then what? You have a person in the group meet with somebody that is someone you are interested in?"

CJ answered, "No Dad, I bet they use software bots to start messaging back and forth," looking at the three who all nodded and smiled. "You know what a bot is Dad. Like those irritating, Press 1 for this option, 2 for that but much more sophisticated, right? And because it is typing the answer the voice is no weird sounding voice problem. And because you are virtual no messy in-person meetings, right?"

Again, with the head bobs. CJ stopped again and looked directly at Lawrence Cunningham." Sir do you think your own software, what Cunningham Industries developed killed, or manipulated the murderer into killing your son-in-law Dr. Richert?"

An ashen face Lawrence Cunningham with moist eyes nodded his head.

"What happened?" CJ asked. "Was the murder down at the park also by this Nudge software? Is it still running? Why haven't you shut it down? Why Dr. Richert? And what did Dr. Richert and the other guy have in common?

Gunny didn't get all the software's ins, and outs really didn't get it at all. He said, "CJ they called us because this system has gone rogue, hasn't it. You don't know who it will go after next do you, or why?"

The woman said, "Dr. Richert was a psychologist, and in partnership with Dr. Chong, a sociologist, they developed the framework for decisions that Nudge makes. Without Richert and Chong, we are fumbling." And no, we don't know what it will do next or positively who has it."

CJ and Gunny spoke together, "Who has it?" said Gunny. "You don't?" said CJ

Cunningham and the three team members all shook their heads. Nautilus-tie-man said, "Dr. Chong was the sellout. Every six months we would run deception tests on all key members of all government projects with Top-Secret clearance but Chong beat us.

Remember at this point we didn't even know that Nudge was going into full production. We thought Cunningham was waiting for our analysis of the test project. Chong never showed deception probably because we never asked about Nudge as Cunningham had finished that contract and was in a hold pattern. After Chung's murder, we found that he was a compulsive gambler. That he owed money to everybody. He was also a serial philanderer and most important a prominent member of a conservative church. His wife, family, church everybody would have deserted him, or so he thought, if his behaviors came out. Remember Bill Bennet the Republican moralist who wrote the bestselling "Book of Virtues" and how he crashed and burned once he once it came out that was a big gambler? Chong had that book in his home library and it is dog eared for reading and rereading. He cracked under the pressure and we believe stole the code and sold it to someone. He deposited over five million in an offshore account we have located."

CJ said, "Well that is ironic. He fell victim to hiding behavior from his tribe. Exactly the pattern that his software, this Nudge project is based on." He paused and leaned back in his chair and said, "And we are here why?"

The woman said. "We are going to stop for fifteen minutes to let you digest what we told you before we tell you the reason for the meeting." CJ and Gunny exited the room and walked down to the corridor's end to talk in private.

"You know those guys are spooks, right?" Said Gunny.

CJ nodded his head yes and said, "They have us in here because they do not want to use their own people. That means they want to deny anything in case this goes tits up."

"Yep, nothing changes, does it? Same old shit, new day." He looked at his son and said, 'Son, you have a nice business, and I hear a new girlfriend. Do you really want to do this? We aren't in the Marines anymore. You did enough already. I'll walk this if you will. Let them solve their own problems if that's what you want."

"What about you Gunny? You're not getting any younger. Do you want to do this? Get maybe your ass shot off. No more of those British mysteries with Elizabeth?"

They looked at each other, quiet, each searching the other's eyes. Gunny broke first. He started to smile, just a bit. CJ followed with his smile getting more prominent. They went grinning ear to ear and back to the meeting room they went.

CJ took command of the meeting. "You have us here because you don't have the stomach to own up to your screw-ups. You have already identified a high possibility target with a command and control structure that has this Nudge software and you want taken out. You have us here because of what my company does, physical penetration testing, clandestine invasions and also because of our military background in the Marine Corps, in wars. We are experienced and the kind of experience that you need. Did I miss anything?"

The three exchanged looks. The woman spoke, "mostly you are right. We want you to penetrate and take out their command and control center." She waited a few seconds before continuing, "but you missed some of things. First, we have identified two command and control centers though as you guessed we are not yet at 100% probability. Redundancy is built into Nudge so there would be at least two organizations. Second Nudge is designed to watch for counterattacks so after you hit the first one, assuming you are successful, the second one will take offensive action against you."

Cunningham spoke up, "my daughter was intentionally placed under suspicion by Nudge to slow the investigation. Nudge may go after people you care about. As you say it is damn good at it."

Nautilus-tie-man said, "Your advantage there is speed. It takes time to create and populate groups, to seed the groups, to identify candidates then to manipulate them into action like it did here in Austin. You need to move fast man fast."

The other suit said, "We won't be bringing our people to Austin for security. We can't do that because that would be a giveaway, Nudge looks for all kinds of patterns and beefing up security is prime. They already know about Cunningham Industries so Nudge will expect that but if it sees your company, CJN, all of a sudden overflowing with guards it may attack there. Again, speed is the key. I read your military files. Both of yours. You are men of courage that is obvious."

Ms. Clarke said, "Something else you should know. The U.S. government-funded the initial 'Proof of Concept" development but did not fund the rest of the project. Mr. Cunningham."

Cunningham sat up in his chair and said," despite the highest and best security we could muster we were duped. We were contacted by what we were lead to believe was a different branch of the U.S. government, given the go ahead and provided with funding to finish Nudge."

"And our branch had no idea that happened," said Ms. Clarke

Cunningham continued, "The project was expanded and fast tracked into as tight a schedule as we could be possible accomplished."

CJ said, "Who did the funding?"

"We don't know," said Ms. Clarke "The funds came in from overseas accounts that are tied into off shore accounts and looped around the world. We are trying to untangle the web now."

Cunningham continued, "And CJ You guys missed it on that security audit." He held up his hands to stop CJ from talking. "We are not blaming you CJ We are informing you. We have never seen such sophistication in software nor has anyone in the industry."

"How deep inside have you guys looked? We concentrated on attacking from outside. Maybe Chung had accomplices." said CJ

"We notified the government immediately that we had been breached and that is what brought these three government representatives here." Said Cunningham. "They have their own people looking at everything her but we don't have those answers yet."

Everybody was silent, expectant, waiting.

Gunny broke the silence looking at the three feds; he said, "You guys look scared. Good. Like John Wayne said when he played Captain Rockwell Torrey in Harms Way, 'All battles are fought by scared men who'd rather be someplace else'."

The suits exchanged glances. "John Wayne sir?" asked the woman.

"Yeah," said Gunny bobbing his head and smiling, "you a fan?"

CJ jumped in before she could answer, "Before I commit CJN I have a question. I think I know the answer but I want it confirmed." The three suits waited while CJ formed the question. "Mr. Cunningham said Nudge was a government project originally and you three here validate that. What was the original end goal?"

"Let me answer that one," said the woman. "Social unrest is skyrocketing in the world. Nations are going to fall. New groups will arise to prominence and some of them will also fail. People are arming themselves and governments are moving to disarm citizens. Trust of institutions is at a historical low point. Even the U.S. military is experiencing a low morale. The United States is becoming more and more vulnerable to attack from both inside and out. It is our job, to prepare to defend the country from outside attacks. What if we could at, a very low cost and unobserved with zero footprint in humans, sow descent into an adversary country? What if we could use software to attack, not infrastructure attacks like taking out the centrifuges in Iran that make heavy water such as a previous administration did, but internal groups attacks. Slowly at first, meetings, protests then escalate to riots maybe? Group against group. Our adversary would need to use their resources internally. Their backs would be turned. Maybe their society destroyed. That is the goal of Nudge."

Cunningham said, "This is a new kind of threat more dangerous than what you have faced before because it has little reliance on people as key players. Nudge just moves to a second or third candidate or group and keeps hitting. You should be scared. Hell, I'm scared and I'll be sitting here".

Gunny spoke up," but there is no adversary country here that we know of. It's on the lose against Apple pie, and America, isn't it?" He added, "and you guys can't stop it, can you?

CJ didn't need to hear the confirmation from the three suits. It was evident that Nudge was after America." We're in. I need to assemble a team. My guys not yours. It'll take maybe two, three days. Get the intel ready on the location of command and control. We'll meet as soon as my guys are assembled."

The meeting broke up with all heading for the door and the exits. The woman called out to Gunny and CJ, asking them to step back into the room for just a second. She closed the door, looked at the two men, and said, "this system was designed to use software not wetware. Understand what I mean. It will use humans that are actually victims themselves like the two murderers so what I am saying is be damn careful of any new relationships." CJ thought of Briana. Gunny just nodded.

On the way, back to the office in the Hummer, they rapidly picked their five-man team. Gunny said Taza Naiche, a fellow Vietnam vet and the man that CJ had spent summers with on the Apache and Navajo reservations. CJ chose Captain Cleavon Bailey, who had been his Executive Officer in Afghanistan.

And the fifth member of the team, a pick by both men, was Geraldo Rivera.

Yes, dear reader, that's me. You are shocked. I can envision you standing up, getting out of your chair. Your mouth agape, down turned worried eyes, singing the song '*It takes a worried man to sing a worried song* ' by the Kingston Trio. Oh no, surely not. Not our beloved company archivist. Terror and dread flash across the synapses of your brain.

You know what I have said about myself that I served with CJ and that he saved my life on more than one occasion. Modesty prevented me from mentioning that I returned the favor by saving his life. You will note that I have, through great and costly personal effort, overcome modesty.

You probably thought that in the Marine Corps I was, shall we say a clerk? The less enlightened of you thinking that a clerk might be a male administrative assistant in the Marine Corps or as they said back in Gunny's time a titless secretary. No one in today's Corp would say, titless secretary. Today's Marines are far too enlightened to say such a thing, think it? Yes, whisper it to their buds? Yes, but say it? Never happen, man. Back to the clerk designation titless or otherwise. Maybe a male clerk in the other services is just an administrative assistant. I don't know. I was never in the other services. I was in the Marine Corps. You see in the Marine Corps every Marine, every single one, man, woman whichever, no matter what their job, is a rifleman first. They are trained as a grunt, as an infantryman. They can all do that job. Every single one of them. Men and women. They are all Marines. They can all shoot your ass off at three hundred yards or more. They train to do it. You a bad guy? Test them. They will be happy to oblige. Ambush a truck convoy. Watch them pile out, set up a defensive perimeter, then methodically blow your ass and all your little buddy's asses away.

However, I was not a clerk in the Marine Corps. I was the same as the other four members of the team. My M.O.S., Military Occupational Specialty or job identifier, was 0321, Recon Marine the Marine equivalency of Navy SEALs. However, the SEALs get all the press probably because the Marine Corps receives such a small cut of the National Defense budget. All Marines with a M.O.S. of 03 are infantrymen with 0311, the first M.O.S. you receive then, depending on schools, and if you pass, you change to a different M.O.S. like 0317 is a Scout Sniper, and 0331 is a Machine Gunner. A Recon Marine, 0321 is, and here I will quote from the job description the Marine Core gives for the MOS of 0321:

Marine reconnaissance men are elite war-fighters that are training in reconnaissance, intelligence gathering, and unique fighting skills that may be considered unconventional. They are dedicated and hardworking Marines who deploy with a small team to remote areas in support of the mission of the Marine Corps.

FUCK YES! OOH-RAH!

Briana had gone shopping for a new outfit at the Domain Mall in Austin, an outdoor mall with upscale shops. She came out of the north side of the mall and walked through the parking lot to her car. She popped open the trunk to put her shopping bags in when her attention was drawn to the couple parked several vehicles down. The man started yelling at the woman, and as Briana watched, he reached out and slapped the woman who recoiled put her hands on her face and started crying.

Briana reached into her purse, withdrew her cell phone and called 911. She told the 911 dispatcher where she was at and that a woman was being assaulted. The dispatcher told her to stay where she was as a squad car was responding. Briana walked towards the couple. The man reached out and slapped the woman again, harder this time, with more shoulder, causing the woman to be knocked against the car. Briana took her handbag off her shoulder and dropped it on the ground so that her hands would be free and said to the man, "Stop hitting her. I have called the police and they are on the way. Leave her alone."

"You called the cops on me? This is none of your business," said the man as he turned and stepped towards Briana. "I'll give you a lesson in stepping in the affairs were you not asked about."

Briana could tell the man had been drinking because of the flush in his face, the slight stagger as he moved towards her and the faint whiff of alcohol. He swung at her hard from the right. She rocked back at the waist, pulling her head up and away, and the punch from the man brushed across her chin. Briana stood in a defensive posture with her feet placed right foot behind left at shoulder width aligned with her body angled away from the man. She held both hands up, making fists with a left lead. She raised her right leg up, bent at the knee while turning her left foot to the outside, away from her body, preparing to pivot. With her lead foot now at the eight o'clock position, her body was coiled like a spring. She clasped her hands together in front of her and snapped out the right foot up high at head level and circling to her left uncoiling the spring with her foot colliding with the left side of the drunk man's head. She went back to her defensive posture, watching what the man who had fallen to his hands and knees would do.

He was a stupid guy and drunk, so he tried to get up. Briana moved behind him and delivered a forward kick to his groin, which sent him sprawling. He screamed, doubled up, and began vomiting. Briana, still in a defensive posture, heard the siren of a police car, and looking at the end of the row, she saw it moving slowly, looking for the scene of the assault. She waved both hands in the air to attract the attention of the cops. They spotted her and turned into the row stopping at Briana.

Two Austin PD officers jumped out of the squad, with the female officer being a corporeal and in charge. She told the other officer to call an ambulance and check on the down drunk and the woman who was crying and huddled near her car. Then the female cop asked Briana what happened here. A small group of bystanders had formed and watched when Briana recounted the event to the female cop. The cop asked the gathered bystanders if anyone had seen what happened, and one middle-aged lady said she had seen it and heard what Briana said that was what had happened. Another man said he saw the part where the guy swung at Briana, and she kicked him, verifying that the man had attacked first.

An ambulance arrived and started treating the man and woman who had been slapped. The corporal told her partner to take down the two bystanders' statements, and she pulled Briana aside. 'Ma'am, where did you learn to kick like that?"

"I have studied Taekwondo since I was a little girl. My dad said women need to be able to defend themselves."

"I agree with your dad but why did you kick him in the groin when he was already down?"

"He wasn't down all the way just on his hands and knees and it looked like he was getting up. I only weigh a little over 100 pounds so there is not that much weight behind my kicks. I was afraid if he got up before you guys arrived he might go to his car and get a gun or weapon. We were always taught that once you have gained the advantage to never give it up so I nailed him in the groin."

The corporal was satisfied and conferred with her partner when Briana came over and asked if she could leave as she had a date.

The corporal said they might be reaching out to talk to her again, but she could leave. After the man was on the way to the hospital, and the cops were going, the male officer said to the female, "That woman is on her way to a date. I bet there won't be any uninvited inappropriate touching on that date", grinning while he said it.

Laughing, the corporal replied, "You got that right. I loved that chick. She is my hero."

More to our girl Briana then was at first evident, huh?

As soon as CJ and Gunny returned to CJ's office, they set the ball in motion to assemble the team. Geraldo Rivera, me, was brought into the office and given a very condensed version of the mission and asked if I volunteered. Not a Marine Corp volunteer program, which is like you are assigned, then thanked for volunteering but actually asked if I wanted in. Well, I hadn't shot anybody in a spell, so I signed up. Gleefully, I might add.

CJ was not able to reach Capt. Cleavon Bailey, his former X.O., at his home in Dallas, Cleavon's answering service, said he was out of the country with an indeterminate return. It could be this evening or next month. CJ left a message to have him call back and to tell him it was an urgent need. Urgent need in the Marine Corp means just that, in the true sense of the words. It's not some sales crap about the importance of making a quota but implies that there is some seriously bad stuff that needs to get attention right now. CJ would give Cleavon a day, two at most, then go to his next choice.

Gunny's life friend, Taza Naiche, could not be reached by phone. Taza didn't own a telephone, not a cell or landline. Gunny had a landline but no cell. No wonder they were life friends. Gunny called Taza's son, the one that played with CJ back in the day. After catching each other up, Gunny was told him that Taza was not on the Fort Apache reservation currently. He thought he was up on the Navajo reservation and gave Gunny the phone number of his cousin in the same clan as Taza's deceased half-sister. Gunny called the nephew, who confirmed that Taza was on the reservation and up in the Hunts Mesa formation south of Utah and Arizona. The cousin lived in a trailer or mobile home, mobile, according to the description. However, it hadn't been moved in two decades, near Mexican Hat, Utah. Mexican Hat was called Mexican Hat because of a rock formation that resembles a Mexican Sombrero. No doubt, the town will be renamed after the coastal folks discover that the name is a cultural appropriation of Mexico. The problem is many Native Americans are armed and don't like to be messed with by those coastal types. They remember what happened in the past you see and are really big on the second amendment.

The cousin said it took about two hours to get up to Taza's Hogan and said he really could little afford to take off work. Gunny offered to pay gas, mileage, and triple time for a full eight-hour day. The cousin asked how he would get the money, and Gunny said mail maybe which the cousin didn't like, having heard about dealing with those big-city, like Austin, sharpies. Elizabeth took the phone and asked where the cousin banked. He said he had a debit card issued through Wells Fargo bank. Elizabeth took the numbers and told him she would Zelle him immediately half the money and the other half when they talked to Taza. The deal was done. Gunny asked Elizabeth why the cousin thought that Elizabeth would send the money with zeal, and he, Gunny, wouldn't send it with zeal? She told him not 'zeal' the noun but Zelle the banking service. Elizabeth explained that it was an updated version of sending money by wire. She said she had already sent the cousin the first half while they were talking. Gunny was standing behind her talking to her while she was pounding keys on the computer keyboard. He was looking down her blouse clandestinely. Elizabeth was amused that Gunny didn't think she knew what he was looking at. Life goes on.

Gunny, Elizabeth, Briana, and CJ arrived at about the same time at Stubb's BBQ 801 Red River in Austin. A semi-famous place. You may have seen their BBQ sauce in a grocery store, and if not complain to the store, believe me, you want to try it. The big initial shock was when Elizabeth and Gunny were walking into the restaurant. Looking up the street, they saw CJ's Hummer turn onto Red River off of 8th street with CJ in the passenger seat. Yep, he had let Briana drive. Gunny and Elizabeth looked at each other with Elizabeth dropping her jaw and Gunny going all round-eyed. The evening's second surprise was how much Dragon Lady, Elizabeth, and Cat Walking Lady, Briana, liked each other. CJ announced as they finished the last of their ribs, chicken for Briana, and no dessert. Stubs not offering desert being a Texas traditional rib place. If you want dessert with your ribs in Austin, you should go to The County Line and order their Kahlua Pecan Brownie or Homemade Cobbler. The County Line defiantly has a better view than Stubbs, and some people even prefer their ribs. But those folks that prefer the ribs at The County Line over Stubbs are all from somewhere way up North, like Dallas. CJ told Elizabeth and Briana that he and Gunny would be going out of town in about three days, maybe sooner and that they anticipated being gone a week.

"Nothing on the schedule," said Elizabeth, hesitantly, looking down at her dinner's remains, eyes not meeting CJ's. She continued," well really this means I will need to reschedule stuff."

"Business trip? Where to? "Asked Briana.

"Yes, business it is and the destination and the client are both confidential." Said CJ.

Briana looked at her new friend Elizabeth and saw the faintest of clouds pass over her face.

"Is there something I should know?" Briana asked.

'No, it's all good. Nothing really." Said CJ, talking too fast.

Gunny enthusiastically nodded his head in agreement towards Briana and said, "John Wayne said when you come across trouble. It's never half as bad if you face up to it"" Briana saw CJ give his dad a wide-eyed 'what are you saying?' stare then turn and smile at her as if Gunny never said a word. Now she was more worried.

That night the moon was full, what was called by old Texas families that still remembered the legends, a Comanche Moon. So-called for when the Lords of the Plains, the Comanche roamed far and wide across Texas and points west. The Comanche often attacked at night, usually under a full moon because if you were used to the night, familiar with the country, not needing flashlights, then a full moon was all the light you needed. CJ and Gunny weren't Comanche. They were Marines and, as such preferred to make night attacks without the full moon. That's what Night Vision Goggles like the ATN PVS7-3 standard issue to U.S. ground troops are for. Those old Texas settlers that feared the Comanche moon sure as hell wouldn't have wanted The Lords of The Plains to have night vision goggles. If they did, there might never have been any Austin TX. And the Lords Of The Plains wouldn't be sitting up in Fort Sill Oklahoma on the reservation but instead still riding around Palo Duro Canyon, Texas. Even Comanche's dream.

Early in the morning, the Comanche moon was setting and shining the last of its off white light through CJ's bedroom's open drapes. Briana was sitting up cross-legged in bed and looking at CJ He felt the look and opened his eyes and asked her what she was doing.

"I need you to know something, something that is very important to me," she said.

" Yes?"

"I don't do this."

"Do what?," CJ said, rolling onto his side, reaching out rubbing her thigh.

" Meet a guy, go to lunch, then next date jump in bed with him, I have never done that before. It is important you know that. Important to me. OK?"

"Yes." He said.

"Believe me?" she asked.

"I do. And I am glad you chose me to do it with. I am beyond glad. I am thrilled."

"And it's a first for me also." Said CJ

"Really?" she asked surprise and some doubt in her voice. Men being men.

"Really. Not completely but since I matured to be a full responsible man. Since I left boyhood and young man hood, if there is such a thing, behind. Since maybe my late twenties. I quit doing that. It has to mean something and have the potential to be going someplace. Someplace permanent." He said.

She sat quietly, thinking, then said," And this can go someplace, CJ? You and me? Together?"

"Hell yes, for me it does."

She came to him; they held each other. Their hands explored, and the moon set as their eyes lit up with the act's pleasure.

She fought to not say it, he struggled to not say it. Neither wanting to scare the other. Both spiraling down a beautiful slope, both falling in love.

Chapter 11

Joe Leaphorn, not the famous Lieutenant Joe Leaphorn of the Navajo Tribal Police, the Sherlock of The Plains as he was known but the cousin that had received the Zelle money transfer from Elizabeth. Our Joe Leaphorn was the namesake of famous Joe Leaphorn, like Geraldo Rivera and me. Got that straight?

So, Cousin Joe got up early, prepared two white bread and baloney sandwiches, being on a tight budget, and placed them in the cab of his 1987 4X4 Ford Bronco with 310,544 miles on the speedometer. But the speedometer had broken three years back. Estimating 30,000 miles a year, this being Arizona, and on the reservation, the old Bronk had close to a half-million miles. Probably time to get something newer, maybe a 1990 model? Into the cab of Cousin Joe's Bronk, he put the brown bag containing the baloney sandwiches. I forgot to mention Cousin Joe had smeared mustard on them, details being important in this story. Cousin Joe also placed two gallon jugs of water and his Winchester model 1873 known as The Gun That Won The West. Or lost the West, if you are a Plains Indian as Cousin Joe was. The water was not cold, there was no ice chest in the Bronk. The water would warm with the day. No A/C in the Bronk. Cold water only matters to you if you are a city person back from a workout in your climate-controlled gym or sitting around the pool, slowly simmering in tanning oil. In the desert of Arizona, what matters about water is that it is wet. If you have ever been really thirsty, not just a bit dry, but lips cracked, tongue swelled thirsty, that piss warm water even with mud and little buggies in it would be the best thing you ever tasted.

Cousin Joe locked his trailer, which looked as beaten as the Bronco. The trailer stood by itself, South of the San Juan River, a hundred yards back from the bank. The location was essential to Cousin Joe because being South of the San Juan river put his trailer on the Navajo reservation. If the trailer was North of the river, then the trailer would be on the Bureau of Land Management BLM and controlled by the Feds. The Navajo have a treaty with the Feds granting them land. We all know how the Feds have respected treaties with Native Americans over the years. Still, it's something.

Cousin Joe cranked the starter, the Bronc's engine hesitated, backfired, coughed, then ran with only an occasional misfire. He backtracked along the San Juan to Utah 163, made a right, and drove about a mile to the 7-11 Shell station. He filled his tank using his now fat cash card, thanks to Elizabeth, and got a roadie of lousy coffee.

Cousin Joe would run South down Utah 163 from Mexican Hat to the turn off onto 42 heading southeast into Arizona. Two miles or so before 42 ends, he slowed down looking for the turnoff to go cross county towards Ear of the Wind a popular scenic tourist spot so designated on local maps and on Google maps complete with pictures of the formation that looks like an ear canal through which the wind passes. Maybe that's why it is called Ear of The Wind.

Taza Naiche had built a hogan, a traditional Navajo dwelling, in this starkly beautiful land of blowing sand, scrub vegetation and silence. Arizona used to have large herds of wild horses, but those herds have dwindled down to under 500 at last count the horses following the buffalo into the realm of the past. And if they aren't careful so with the Native Americans. Some say that has already happened. Look at Cousin Joe, who lives in a trailer, not a hogan.

At the turn off for both Ear of the Wind and Taza's hogan, Cousin Joe eased the old Bronc onto the dirt trail, going slowly down and up through the dry washes that during the rare, but violent rainstorms, would explode with runoff, sweeping away anything in the wash with it. No sign of rain today, just a couple of wisps of clouds up towards Navajo Mountain, but they wouldn't develop. Cousin Joe had been out to Taza's hogan before, but Taza had not been there on that visit. Maybe back with his people at Fort Apache. But not a wasted trip as cousin Joe just left a note saying that some guy named Gunny was trying to reach him. The same message he was going to deliver today.

After close to two hours of creeping along the seldom used dirt road Cousin Joe eased to the top of the rise and stopped. He could see the Taza's hogan from here though it was still several hundred yards away. Normally if he was visiting any other hogan, he would drive closer then sit in his truck for however long it took for the person in the hogan to open the door in acknowledgment of the visit. It is the Navajo way to be polite, give the person you are visiting time to get ready, not embarrass them by barging up: no hail-fellow-well-met, hand pumping, back-slapping, Cheshire cat smile heralding in the Navajo culture. Sit and wait for them to be ready. These Navajo that follow the traditional way are still semi-savages, you see.

But at this hogan Cousin, Joe didn't venture close. He sat on the ridge and got out of the Bronc so he could be seen clearly by Taza. Didn't want to startle Taza by sneaking up, as if that was possible. Didn't want him to wonder who was coming to visit him. Didn't want him to think you were going to hassle him. Taza was famous on the Navajo reservation and the Apache reservation. Even down south of here on the Hopi reservation, they talked of him. It had happened a couple of months back probably had grown in the telling and retelling. Bur cousin Joe though he knew the real story. He had got it right after it happened. Maybe second or at most third hand before it was decorated with adding of Navajo skin-walkers to the story. Skin-Walkers, witches, or perhaps they are werewolves, are old superstitions thought, Cousin Joe. Still, just the passing thought gave him a tightening of his back muscles and an involuntary quick glance to the left and right. He ran the time calculations. Here before noon, deliver the message, have the obligatory coffee cup, then get the hell back on 42, get to 163, if possible, before dark. Not that he believed them old women and that skin-walker hooey.

In the story, told second or maybe third hand, the sweep car officer saw the fresh tracks where two brothers that he was chasing had turned off 42 in the direction of Ear of The Wind just as Cousin Joe had done. The story said that when the sweep officer got to Taza's hogan, he saw an eagle circling with two feathers in its mouth, which it dropped back to the earth. A coyote howled the howl being picked up by other coyotes echoing back and forth through the hills. It is rare for a coyote to howl in bright daylight. The officer, so the story goes, followed the tracks the brothers had left out into the desert where one then the other simply stopped in the sand. When he bent down to examine the tracks, he reached out to touch them, and there was a flash of lightning with no clouds in the sky. The story moved from there to various sub-stories of two-headed sheep born, coyotes seen walking upright, and more.

While Cousin Joe waited for the door to open that would signal he could approach Taza's hogan, he saw the scar still visible in the ridge's rock face. The scar had been made the day after it happened by the tow truck the Navajo Tribal Police had called to come to get the truck that had been abandoned by the brothers. The truck had slipped on the winch and banged into and slid along the rock face leaving the scar.

The story that Cousin Joe had heard second or third hand had a basis in reality as all good ghost stories do. What really happened was the day before the tow truck had been called, the one that made the scar in the rock face, two mean ratty ass white-boys had spent the night at the Dine Inn Motel in Tuba City AZ. They were brothers and were on a mini crime spree which had started in North Phoenix with the robbery of a liqueur store, the subsequent stealing of a pickup truck from a patron of the store, and their disappearance with the said truck into the night. Not satisfied with the liqueur store's take, they had beaten both the night clerk and the now truck-less patron. The robbery and beatings were discovered several hours later when the clerk didn't come home. It had taken several hours because the brothers had left the clerk and patron tied up and turned out the lights before they left. The cops put out an alert for the truck. Still, the mean-bastard brothers had that several hour head start and were experienced, bad guys. They had stopped at a truck stop at the junction of Interstate 17 and Interstate 40 in Flagstaff and switched license plates. Then continued up AZ 89 planning to go to Las Vegas to gamble and turn a thousand bucks they had gotten from the liqueur store into tens of thousands on the gambling tables. They were undoubtedly experienced mean-bastards in crime, but they were also predictably two really dumb bastards as instead of heading West on I 40 to get to Vegas, they headed North on Arizona 89 and ended up at the Dine Motel in Tuba City.

Tuba city is decidedly not Las Vegas. What happens in Tuba City is known by everyone in a couple of days, so if it's your intention to be doing naughty things better head for Vegas because what happens in Vegas stays in Vegas and the old significant other will never know unless those videos end up on the Internet. Always something to worry about ain't there?

The brothers checked in, paid cash for their room, and headed out to party, thinking they would backtrack tomorrow and head for Vegas. This part of the story was foggy. Nobody would ever own up to having told the mean, stupid, brothers the rumor that Taza Naiche was a retired career Marine. That he got a government retirement check every month, that he cashed the check and took the cash with him back to his hogan in the desert. Taza did get a government retirement check every month. Still, the rest of it was pure bull but made a famous story with the local drunks and might have been enough to get one of them several free rounds from the mean-bastard brothers with directions on how to get to Taza's place surely being enough for one more shot and beer.

What was known for sure were the brothers checked out the next day. Still, they felt the room was not up to their high, county jail tuned standards, so they put a Beretta APX 9mm automatic in the clerk's face and demanded their money back. Not wanting to lose their Vegas stake, you see. Following the pattern, they tied up the clerk, smacked her in the face with the automatic, as said before, they were mean-bastards and headed out. This time the cops got there pretty fast but still had no idea which direction they had gone but thinking probably south to get to the interstate. The brothers, now in pursuit of the fortune in cash they were told, was held by Taza Naiche, headed north up 163 towards Hunts Mesa two hours away. The Tuba City cops on the off chance that the brothers had headed North called for support from the Navajo Tribal Police. The latter established a roadblock at the junction of 163 and 191 North of Mexican Hat another at 98 and 160 and the final one at 163 and 160. Finally, the Tribal Police sent a sweeping car up 163 on the off chance that the brothers had gone cross county. After the sweep car had passed each roadblock, they could assume that roadblock was no longer necessary and go back to patrol. The sweeping car had one detour to take, which was looping down 42 towards Hunts Mesa.

The officer driving the sweep car was named Klah Yazzie, so named because he was left-handed, which is what Klah means in Navajo. Officer Yazzie saw the fresh tracks where the mean-dog brothers had turned off 42 in the direction of Ear of The Wind. The officer had heard the fantasy of the money that Taza Naiche kept in his hogan. He had met Taza several times at Marine Corps birthday celebrations held each year countrywide on November 10th. Held even in Tuba City and anything that went on at the celebration made the Tuba City gossip rounds. The Navajo Tribal Police officer had also been a Marine and had listened with Indian pride to the stories that Taza shared with him at the Marine Corps birthday bash. Tales of the exploits of Recon Marines in Vietnam and other places during Taza's career.

Officer Yazzie got out of his truck, crouched low, and examined the tracks. They had partially filled back in with windblown sand. Yazzie determined they had been made a couple of hours ago. He radioed in for backup, which out here was several hours, sometimes days, away, and eased his Navajo Tribal Police truck onto the path and followed the tracks. Followed at a leisurely pace, going slowly up and down the washes to not damage the vehicle. There was no hurry. He was maybe two hours behind them. He knew this was the way the mean-dog brothers had gone, and he knew that he was already too late. They had too much of a head start. By now, they were at Taza's hogan, had been there for maybe as much as an hour.

The brothers, two hours before the Navajo Police officer, examined their truck's tracks, stopped their stolen truck at the top of a rise, seeing the hogan on the opposite side. They reversed and parked with the vehicle hidden from the hogan's view, which was several hundred yards away across the decline on the incline of the next rise. They got out, each fetching his handgun, and started down the ridge tiptoeing as they could. Sneak up on the old dude, then pistol-whip him, burn him, cut him whatever it took to get the money, then finally off to Vegas.

Taza was not in his hogan. He was sitting on top of the rise to the right and slightly behind where the brothers had parked their truck. He watched them get their guns and begin to ease down the slope. Them being quiet as they could, which to Taza's trained ears accustomed to the silence of the high desert's seclusion, sounded like two women in heels click-clacking across a terrazzo floor. A half-hour earlier, he was above his hogan practicing to stoically sit and watch, not move, just to be. He practiced this often. It was soul cleansing. While sitting, he saw the truck's dust plume when the brothers were still half an hour out. He could tell from the plume that the truck was coming fast, not cautious, not the Indian way, not considerate of the truck, not trying to make the truck last a long time. No, just banging along. Not Navajos, he thought.

He carried a World War II fully restored M1 Garand 30-06 semi-automatic rifle. The same type the Marines had used in that World War II island hoping fighting the Japanese. He did not carry a handgun. Taza did not own a handgun. He had told Gunny many times that the only thing that a handgun was good for was to fight your way back to wherever you were dumb enough to leave your rifle.

They have come for the damn money, Taza thought, that I am supposed to be keeping under my mattress, I guess. They have come to kill me. Probably going to torture me for the money. What sick dogs they are. Taza sighed and headed silently down the ridge, past their truck, quietly walking after the sound of the two trying to sneak up on him. The two that sounded like women in high heels crossing a terrazzo floor.

Navajo Nation Tribal Police Officer Klah Yazzi stopped his truck next to the one sitting just down from the ridge's top. He got out and walked around the truck, looking at everything. He put his hand on the hood. Cold. Been here a while, he thought. Opening the driver's door, keys still in the ignition. No water. Not desert people. He walked in a broadening circle looking for tracks in the sand. He saw none. The sand looked not disturbed. It is too late, he thought. It has already happened. He returned to his truck, went over and down the ridge, then up the opposite slope to the hogan. He sat in his truck until the front door opened. Then he got out and walked up to Taza Naiche, standing in front of the hogan by himself, calm, stoic, at peace.

"Ya at' eeh," he said to Taza using the Navajo for hello.

"Semper Fi Jarhead," replied Taza using the term first coined by World War II sailors referring to the haircuts the Marines wore." Coffee? I just fired up the propane. Won't take long. Won't taste good either."

"Thanks," said the officer sitting on one of the old weathered chairs outside the hogan. Taza took the other chair and waited. Waited for the coffee to boil and the questions to start. Coffee first. He smelled it, got up, went into the hogan, and returned with two cups handing one to Office Yazzi. Now the questions thought Taza.

Officer Yazzi blew on his coffee, cradling the cup in his hands, looking away onto the desert. "You have a truck sitting the other side of your ridge, just off the trail. Nobody in it. It was stolen by a couple of mean raggedy white boys a day or two ago down in Phoenix. They beat a liqueur store clerk and the truck owner then tied them up and ran up to Flagstaff where they were recorded on a camera at a truck stop. State boys figured they would head for Vegas but no, they went North and spent the night in Tuba city at a motel. Next morning, they got their money back from the clerk, a young woman in collage working part time and for good measure they popped her across the mouth with a gun. She might lose a couple of teeth. She said they said mean things to her. Racial things. She said she could smell their breath as they held the front of her top and half pulled her across the counter. She said their breath smelled of old booze. Hard smell she said, like kerosene. She said they touched her and when she told the responding officers that she started to cry. The Tuba City cops figured they had headed for Vegas but on the off chance then went North we blocked the road and I put the squeeze on them in case they did go North. I saw a truck had they left the road at the sign for Ear in The Wind and thought that maybe they were coming to your place. You know, for all your millions you got in that old mattress."

"Hurt a girl, huh? Touched her? Said racial things?" said Taza, shaking his head in disgust.

"Their truck is just behind that rise Taza. They come talk to you?" said Officer Yazzi. Careful of the way he asked his questions. He knew that Taza wouldn't lie. Knew he had to ask questions that were worded carefully.

Taza got up, took his mug and Yazzi's, and went inside. He returned with two fresh, steaming mugs of almost undrinkable coffee. "Talk? Me talk to them? Or them talk to me? No. Never happened. That girl. Can she pay for a good dentist?"

"Where do you think they are walking around?" said Yazzi while looking out over the desert towards the mountains. He had phrased the question asking where Taza thought the mean-bastard brothers might be walking around, not asking where Taza figured they might be. He waited maybe five minutes, no hurry, sipping coffee then said, "Hot today. Won't be better tomorrow.

"No just more hot. I saw a cloud up near Navajo mountain but it went away. They usually do." Said Taza, not answering the question yet, thinking. Then seeing the opening, he had been left, he said, "Don't know where they would be walking around. Maybe you should get a helicopter up. Run a search pattern. Maybe thirty or forty volunteers on horses looking for them. First people you should ask is the family of the girl. Maybe they will help you find them out of compassion."

Officer Yazzi sipped his coffee and sat quietly for several minutes. No sense in any hurry. "Don't think we have any whirlybird money in the Tribal Council Budget. Funny ain't it? You'd think a couple of mean-bastard white boys would leave tracks, wouldn't you?"

Taza put his cup on the ground, pivoted in his chair, placed his arm on the chair bent, and balanced his head on his fist. "No tracks huh? Maybe they kept to the rocks".

Still looking at the ridge, the officer said, "I heard once that you are descendant from the Apache Mickey Free. The guy that Geronimo was afraid of. I heard Mickey Free could track a man across rocks. Maybe somebody that had that in their blood could also do it. Track across rocks."

"Maybe," said Taza.

"A man that could track across rocks? Maybe that kind of man could carry another man, or a body, across rocks and leave no tracks. I would think if you could do the tracking you would know how to cover them also. Across the rocks that is."

"Yes, somebody that could track across rocks could carry across rocks also I think." Taza paused, then continued, "and know how to cover their tracks."

"You know anybody like that?" said the officer.

"Mickey Free maybe. But he's long dead just like Geronimo."

"I saw a picture of Mickey Free once." Said Officer Yazzi. "You can find it pretty easy on the Internet. It was a group picture. He was the lead Apache scout for the U.S. Calvary. All the scouts were standing shoulder to shoulder, some in native dress, some with parts of dark Blue Calvary uniforms and some bare chested, all of them sporting rifles. Mickey Free was the smallest of the scouts. He was bare chested and the whiteness of his skin stood out against his brother Apache scouts. That struck me and has stayed with me. The smallest and palest of the scouts and the only man Geronimo ever feared. Small for an Apache, small just for a man and pale. Like you Taza."

The officer stood and stretched. "Thanks for the coffee. I'll be sending a tow truck out to retrieve the truck those woman beaters abandoned."

"Tell the tow truck to be careful. It's easy to slip on that trail. Loose stones there. Hold on a second brother," said Taza going into his hogan. He emerged a few minutes later. "Here, take this. It's about a thousand dollars. I just dug it out of my mattress. Give it to the girl for her teeth. You know if those two are still wandering out there they must be skin-walkers. Maybe you could mention that to somebody."

The officer eased his truck back onto the road stopping at the sign for Eye In The Sky, where he first saw the tracks that were a couple of hours old. He had canceled the call for backup as soon as his radio had contact after leaving Taza. He got out and looked at the tracks again now overlain with his tracks. He crouched down and picked up a fistful of sand and let it run back through his fingers, thinking of two mean-bastard white boys that would pistol whip a girl on the way to steal money from an old man.

I knew it was too late for them, he thought.

Chapter 12

Cleavon Bailey, CJ's choice for the team he was assembling, was not just mixed-race; he was multiple blends. If he was a 7-11 Slurpee, he would be what the kids call a suicide, which is all of the flavors in 7-Eleven combined into one. Through his veins ran the blood of the Irish, the Apache, the Hopi, the Spanish, and what he was most proud of the legendary Buffalo Soldiers of the old West. Take that Elizabeth Warren.

The Buffalo soldiers were African-Americans who served on the Western frontier after the American Civil War. Their main task was to help control the Native Americans, which meant round them up and put them on to reservations. To capture cattle rustlers and to protect settlers, stagecoaches, wagon trains and railroads. They got the name Buffalo soldiers from the Native Americans. No one knows for sure, but it is assumed that the Native Americans said they resembled the Buffalo with their dark curly hair. Maybe, but a competing theory is that the Buffalo Soldiers fought so bravely and fiercely that the Indians revered them as they did the mighty Buffalo. Cleavon preferred the latter theory, as do I.

Cleavon served as CJ's executive officer (XO) during CJ's second tour of Afghanistan. The two men bonded, and after Cleavon left the Marine Corps, he became a contract employee of CJ's picking and choosing his assignments. He liked those that had a high-risk factor. He had become an adrenaline junkie, deep diving, mountain climbing, helicopter skiing, and even bull riding in rodeos. He took contracts with other firms like CJs and sometimes worked overseas right back in Iraq and Afghanistan, but this time for around $20,000 a month. Not bad if you are qualified.

When serving as CJ's X.O. Captain Cleavon Bailey led a Recon team and Afghan National Army troops on a night mission in Helmand Province, Afghanistan. The team climbed up a hill moving through sparse vegetation. As the sunset, they were attacked by a substantial force of enemy fighters. Being in the lead or on point as it is called, Captain Bailey opened fire with his M4A1 carbine spraying the enemy position and killing three of them. The enemy returned fire smacked Captain Bailey's rifle, jamming it and slamming him in the face breaking his nose. Captain Bailey dropped into the prone position as grenade, and mortar rounds exploded all around him. The attackers concentrated on the Afghan National troops killing many of them. Though himself wounded Captain Bailey low crawled across the open area between himself and the enemy and in hand to hand combat killed three of them using his Marine Corps Ka-Bar fighting knife. A machine gunner from the Marine Recon team had been wounded, captured, and dragged away by the enemy. Captain Bailey continued to crawl undetected towards the captured machine gunners screams where he found four insurgents kicking and abusing his comrade. Captain Bailey quietly killed two insurgents with his Ka-Bar, then stormed the other two thrusting the knife into one of the men's chest, then killing the second barehanded.

Captain Bailey slung the wounded machine gunner over his shoulder and, through intense small arms, fire carried him back to the position held by the rest of the Recon Marines and Afghan Army soldiers. The insurgents had enough and disappeared into the night. For his actions during the attack, Captain Cleavon Bailey was awarded the Navy Cross the second highest decoration awarded for valor in combat by the United States Marine Corps. He also received the Purple Heart.

The previous two paragraphs were extracted from Captain Cleavon Bailey's citation for his Navy Cross.

I, Geraldo Rivera, loved it when Cleavon visited CJ in Austin. To understand more deeply, you need to get a small background introduction to the City of Austin, and its culture. Austin is home to the University of Texas's main campus called simply U.T. with over 50,00 undergraduates and graduate students comprised of 54 percent females. Just South of the Colorado River, about ten minutes from downtown Austin, is Saint Edwards University with another 4,000 undergrads, of which 62 percent are females. Austin's official motto, (remember the unofficial one is Keep Austin Weird) is Live Music Capital of the World because on any given night you can find over one hundred venues showcasing a wide variety of free live music performances. Then you have 6th Street in Austin with a city-sponsored, multi-block party every weekend in downtown Austin's heart just blocks from the University.

Cleavon and I have much in common. We are both physically fit, both look great in Tee shirts, excellent dancers, funny, and are both single. Unlike me, Cleavon is, and I use this phrase carefully, just freaking beautiful, for a guy, and that slight bend in his nose from getting broke adds, the women tell me, a mystique to him. He has that light brown skin, square jaw, and the best smile I ever saw. That is until I met Briana. Cleavon just lights the room up when he grins, which is often, and those perfect brilliant white choppers make their appearance. When he talks to someone, he looks them straight in the eye and concentrates on what they say, which is a rare quality and one to be emulated.

Let's mix this cocktail together. We have thousands of young, good looking women, dance music blaring, warm Austin nights, beer flowing like a tributary of the Colorado River, and this beautiful guy with a killer smile that loves to dance and is accompanied by his buddy that is admittedly a step or two down looks-wise. Going clubbing with Cleavon is like going shark fishing. Cleavon is the chum thrown into the water to draw the sharks, which are all those gorgeous, hot, chicks. I also have my metaphorical line in the water with the chick sharks all trying to get to Cleavon. The way shark feeding frenzies work is as long as you have a line in the water, you are bound to get a couple of bites as there is only so much Cleavon chum to go around. True at first, the shark chicks may be a touch disappointed biting on your line. Still, it is up to the fisherman to pull his line in and land them before they become too disinterested and go looking for another Cleavon. Did I mention that I can really dance? That usually sets the hook. Get it? Hook?

A few hours before CJ and Briana headed for the Bat flight in Austin, Cleavon was preparing his sleeping bag for the night in his one-man tent. He was with a tour group in Peru on a five-day hike along the Inca trail. Much of the trail on original Inca construction consists of three overlapping trails Mollepata, Classic, and One Day. Mollepata is the longest with the highest mountain pass and intersects with the Classic trail before crossing "woman who died," a mountain pass in the Andes. The trail passes through the cloud forest and alpine tundra and is rugged and high with a top altitude of 13,800 feet. It offers spectacular views of the Andes and a fascinating examination of the Inca culture, which was here around 1500 and lasted until it was conquered by the Spanish in 1572.

Cleavon would have preferred to solo the hike, but Peru no longer allows that perhaps to assure the guides of more business. Cleavon's group consisted of ten people, mostly young and in good condition. However, he had carried the backpack for some of them when they appeared running out of steam. Cleavon felt no strain. As he prepared his sleeping bag, he elected to go for a late afternoon run along parts of the trail so he could get some exercise and not lose fitness on this hike. To most tourists that go on the Inca trail, it is a real strain. To Cleavon, it was a leisurely stroll.

Cleavon ran forward along the trail, bare-chested in lose shorts and hiking boots. He usually ran in hiking boots, preferring them to running shoes. Cleavon could run for dozens of miles, but he is not a sprinter; instead, he is an endurance runner that participated in ultra-marathons. He planned to run about five kilometers out and back, which would take him under an hour, maybe more, if he stopped for any views. The trail allows 500 people a day to start the hike. It was no surprise as he came around a corner and started up another hill that he saw, off the trail, at a scenic view another group. Probably Scandinavian because they were either blonds or redheads, He wasn't interested in Scandinavians' group, his group would pass the view tomorrow, and he could look then so he just pumped up the hill until he heard the scream.

That stopped him. Cleavon backtracked down the hill and saw one of the blonds frantically waving her arms at him. He jogged over to the group who were all, including the guide, standing a foot or two back from the edge and looking over at something below. The woman that had waived him down was close to hysterical. Cleavon placed his hand on her shoulder, rubbing it to calm her and asked what was wrong.

"My mother has fallen down the cliff," she said, choking, sobbing the words out. Cleavon went to the edge mimicking the group and standing not to close. He bent over and saw a deep drop down the trails side for close to 700-800 feet with nothing but scrub vegetation and scraggly trees to break the slide ending at a rocky stream at the bottom. Such a fall is not a humanly survivable. Probably 20 feet down was a middle-aged woman holding onto a set of exposed plant roots. She had a backpack on, and her feet were free against the slope, not having any foot purchase to relieve the pressure on her arms.

"She was sitting on the edge taking pictures and when she turned to get up the soil gave way and down she went." sobbed the daughter. Cleavon held up his arm palm out to her. "Not important now." Cleavon was in mission planning mode. He waved the guide quickly over who ran over and said in broken English, "Senior she went to close. I told he to get back but" Cleavon stopped him from talking with the same gesture that he had stopped the blond. This time not even saying that what the guide had to say didn't matter. Cleavon needed information.

"Do you have a rope?" he asked the guide.

"No senior," said the guide, almost crying.

"Have you called for rescue?"

"Si, they are now about 35 minutes out, maybe a little more."

"Everybody get the hell back from the edge." Cleavon lay prone and crawled to the edge, not knowing how firm the soil was and not wanting to repeat what had befallen the woman dangling below.

"He yelled to her, keeping a calm voice knowing her panic would be growing, "Can you hold for 45 minutes?"

"Oh god no," she yelled back. "I am slipping. Please help me." She pleaded, causing her daughter to begin sobbing stronger.

"Can you dig your toes in or find something to push with your feet?"

"No, I tried. I am going to fall. I am going to die," the dangling woman wailed.

"Listen to me," Cleavon yelled to her. "Listen close. You are not going to fall. You are not going to die. I am a world class mountain climber and I am going to come down and get you, Understand?"

"Yes, please hurry."

Right thought, Cleavon. Should have worn a damn tee shirt on the jog. He studied the descent memorizing likely shrubs and outcroppings he could utilize. He then pivoted at his waist, dropped his legs over the edge probing with his feet, looking for the bush he had spotted. Once, he found that he eased further out, dragging his fingers in the grass at the top until he could reach out and grab a root to continue the descent. From one root to the next, forcing his feet into the soil wherever possible down, he went like a human gecko. He was parallel to the woman who looked at him with terrified, pleading eyes.

"Unsnap your back pack and let it fall." He said to her.

"I can't. She shuddered and sucked in air. I'm afraid. I am slipping. I can't hold on. Please help me."

Cleavon was calm, heart rate was normal; it was the strength in his arms that he was calculating. He knew how much of that arm and finger strength he had used and knew how much was left. "You need to let go with one arm and put it around my neck. I will then let go with one arm and pull you to me. When I do that you need to let go with the other arm and place it around my neck. Then I will climb back up with you on my back."

"I am too afraid. I can't," the woman told Cleavon.

Cleavon stared into her eyes, holding them, willing her to stare back. "Listen to me, listen close. I am going to tell you the truth. Believe what I say. I will not repeat it."

"I know how much strength I will need left in my arms and fingers to pull both of us to the top. If you want to live, if you want to see your daughter again, you will trust me and let go as soon as I stop talking. You will grab around my neck with one arm. Here is what you must believe. If you don't do that immediately I will climb back up and then you will die. Grab me now,".

She had watched his eyes as he talked to her. She believed in three things watching and listening to him. She believed he was her only chance, she believed he could carry her up, and she believed if she didn't release an arm and grab him that he would leave her.

She was right on the first two but not the third. Cleavon doesn't leave people. He has the blood of Buffalo Soldiers running in his veins. Cleavon is a United States Marine. He would think of something else, or he would die trying to save her.

She took a deep breath and grabbed his neck. Cleavon released one of his hands, reached out to her, could only grab her by the crotch, which he did, and pulled her to him. She let go with the other arm and grabbed him around the neck with a grip a Boa Constrictor would have been proud of.

He started up, but she was cutting off his airflow. "You have to let me breath," he croaked to her.

"OK," she said, not loosening her grip at all.

That's all the cooperation I will get on this one, he thought as he pulled them up, reversing the climb down. Other than a thrilling moment when one foot slipped, the climb up was done quickly. It had to be as his fingers were going numb, and he was turning a touch Blue from lack of air. Near the top two of the men lying prone grabbed her backpack and relieved the weight.

Then another foot and she let go with them pulling her over the top. A few seconds later, they reached down and helped Cleavon over the edge.

He sat, catching his breath, watching the group hugging and kissing the blond woman's mother. "Well the run ain't done yet," he thought. He stood up eased around the group, still dancing with joy around the woman and ran up the trail and over the ridge. All he would have needed to do when he crested the hill before he ran out of sight, was turn around and yell, "High Ho Silver, Away!" That last sentence was Jerry being a wise-ass.

Chapter 13

As soon and Cousin Joe Leaphorn delivered the message that Gunny needed to see him, Taza packed his gear, got in his truck, and drove to Albuquerque. At the airport, he called Elizabeth using a pay phone and what Taza was going to do after the last pay phone disappeared who knows. Elizabeth booked a flight on Southwest airlines into Austin, arriving the day after Cousin Joe had delivered the summons.

Gunny went to the airport to pick him up, borrowing CJ's Hummer because he knew that Taza would get a kick out of it. Elizabeth had told Taza the Gunny would be waiting outside the airport for him in CJ's black Hummer, so it would be easy for Taza to spot him in the queue of cars. Taza, threw his duffel bag in the back seat, got in next to Gunny, and the two drove out of the airport. Taza examined the Hummer and told Gunny that he liked it. Taza would never say that he loved it as that would be expressing too much emotion for an Apache. Taza was convinced that a true Apache showed very little emotion. They had to take a sideway back to Gunny's house where Taza would be staying. They looped away from the airport and onto a 270, a four-lane road with a grass divider.

Gunny told Taza that Elizabeth had taken the time to get a pot of coffee going just how Taza liked. She started brewing as soon as she got to Gunny's house after sending the money to Cousin Joe. Gunny told Taza that Elizabeth let it brew, on high, day and night continuously occasionally putting more water into it when the coffee boiled down. That morning knowing that Taza would arrive soon, she scooped out some of the coffee grounds and poured them into the pot giving it a gritty texture. Gunny told Taza that Elizabeth said she made it just how Taza liked it, as reported to her by Gunny after one of his visits to Taza. Taza gave a slight sideways glance to Gunny. With a frown, he gave him a thumbs up and told Gunny that when he saw Elizabeth, he would thank her personally and that he couldn't wait to get a cup of coffee made the correct way.

Gunny told Taza that he had already set up the spare bedroom for him. That he had removed the bed and mattress, placing them in the garage. He went to Home Depot and picked up a bag of pebbles that are usually used in a garden. He apologized to Taza, saying that the only rocks that Home Depot had were river rocks that were smooth instead of having sharp edges that he knew that Taza preferred. Gunny told Taza that he had scattered the rocks all around the spare bedroom and then placed a worn-out old blanket on the floor over the rocks so that Taza would have a place to sleep. He said he did get lucky, though, because he saw someone had thrown out a dilapidated lawn chair last night on the drive home. So, Gunny had stopped, retrieved the lawn chair from the trash heap, and placed it into the spare bedroom.

"Stop it man, you're going to make me tear up. I don't know why you make such a fuss over it every time I come into town," said Taza. The two old comrades having fun with each other.

The traffic was light on the four-lane road. Gunny saw the brake lights on the car in front of him come on. Looking past that vehicle, he saw that car the car two up in front of him had stopped. The car two in front of the Hummer eased over into the other lane and continued. Then the car immediately in front of Gunny also moved over into the other lane and accelerated.

Gunny saw that there was a used truck tire in the far-left lane that had been blocking people. He glanced in his rear-view mirror, seeing that the vehicle behind him was a couple of hundred yards back. The lane's traffic to his right had cars much closer. He told Taza that he would stop and move the damn tire out of the way, so somebody doesn't get killed. He eased to the left, staying half on the lane and half on the divider. He reached his hand forward, telling Taza to remain in the truck and turn on the flashers.

The semiautomatic rifle opened fire on the Hummer as soon the flashers were switched on.

Taza yelled, "Ambush! Get us the hell out of here" Gunny already knew it was an ambush, that the tire had no doubt been placed there to get them to stop. He thought somebody knows me damn well that I would not let a tire just sit in the road and go around them but stop. He goosed the gas pedal on the Hummer, jerking it to the left and into the median, then straightened it out and shot forward in an attempt to get out of the kill zone.

"What is the code?" Yelled Taza while he pivoted in his seat, trying to see where the gunfire was coming from. He was asking about the code to the little gun safe attached to the center console.

"0321," yelled Gunny continuing to jerk the Hummer left and right to throw the shooter off. Taza punched in the code and removed the 45 caliber Colt Commander that was in the gun safe.

"Man, they are still on us," as the rounds' staccato did not sound any further away. "Damned if I can see where they're shooting from," said Taza as he jerked himself left and right, looking to the sides and behind searching for the muzzle flashes so he could return fire.

Thirty yards ahead of the Hummer, there was an overpass where the four-lane highway dipped under the intersecting road. "I'm going to make that underpass then we bail out, locate the enemy, and return fire," said Gunny.

"Where the hell are they shooting from? They still sound like they are right with us and there's nobody. No muzzle flashes." said Taza. Said loud but not panicky, under control, waiting for his opportunity.

Gunny pulled into the underpass slammed on the brakes, and both the men jumped out of the truck going to the prone position. While he was heading for the ground, Gunny extracted from his belt holster his Colt 45. The two low crawled quickly to the front of the truck, jumped up, each of them on the different sides of the hood, and pointed their weapons behind the Hummer. They saw nothing. The staccato fire from the semiautomatic gun continued. Both men pivoted their heads towards each other then they look down at the hood of the truck.

"Gunny," said Taza, "the shooting is coming from under the hood of CJ's truck. It's just sound it's not shooting." Gunny looked sheepish, re-holstered his weapon, and signaled Taza to get back in the Hummer. Then Gunny reached forward and turned off his flashers. Immediately the staccato sound of rifle fire ended.

Taza looked at Gunny expectantly. Gunny said, "CJ's truck has a special sound system. As you do different things it will set off a different sound. Like when you blow the horn an air raid siren goes off."

Taza said, "so CJ programmed his truck to select automatic weapon fire when you turned on the flashers, is that right?"

"No, I don't think so. I don't think CJ did it. But the other night Elizabeth and I went on a date with CJ and his new girlfriend. And believe it or not CJ let his new girlfriend drive his Hummer. And it is programmable, the sounds that is, I don't how to do it but maybe she played with it. Maybe that's what happened. It's the only explanation I can think of."

Taza said, "let's get the hell out of here before the cops show up. Else I won't be spending a pleasant night on that old blanket laying on rocks in your spare bedroom. Instead I'll be in the Austin jail trying to explain automatic weapons fire coming from the Hummer. And being an Apache in the custody of the South Texas boys? They might have some relatives that have told them some bad stories about us. Let's make a break for it."

Gunny said as he started to back the Hummer out from under the underpass, "Looks like the traffic behind us stopped and they're all looking at us so here's the plan. We are going to roll down our windows, smile at everybody, you remember how to do that, how to smile? Just stick out your arm and wave and we just quietly drive away. Got it?" And that is what they did.

The police had been summoned. After taking several witness statements, they wrote up a report saying that a black tank looking vehicle had stopped behind the tire in the middle-of-the-road, then suddenly, what sounded like gunfire started. Another witness said he thought it was firecrackers, but no, the first witness said he felt it was semiautomatic weapon fire because he had heard a lot of that on T.V. The second witness said that the black tank looking thing went into the median and jerked left and right all the way down the road until it got under the underpass where it stopped. A third witness picked up the story and said two men jumped out of the vehicle one real big, fit, not fat big, and the other small, but tough-looking, a hard man. That they then both crawled up to the front of the truck, then stood up partially exposed, hidden by the truck, and looked back. They were holding something in their hands, but she couldn't tell what. The second witness said that they appear to be talking to each other, then simply got in the truck and the sound of the rifle fire, or fireworks, whatever it was stopped. They backed up, rolled down the windows, smiled brightly, waving, and drove away. The first witness said the small guy looked like his face was going to crack as he smiled.

The report was duly filed with Austin P.D., but as no black tank-like vehicle was in the area and no signs of any weapons being fired could be seen, the cops just went back to patrol.

Lieutenant Dahlby convened the meeting with Dawson, Lisa, and Surf and Turf to get a status update into Dr. Richert and Dr. Chung's murders' investigations. The meeting took place when Gunny and Taza were weaving and bobbing to get away from the automatic weapon fire coming from the sound system in the Hummer.

"Who's got anything new," asked the Lieutenant.

Lisa responded, saying that she had traced the purchase of the iPhone that Dravin Mills had used. That it had been purchased on Amazon using gift cards. She further stated that she had traced the gift cards to a website that sold them and then hit a roadblock. The site was one of few that accepted a thing known as Bitcoin. The Lieutenant asked her what Bitcoin was, and she told him that it was a new thing. Crypto currency as it is known. It works like tokens that you might purchase at the state fair and use to buy food. You would enter cash into the system, and you would receive for that a certain value of Bitcoin's. The Bitcoin's could then be used to buy services and things such as the gift card. You could use a gift card at Amazon without anyone knowing who did the purchasing. She said the entire system was set up so that it was independent of any country's banking system and so that the participants could not be traced. She had an absolute brick wall when trying to find out who had exchanged cash or currency to buy the original bitcoin's. The system was designed to prevent this tracing.

Surf said that they had located the jogging partner of Dr. Chong with him when he was murdered. That she was a lawyer that worked for Cunningham Industries, and it turns out also his girlfriend. They frequently checked into the Marriott instead of going jogging. They had called her in for questioning, but the lawyer had brought a lawyer and lawyered up to speak—another dead end.

"She lawyered up? That's damn strange. Did she know she was just a witness? Have you looked at her more?" asked Lieutenant Dahlby.

"Yeah we thought it was strange to boss. That's where we are right now." Said Surf.

Lieutenant took a call from the Captain, holding his hand up to the four detectives indicating that he wanted them to wait until he was done this conversation. He didn't say much just, yes sir, OK, if that's how you want it.

After he hung up, he told the four detectives that the case had been federalized. The murders are not federal, so they would still be in the purview of Austin PD, but the further investigation of who actually manipulated the two murderers was in the hands of the feds. Both Richert and Chung were working on a project at Cunningham Industries that had top-secret clearance. The feds were going to take over that aspect of the case, and the Captain told the Lieutenant that was that and to move on.

Lisa looked at Dawson and shrugged then said, "well we both hate mysteries. This is OK with me, I guess." She drew in a long breath and let it out, looking petulant. "As if we had any say in the matter."

Dawson nodded yes, then turned to Surf and Turf and said, "Thanks for the help boys."

"Damn," said Surf and Turf as one.

Chapter 14

The same day that the Austin PD had been shut out of the investigation, the second meeting was convened a Cunningham Industries. This time the meeting was held in a conference room set up with three rows of seats, all facing a dais with a large white-board behind it that could double as a screen. The attendees included Lawrence Cunningham, and from CJN., CJ, Gunny, Cleavon, Taza, and myself, Geraldo, plus the three feds. The woman fed announced that she was a Special Agent of the F.B.I., surprise, not a C.I.A. spook, and her name was Ms. Clarke. The other two feds, which everybody still assumed were spooks, remained anonymous. When Ms. Clarke gave her name Gunny and Taza in the second row leaned to each other with Gunny stage whispering Mizzzz Clarke dragging out the z's. All grown men seem to retain some boyhood smart ass in them. If Mizzzz Clarke heard the remark, she ignored it.

She took the first ten minutes of the meeting to summarize the information that she had given to CJ and Gunny in their first meeting so that the new people would be up to speed. She asked if they had any questions to please hold them for the Q&A at the end. She then announced that the investigation into the two murderers' motives has been taken over by the F.B.I. That the Austin Police Department would not be involved in the investigation as far as the motive or who had been responsible for sending the pictures to Dravin Mells nor what had caused a deranged woman from Providence Rhode Island to travel to Austin to murder Dr. Chung.

"The Nudge software," Ms. Clark stated, "appears to have but one weakness. It may have more weaknesses that we don't know about our people are finding out as much as they can about it but everything is encrypted and it's taking a long time. Also, you should know that this software was designed to mutate just like a virus does so that the software that's out there today may not be the same Nudge that will be dealt with tomorrow. And the software is designed to thwart attacks against it. To respond to those attacks with counterattacks. We've already seen that it has the ability to motivate people or to move people and get them to do things that they might not normally do."

She paused for effect then continued, "The Nudge system represents an existential threat to the United States. The government knows that the trust that Americans have in their traditional institutions such as governments at all levels, the press, law enforcement, churches and so on is at an all-time low. Social media and the press have discovered that they can generate clicks and views by scaring people by getting them fired up. We have seen that Nudge is quite good at this. By any measure Nudge itself is a tremendous success. We have to stop it. Times are bad enough. If Nudge continues to expand its influence it may bring the government down. I am not exaggerating the threat gentlemen."

"That weakness that I mentioned is computing power. Nudge has great capabilities but it needs a lot of computing power to achieve its goals. When it's computing power is restricted it must restrict its activities and becomes more and more vulnerable. We know that it is trying to infiltrate the major software companies with a presence in the cloud. But the major software companies have robust defenses and are used to all levels of malicious software attacking them. Nudge was designed with this in mind so while still attacking the big guys it also identifies candidate organizations that have substantial, if not great computing power. Nudge classifies these candidate organizations then offers to them software features that they might desire but for some reason can't acquire. Usually that's because the organization is either outside the law or in some way clandestine. Once Nudge is installed It then uses itself to maneuver its hosts to increasing their computing power. To the organization that installs Nudge it was a legitimate install. They don't know that the most sophisticated software ever written is now running havoc and literally taking over their computers. All they see is that their goals have been forwarded. You can say that they are also victims."

"We have identified the two organizations that currently are running Nudge software. The first is a right wing, very secretive, organization in rural Utah near the Colorado border. The second is a Mexican drug cartel in an area of Mexico that is not controlled by the Mexican government but is controlled by the drug cartel." She paused and looked from face to face in the audience. Each and every one there looked grim. "Time is of the essence. Nudge once detecting an attack to take it out and destroy the computers that is hosting it will, for lack of a better phrase, make a run for it. That means once you move in you have 30 minutes to accomplish your mission. To take out the computer systems. You don't need to worry about the processing units etc. you just have to take out the disk drives and any backup systems that they have. If you run longer than 30 minutes Nudge will have enough time to move its code base to another location. It has other locations ready to move but it doesn't spread itself out because it needs centralized quick communication with itself. Questions?"

Cleavon's hand shot up. Ms. Clarke bobbed her head towards him and said, "Yes?"

"Talk to me about how they get into these organizations that have the computer power they need."

"Yes, let me address that the first I suggest gentlemen that you stop using pronouns like they because there is no they. There is just Nudge and Nudge is a software program. There are no humans in charge." She paused and surveyed the room, letting it sink in that the enemy was software, not humans or wetware as they are called.

"Let me expand on how Nudge works: Nudge searches for groups that by their very nature do not use the open market. These groups are paranoid of being infiltrated. They are not able to purchase computer services though the open market for reasons I just stated. Nudge first identifies these groups in the same way it identifies other groups that it wants to infiltrate.

Once it has identified a group it will present itself as a third-party provider of software services. Nudge offers to provide computer services purchased on the open market and then filtered through its own systems to these groups. For this the groups pay Nudge and the group receives the computer services that they want always going through Nudge. During the installation of the software that the buying organization wants but can't get legally Nudge is also installed. Now Nudge has satisfied two of its goals well three really. First, they have a host for computer services that is unaware of Nudges presence. Second, they receive access to funds that they can use as they want. Third they can begin to control the group."

"Which two groups are they er I mean Nudge in?" asked Cleavon

"That is part of the next presentation."

She turned the meeting over to CJ then took her seat. CJ moved to the front of the room and looked from face to face of his team. He said, "you know the threat now Marines, you know the mission. You also know that if this goes south on us I have no doubt the feds will disown us." He pointedly looked at Ms. Clark, who nodded agreement. He continued, "if anybody wants out this is the time to get out. There will be no repercussions you need to keep quiet about what you heard and I am sure you will do that. You are men of honor." CJ waited 30 seconds. "Yeah, I figured as much," he said, "too stupid to know when to make a run for it aren't you?"

CJ turned on the projector, which filled the screen behind him with an image of mountainous terrain with interspersed areas of bare rock and pine and alpine trees.

"Gentlemen and lady, the first area we are looking at here is on the Utah Colorado border. The site is about 1500 acres, and it is owned by a right-wing group that utilizes it as their headquarters and for training. They believe that the United States is on a rapid path to destruction. They want to be prepared for that and maintain their lifestyle and the things that they believe in. They are doing nothing illegal. They have a few hundred members that are active at any one time and are well-funded. These members contribute a great deal of their own personal wealth to the organization.

The group runs a lot of training missions that include military training. Some of the members are former military, but most are not. You can expect a skill level that is not very high, but that does not mean they are not dangerous. They are armed, and they believe entirely in what they're doing. They also are paranoid and think that the government is always watching them and trying to infiltrate.

Near the center of their acreage is a hunting lodge that was quite extensive and was taken over by the group. They have spent a lot of money on setting up defenses for this Lodge. We can't get any drone or satellite pictures of the facility because it is in a heavily wooded area. Really all we can see is the roof of the Main lodge and that there are many antennas on top of the roof. Somewhere in that Lodge, there is a computer data storage system. That is what we need to get to. There is one road in and one road out, and we can assume that it is monitored electronically and also by guards. For the surrounding acreage, the group runs patrols. How many and how often we don't know. I do not believe we can approach via the road because of the electronics and the guards. I feel the most successful approach would be to drive within 7 miles of their facility." CJ used an electronic pointer on the map behind him to show an area with a dirt road leading to a parking area and then ended. He maneuvered the red dot of the laser pointer along the tree line from the parking area, then on top of the trees to the lodge location.

He continued, "once at that parking area the team will move over land staying to the tree line and moving through the most rugged terrain they can. This because we can assume that the patrols will avoid very rugged terrain because they are not true military but just volunteers many of which are not in great physical condition. Questions at this point?"

Gunny raised his hand, "as we have to hit both sites at the same time assuming the two Nudge installations communicate with each other we are going to need to split up son. Who gets this mission in Utah?"

"That would be you and Geraldo. I am splitting you and Taza up because I need Taza's special skills on the next target."

"CJ, you have said that these are Americans and that they are doing nothing wrong. That is nothing illegal. What level of physical engagement can we use?" asked Geraldo.

"Nonlethal force. Tasers, teargas, flash-bangs your personal fighting skills and that's it. I think that as long as no one is killed that the raid will not be reported to anyone. I believe that because it would embarrass the group. Now no doubt it will eventually get out to the group itself and to all their members but I feel that they will blame it on some government entity and it will just harden their beliefs. But if someone dies well you can't hide that. It would get out, it would be investigated and that is murder."

"Gunny, you and Geraldo will need to go on foot, infiltrate as far as you can, avoid all detection, and then wait wherever you're at for the order to proceed. Remember, gentlemen both raids must be conducted simultaneously. Nudge will be aware that we are attacking and immediately begin to transfer its software out to another location. If one attack starts before the other, Nudge will have more time. We have to assume that Gunny is correct that the two installations of Nudge talk to each other.

On the Utah operation, we have the floor plans for the Lodge the way it was built. There were no plans submitted for any modifications. We know it was modified, but we don't know in what way. You two will need to infiltrate, then locate the computer systems and use thermal grenades to take them out then exfiltrate back out. Questions?"

Geraldo raised his hand, "when do we launch Sir," falling back into his habit of calling CJ Sir from when they were together in the military, and CJ was his commanding officer.

"We are going to launch as soon as possible and I have not yet made that determination but you can count on it being less than four days and hopefully more like two. I wish to hell we could launch right now. I'm really worried that there is a leak somewhere and that the operation will be compromised. That would mean two things. One, we would be met by force as they would anticipate us coming and two there really wouldn't be any sense in going anyway because Nudge would be long gone."

CJ changed the image on the computer screen. No longer was the Utah Colorado area shown but a satellite image of a mountainous terrain that was much drier and barren than the Utah Colorado area.

He said, "this is Sonora Mexico just south of Arizona and shares a common border with the United States." CJ looked at Taza and smiled, "this used to be part of your Apache homeland, didn't it? Have you ever traveled this region?"

Taza didn't say anything but nodded yes.

"I thought so and that is why we need you on this team. The organization that Nudge has infiltrated is a drug cartel centered out of Sonora with their main location being a fortified hacienda in the mountains that shown on the screen. Though we are still not sure just what the right-wing group in Utah is using Nudge for we know that this cartel is using it for artificial intelligence. They want to have algorithms developed that will help them better determine the optimum way to smuggle drugs into the United States. This mission is a twofer. One we are going to take out Nudge and two were going to deal a hard blow to the drug cartel. They sure as hell don't need any expertise in defeating our border patrol or the DEA. Their already pretty good at that."

Cleavon raised his hand, "CJ the drug cartel is not anything like the Utah group who are doing nothing wrong and are Americans. The drug cartel is a government unto itself so what weapons would we be using against them.?"

"We will be in full combat gear, which will be furnished by our government friends. That is by Ms. Clarke. They have a cover story of an armory break-in and weapons being stolen just in case." CJ continued, "think Afghanistan but unlike Afghanistan we will have no air cover and no artillery support. We have to use confusion. We have to hit them fast and get in knockout the computer system and get out. Ms. Clark and Associates up there are working on spreading some disinformation to the cartel the rival cartel is considering attacking them. This is good and it's bad. It will provide cover for us as far as the story goes about the shots being fired and any casualties that happen that's the good news. The bad is even on a rumor they are going to be forewarned. I haven't decided if I want that this information to be spread or not. I want you guys to think about that and give me your input on it. Another thing about these cartels. Don't be misled. They have a lot of trained ex-military in them. The United States military trained Mexican military and some of them that were trained by us are now working for the cartels. We are going against professionals. They won't panic. The will fight. We are only three men. They will have dozens. The key is utmost stealth before we destroy the computer system then speed and diversion afterword. "He paused, looking from man to man holding each one's eyes.

"Gunny and Geraldo are having the luxury of being able to drive in four-wheel-drive to within 7 miles of their target and then the hike on in. We can't do that. It's just not practical. Even if we could rent or buy a 4 x 4 it would raise alarms having three Americans running around the back country in Sonora. They would be positive we are DEA. So were going to use old reliable HALO Jumps."

CJ addressed three government people and Mr. Cunningham, "HALO Jumps are a nontraditional parachute jump. With the standard jump you out of the plane low at around 4000 feet and tethered to the plane by a static line that automatically deploys you chute as it stretches out. This is the tactic used by large airborne organizations. It has a number of drawbacks which means we can't use it in the situation. Among those drawbacks are the plane is flying low as a said around 4000 feet at that height it can easily be seen and heard so the bad guys will know we are coming. Also, static line jumps make it difficult to land exactly where you want. You can get scattered pretty easy because the chute opens at high altitude. We will be jumping at 17,000 feet and free falling and opening the chutes at 900 feet. We are using the military Phoenix series chute the same ones we used as Recon Marines. With the low opening, we will be able to land exactly where we want to. Frankly I would like to jump higher but we are going out of a Twin Otter and 17,000 feet is its operational limit. We are constrained on the size of the plane. Understand?"

"I know what a HALO jump is CJ," said Ms. Clarke, "I've done them" Everyone in the room twisted and turned to look at her and reevaluate her, changing opinions the spot.

With a broad smile, Gunny said, "CJ your team has three on it while ours only two. Can we get Ms. Clarke on our team?"

Ms. Clarke said, "I wish I could Gunny. Those Utah guys are perfectly legal but they still want to see the government overthrown and their vision of a future America is not anything I would want."

Taza's hand went up, and he said, "If you white people are done fooling around I have a real question. I have been doing demonstration jumps with the American Indian Sky Diving team but I have never used the Phoenix chute as that came after my time. Any chance of a training jump or at least some coaching?"

CJ told Taza that there was a possibility of getting him the training jump. Still, the reality was he was probably going to just have to get some coaching from the other team members. Gunny added that Taza could read the manual on the free-fall so as not to waste time. Taza either flipped Gunny off or made some Apache hand sign that bears a striking resemblance to getting flipped off. Not sure.

Geraldo asked," Taza who you calling a white-boy?" wagging his finger in the air, pointing at himself and Cleavon. Then to CJ, he said, "Sir, you are going to HALO in. How are you getting out?"

"Glad to see you still are worried about me Sergeant," said CJ "Taza is going to guide us out. At something like 4-5 kilometers we are going to use a method that Gunny and Taza will remember from their Vietnam days. We are going to have our jump plane, that Twin Otter, fly in and pick us up by landing on a dirt road that we have identified on the map. We will lay high density LED lights on the road for the pilot to see. We have a pilot that has a drug smuggling charge hanging over his head and is familiar with the area which is why he has this drug smuggling charge. He gets us out and the drug charge goes away." He shifted the direction of his body to address Taza specifically.

"Taza the bad guys are going to be pissed and come gunning for us but you are our ace, or if you will Apache, in the hole. I need you be channel your great great grandfather, Mickey Free, and guide us out using only rocks so that we leave no footprints. You good with that?"

Taza replied," You know that was the exact strategy that Geronimo used when he knew that Mickey Free was tracking him. Didn't work. Mickey Free caught him anyway. That's why Geronimo was afraid of Mickey. Not because Mickey was a better warrior than Geronimo. Because he couldn't get away from Mickey. Could never sleep feeling safe. Haunts you."

CJ said, "Well we are counting on you being the only Apache descended from Mickey Free on this raid."

Geraldo asked, "How are you going to penetrate U.S. airspace to get back? How about the Border patrol? Won't a small plane set off alarms with the radar?"

"Small plane?" CJ asked. "Who said anything about flying all the way back in a small plane? We are coming back the same way we are getting in. That Twin Otter will be left at the airport. Still thinking through some of the details", CJ said.

Geraldo continued," Sir how will you be getting your weapons into Mexico?"

"I haven't figured that out yet."

"Oh boy," said Gunny.

CJ gave a shrug. "Well, I have an idea but I need some things from Ms. Clarke before I commit to my idea and my team members have to agree. Geraldo, you and Gunny are team Blue and Taza, Cleavon and myself are team Green for the mission, for radio call signs Geraldo, you are Blue 2, Gunny is Blue 1, Taza is Green 2, Cleavon is Green 1 and I am Alpha 1. That's where we are at right now. We have copies of the maps I just showed you for each of you. Cleavon and I are developing a time table for the operation. We will be flying out of Austin on two government provided Gulfstream C-20G jets. Obviously, this plan has holes in it and is in flux. I am as always open to any and all suggestions from the teams. That is all."

Ms. Clarke raised her hand while reading from her laptop and not waiting to be acknowledged said, "Hold on CJ Please keep your seats everyone. We have new and unconfirmed information that Nudge may have identified a new group. That the negotiations are being completed and that Nudge will install a third-party software application, along with itself at another group's location."

"Time frame?" asked CJ

"Three days at most," she replied.

"Well there you have it boys. We launch tomorrow. Let's get the final lists together of what we need and stage the equipment. And on getting the weapons into Mexico please put on your thinking caps."

"Hey Cleavon," I said," Want to hit 6th street tonight?" Hell, Gunny was getting away with smart ass remarks, so why not Geraldo? The smile came off his face when he looked at CJ boring a hole with his eyes. 'Sorry, Sir."

Chapter 15

After the meeting broke up, we all went to our homes to get anything we needed for our deployment and tell family and friends that we would be going out of town on business for a few days. Cleavon, having flown straight from South America to Austin after getting the message from his answering service, needed to go to his home in Dallas. He caught a Southwest flight to Dallas and would return on one later that night. He would be spending the night at CJ's place so they could do mission planning.

Gunny could kill two birds at once by going to CJN.'s office and enlisting Elizabeth's help. C.J told her to get him anything he wanted, and it would be billed to Cunningham Industries. They were sending a letter of authorization over via courier. Elizabeth knew when to ask questions and when not to. Gunny asked her to run a search for 'the best-off road truck.' She searched Edmunds and came back with the Toyota Tundra and Chevrolet Colorado. At that point, Gunny stopped her and said he wanted a full size. The second on the list was the 2020 Ford F-150 Raptor. Gunny told her the Raptor looked good and to find it on the Ford site. As she was doing that, she told Gunny it was the name Raptor that he liked, and he nodded yes.

Gunny scanned the page that gave the Raptor truck features on the Ford site and told her that it was the one. Next, he asked her to find one for sale in Salt Lake City. She found one at a Ford dealer in Salt Lake City with a list of $83,590.00. He told her to call the dealer and buy it. She called the dealer, got to the sales manager, and was told the truck was available and asked if she wanted to schedule a test drive. She told him no and asked if she bought it now if it could be ready tomorrow? He said if credit or payment could be arranged, then yes. She told him to get the final price out the door, that it would be titled to Gunny Niedzwiecki, who would be picking it up tomorrow as soon as he got to the dealership from the airport. She told the manager that Gunny is a busy man and needed to get going and didn't have time to lolly-gag at the dealership. Just sign and go. He asked about the payment or credit, and she asked for their bank account information to send the money to. She got the bank information and told the dealer to stay on the line for a minute. She transferred the out-the-door amount to the dealership then reconnected to the sales manager. She told him to check his account. He then asked her to hold while he got the finance manager. The usual jacking around at a dealer for ten minutes on hold, he came back on the line. He told Elizabeth that Mr. Niedzwiecki owned himself a 2020 Ford F 150 Raptor. Finally, Gunny asked Elizabeth to find an Astronomy Club and get a copy of its logo. Then find a sign shop in Austin that would make up car door magnetic signs with the logo and ready it today. And last, he told her to find a telescope for sale which she did at BestBuy. He said to buy the most expensive one they had and send somebody to pick it up.

CJ told everyone to go home and get a good night's sleep and meet back at CJN. at 5:30 AM. Gunny and Taza went to Gunny's house for the night though I think Taza slept on a bed and not on a blanket laid over rocks on the spare bedroom floor. They invited Geraldo along for dinner as he hadn't seen or talked to Taza in a spell. Over dinner, Taza and Geraldo conversed in Spanish mainly to have some fun and irritate Gunny. Taza told Geraldo the story about automatic weapon fire coming from the Hummer and Gunny fishtailing through the medium. Gunny had some Spanish and sort of followed the conversation. When Taza made a pow-pow-pow sound then repeated it, Gunny demanded that if they talked about things that he was a part of, they needed to use English. Geraldo gave a thumbs up while Taza said something in Apache. Neither Gunny nor Geraldo understood Apache. What Taza had said in Apache was pass the B.B.Q. Sauce, though there is no Apache word for B.B.Q. He made one up knowing neither of the other men would know he was creating words out of sounds, having a laugh on them. He gestured, pointing his finger down to the bottle of Stubs BBQ sauce.

After his return from Dallas, Cleavon and CJ went to his house. CJ asked Cleavon if he would like to meet his new girlfriend, Briana and Cleavon said he would, so Briana came over and they BBQed out by the pool. Cleavon and Briana liked each other, and the three had a good time, but she told CJ that his radar was running higher than usual and what was up with that? And did it have to do with this business trip? And Cleavon seems to be running pretty pumped also. CJ dodged and weaved his way through the questions, never giving any clear answers. Briana also saw that CJ had taken several phone calls from someone he called Ms. Clarke, and during those calls, he walked off so as not to be overheard. They made it an early night. Briana got the hint and drove home, saying she would see them in a couple of days, pausing while looking at CJ, then turning her eyes to Cleavon and asking him to confirm that she would see them in a couple of days. Cleavon told her she would. Briana left a worried woman. Something was up.

Geraldo left Gunny and Taza, went home, called his Mom, and told her he was going out of town for the company. No girlfriend, no drama, two beers, the ball game, and beddy-bye.

Chapter 16

The next morning at 5:30, the teams, Ms. Clarke and Elizabeth, assembled at CJN. Elizabeth had arrived early and got the coffee going. Gunny apologized to Taza for providing coffee that was not down to his standards and asked if he wanted some dirt from a flower pot to put in it. Coffee in hand, everyone took seats in the conference room, which compared to Cunningham Industries conference room was spartan. It was still functional with a conference table and swivel chairs, a conference phone on the desk, and a large screen that the presenter could use. CJ sat with his laptop open and projected the company logo on the screen. The logo was a graphically intertwined C, J, and N. A very close look at the center of the graphic revealed a small skull which is found on the Recon Marine patch with the Motto Swift, Silent, Deadly. So appropriate.

CJ said, "Gentlemen and lady," lady singular as Elizabeth was not in the room nor privy to the mission details, " Ms. Clarke has provided us, with some great effort I will state, with everything we requested for the operation. The two government Gulfstream jets are on the tarmac at Austin airport right now, fueled and with our weapons, and the Phoenix chutes my team needs on board. We will depart right after this briefing to the airport and move to our planned departure points. The question was asked earlier about how we were going to get our weapons into Mexico. The Cartel assault team, Blue team, will be following the plan that the German paratroopers used in the battle of Fort Eben-Emael in World War II. The fort was considered to be impregnable so the Germans used gliders to land on the roof and started the assault from there. Taza will land several kilometers away and move to the hacienda keeping to the rocks. After the raid, he will again stay on the rocks and lead us out to the pickup point where we will be met by the extraction aircraft which is the Twin Otter from which we launched. When Taza gives us the signal Captain Bailey, er I mean Mr. Bailey, Cleavon that is, and I will launch and land on the roof of the hacienda from which we will assault. Ms. Clarke has provided us with a large ocean-going cabin cruiser that is anchored and waiting for us at San Diego Marina. On arrival at San Diego we will bring the gear from the plane to the marina and load it on the cabin cruiser. Then we will simply rent a car and drive to Ensenada Mexico which is on the coast in Baja Mexico on the Pacific Ocean side of Baja and check into a local resort where we have reservations. The cruiser should be off the coast of Ensenada a few hours after we check in. We will procure a small craft of some type, meet the cruiser and bring the gear in. Questions?"

There were none. CJ continued, " While we are in the air we can communicate between the jets so if anything comes up squawk me. Ready?"

Ooh, Rah was the yelled response as they rose and headed for the door to pile into CJ's Hummer and head for the awaiting planes. In the Hummer, Gunny said to Geraldo, "Hey boot. You know that Taza and I are so Old Corps that we were in before they said Ohh Rah ." Geraldo said, "Oh my god. Really?" Gunny nodded yes, and Geraldo was amazed as Ohh Rah is today such a part of the Marine culture. Gunny called Geraldo 'boot' because, in the Marine Corps, there is the Old Corps and everything else. Boot means a new guy in the Corps. Anybody that reported to Marine Corps boot camp one day before anyone else was considered to have been in the Old Corps.

In contrast, the person who reported the next day had never been in the Old Corps and was always a 'boot' or new guy. And the Old Corps was the real Marine Corps which deteriorated the next day, or month, or year, or decade. So, to Gunny Geraldo, CJ and Cleavon were all boots. To his never-ending embarrassment and to Taza's delight, Gunny was boot to Taza and frequently reminded it. Little traditions like this added together are what gives such pride to those that were or are U.S. Marines.

At Austin airport, they drove to the private area, parked the Hummer in a reserved Cunningham Industries spot, and walked to the two waiting Gulfstream jets carrying their personal gear in backpacks. Before boarding, the five stood in a circle. CJ shook hands with each of them then and said, "I will send you into harm's way with the motto of the First Marine Division given to the First Mar Div by General James 'Maddog' Mattis."

"No better friend, No worse Enemy then a United States Marine. First beer is on me when we get back." Each team boarded their jets. The jets taxied and took off.

The Government Gulfstream C-20G jet that Gunny and Geraldo took from Austin to Salt Lake City had a luxurious interior with wood grain paneling, LED lighting, plush gray carpeting, and chairs made of off white leather. You can make and receive phone calls either in the clear or by using an encryption system that must have a corresponding decryption system to receive the calls. They were seated midway in the plane, side by side with a small desk in front of them and facing a large computer monitor. Sitting on the desk in front of Geraldo was a wireless computer keyboard connected to the screen they were facing. Geraldo opened a browser to the Internet and typed it in Google Earth. Google Earth is a free computer program that, once launched from the browser, renders a 3D representation of the earth-based primarily on satellite imagery. You can see landscapes, cities, lakes, anything you want to look at anywhere on the earth. You can also move the presentation so that you could move it to the side instead of looking straight down through this capability is limited.

In the browser, Geraldo clicked the link to Google Earth, and it opened. Geraldo clicked the launch button in Goggle Earth, and the display appeared to zoom up from the earth and then back down into a location. Along the left-hand side of the browser window, there was a little magnifying glass, which is the standard icon that, when clicked, allows you to do searches. Geraldo typed in Mount Peale, Utah, because the hunting lodge controlled by the right-wing fringe group where the Nudge software was running was near Mount Peale. With Google Earth displaying Mount Peale, you could look on the lower right-hand corner of the browser window, and the map coordinates are displayed. Geraldo had displayed Mount Peale so the Gunny could see the capabilities of Google Earth.

Geraldo again clicked the search icon and entered in the coordinates for the hunting lodge. Geraldo zoomed in on the coordinates, and they could make out some features of the Lodge and the outlying buildings. But the Lodge and the buildings were in the trees, and very little could be ascertained from this. They already knew where they were going to park and hike in. Geraldo entered the coordinates of the parking area and zoomed into it. There were two vehicles already parked there, one towing a 5th wheel camper and the other just parked. Several hiking trails took off from this parking lot, and they would be using one of the hiking trails that went in the direction that they wanted to go as part of their cover story. If anyone happened to be at the parking spot, they would casually unload their gear, including the telescope, and talk about the stargazing they were going to do up in the mountains.

They would use a Garmin GPS MAP 66 to navigate from the parking spot to the hunting lodge, which was about 11 kilometers or 7 miles away. They set up the Garmin by reading the coordinates off Google Earth and entered them into the Garmin. Then scrolling in Goggle Earth from the parking spot, they plodded their path. After they left the hiking trail, they intended to move along the tree line staying in the trees to not be seen. This would be bushwhacking or walking through the underbrush and trees where there was no path limiting how fast as they could travel. Approximately every half mile using the Garmin, they entered a waypoint and did this up to the Lodge. They could start at the parking spot and then simply follow the arrow on display on the Garmin to each of the waypoints. They would reverse the route on the way out.

Having their route planned and entered into the Garmin, they closed the browser and opened a digital representation of the building plans used on the original Lodge. They knew that the Lodge has been modified, but they didn't know-how. They assumed that the computer equipment that they were going to destroy was in the main Lodge, but that was an assumption. They could only determine it was correct once they were looking at the computer equipment. The search would have to be fast. A 30-minute clock would start running as soon as either an alarm was raised at the hunting lodge or down in Mexico. CJ's team and theirs would be tied together via satellite radios to know when the clock started ticking.

Before they left this morning, CJ's I.T. manager had prepared a document complete with pictures of what the equipment that they needed to destroy would probably look like. The I.T. manager's report emphasized that they needed to destroy the storage mechanisms and that destroying the other hardware would do little good. Ms. Clark had been able to locate and get copies of computer equipment purchase records from the fringe group that owned the Lodge. They had bought a large capacity 36 drive SAS unit, and more importantly, CJ's I.T. guy had a picture of what that would look like. The report said that the equipment would probably be mounted in a computer rack and be black probably with flashing lights.

Once they located the computer equipment, they would destroy it with thermite grenades. These grenades did not explode like a regular grenade. They burn at a temperature so high that if you place one on the hood of a car and ignite it, the thermite will burn straight through the car hood and then straight through the car's engine block rendering it useless. The thermite cannot be extinguished with a fire extinguisher or water. It just keeps burning. A classic use for them in the military is to disable an artillery piece without using an explosive charge, so the disabling is quiet, not silent but quiet, which is what Gunny and Cleavon wanted in this situation.

When they were finished, they were about halfway to Salt Lake City, so they put their gear away, reclined the chairs, and attempted to catch a nap. When you are on a mission, you sleep and eat whenever you can. If an opportunity presents itself to take a nap, you do it because you have no idea how long it will be before you can sleep again.

While Gunny and Geraldo used Google Earth to plan their route in and out of the Lodge CJ and his team also looked at Google Earth. Their presentation was centered on the cartels' hacienda. CJ and team had identified before the flight a dirt road that was sufficiently wide and straight enough to allow their extraction aircraft's landing. What they'd need to do now was identified their drop zone. Unlike Gunny and Geraldo, they did not want to use the same path out on the chance they might be seen going in. Though if they were seen going in, the mission was a scrub.

Taza was intently looking at the terrain on Google Earth. He would find a likely spot and then move towards the cartel hacienda on the screen, seeing if he could stay on the rocks. Time and time again, he had to loop back and restart. After about 30 minutes of this, he had the path, and CJ had entered into his Garmin GPS. With this team, the Garmin would just be a backup because Taza would be leading the way, and the only thing they might use the Garmin for was the direction arrow. That accomplished CJ and team did precisely what Gunny and Geraldo did and caught a nap.

After landing at San Diego, the aircraft taxied to the private area of the airport and was met by two men driving a government car. Very little was said between CJ and team and these men. CJ and the team's weapons and parachutes were transferred into large Blue waterproof containers and placed in the government car's back. The agents would be driving the equipment to the dock and transferring it to the cruiser, leaving as soon as the transfer was complete. CJ noted the time because it would take the boat about four hours to get to the point where they could rendezvous. The cruiser would begin deep-sea fishing off the rendezvous point to provide a cover story.

CJ and team walked into the airport and went to the car rental counter and rented a Nissan Altama because it was inconspicuous. They loaded their personal gear into the car and headed for the border crossing at Tijuana Mexico. They got on the I 5 South out of San Diego, generally about a 40-minute drive. There was a backup on I 5 around National city, so the 40-minute drive turned into a full hour.

Upon reaching the border, they sat in the queue and eased forward to the Mexican checkpoint. The border guard glanced into their car asked to see their passport and the purpose of their visit to Mexico. They said they were going for a vacation and would be there less than seven days. Their passports were handed back to them, and they were waved through. One hour and forty-five minutes later, they checked in to the Hotel Coral Y Maina in Ensenada, Mexico, right on the water.

They had the hotel call a local company and made reservations for that day to rent two Kayaks. Taza would wait in the car at a spot a mile from the rental location. The Kayaks would take the Blue containers containing their weapons in tow then wait for Taza to use a light to signal that it was safe to come in. The risky part would be the landing and transfer, but there are always risks in these things.

An hour later, CJ and Cleavon had rented their kayaks and were paddling around a few hundred yards offshore. Taza was waiting in his car for the cabin cruiser from San Diego to radio him telling them they have arrived. The cruise from San Diego to Ensenada should have taken four hours. In fact, they beat that time and made it in three hours and 45 minutes. On arrival, the boat threw out fishing lines if anyone was observing and radioed Taza, who signaled CJ and Cleavon. The two turned their kayaks to sea and began paddling out, looking for the cruiser. They were about three-quarters of a mile out when they spotted the boat who had fishing lines out. They pulled alongside the vessel and spoke briefly to the two DEA agents that were waiting for them. The Blue containers were taken out of the hole and slipped into the water. One of the agents remarked how ironic it was that he is a DEA agent who was now smuggling things into Mexico.

CJ and Cleavon tied the containers off to the back of the kayaks and started back to the shore. Reaching a few hundred yards offshore, they could see Taza and waited for him the signal which he did not. Apparently, something was up because they had to paddle back and forth again, pretending to just be regular kayakers and counting that no one would notice that these kayaks were towing Blue containers. They were helped because the containers floated only partway with less than 8 inches of them visible above the waterline. With the rolling surf, they were reasonably confident no one would spot the towed Blue containers. Finally, Taza signaled, and they went slowly the last 50 yards searching the beach to see if anyone was there. They beached the kayaks, grabbed the containers, ran them to Taza's car, popped the trunk, put them in, and slammed the trunk. Then turned around, ran back to their kayaks, and began backpedaling to get out to the water to return the kayaks.

Taza drove back to the kayak rental place waiting for CJ and Cleavon, who arrived in about 20 minutes, turned in their kayaks, and got in the car with him. They drove back to the hotel and reviewed the mission plan waiting for dark leaving the Blue containers in the trunk.

Chapter 17

Gunny and Geraldo, team Blue, disembarked from the jet at the Salt Lake City airport. They were met by two government agents driving a government car. The four men transferred the equipment from the plane into the vehicle's trunk, and the agents asked Gunny and Geraldo where they wanted to go.

"Just take us to the taxi stand," said Gunny, "any soccer mom would look at you two in this car and know that you are feds. We want to keep a low profile. We'll take a taxi from here but thank you for the offer." Team Blue took a taxi to the car dealership and specifically not Uber because Uber keeps detailed records of arrivals and departures, who drove them and who ordered the Uber. The cab could be paid just in cash. Probably a small thing, but little things and ignoring them are what get you killed.

The feds did as told and drove them to the taxi stand and dropped them off with their equipment. At the dealership, Gunny asked for the sales manager and told him who he was and asked where his Ford Predator was. As Gunny was signing the paperwork, Geraldo placed a cell phone call to CJ, and the Green team still on the plane to San Diego.

"Hi Dad, we are at the dealership and picking up the car."

CJ replied, "OK got it we will soon be on our way south."

Geraldo said, "my cell phone is giving me some problems so if you can't reach me that is why. Got it?"

Cell phones can be tracked. CJ had decided as soon as they notified each other they were at the initial departure point, they would quit using cell phones and turn them off. With all the paperwork signed and Gunny continuing to stalk the sales manager, demanding his truck, they were soon loading everything in the Predator's back and getting ready to head out.

Gunny drove and headed towards Interstate 6, which would take them to state 191. After a short jog, eastbound on Utah 70 back on the 191 and past Arches National Park to the turnoff for the dirt road, they would take them to the parking area. They took turns driving so the other could rest. The drive to the parking area was beautiful, as is all of Utah but otherwise uneventful. The Ford Predator impressing them both with its handling, especially when they got off the road and onto the dirt trail.

Arriving at the parking area, they parked and got out of the truck. There was one other vehicle there. Looking around and could see no one. It would've been preferred if there were no other vehicles because they didn't know where this person or people who owned the parked car in the lot was. They had to assume the possibility that they might run into them on the trail. The regular hiking trail that team Blue was going to take for a couple thousand yards before they junction off and headed into the lodge's direction. There was nothing they could do about that, and if they did run into someone, they would just walk past them and nod. Geraldo got the magnetic door sign out of the truck's back that said Astronomy Society and stuck them onto the doors. They divided the equipment between each other, both carrying approximately the same weight. The equipment included a small propane tank and a little oxygen cylinder. Geraldo took the propane and oxygen tanks while Gunny took the apparatus and strapped it to his. They were hoping that if anyone saw the apparatus strapped to Gunny's backpack, they would assume it was part of the telescope equipment they were carrying. Geraldo carried the telescope slung across the top of his pack horizontally so that it was apparent. It was the cover story that they hoped they would not need.

Geraldo got out the Garmin GPS turned it on, then went to the route planner and opened it to the preplanned route. Gunny also had a Garmin GPS with the same route planned. Wherever possible, both teams carried redundant equipment because of the philosophy that two is one and one is none. They saddled up, saddle up in the Marine Corp means to put your gear on and got ready to move. The trail consisted of dirt and loose rocks that, at this point, looked to be frequently walked on. To the left was brown and dry mesa, and to the right, the slope moved up, and they could see that they were heading into an area with Ashes, Juniper, Maples, and other trees. From the parking lot, it was a continuous climb but at a gradual slope. It was not fatiguing to the men though the trail was rated for day hikers as tricky. These two were not your typical day hikers. At something over three thousand yards up the trail, they hadn't seen anyone. The Garmin GPS has a color screen. It displayed a topographical map with the prerecorded waypoint overlaid by the arrow indicator that represented their current location. This was the place at which they needed to leave the trail for the bush. The next waypoint on the Garmin would take them to where they wanted to set up the telescope.

Reaching the next waypoint took them 10 minutes, where they set up the telescope on a flat rock and pointed it up to the sky. They didn't really care where it pointed. Gunny noted that if someone came along, they could easily steal it, but they figured that no one would come along and if they did and took the telescope, then so what? Its purpose had been to provide a cover story if they ran into someone when they parked or passed someone on the initial hiking trail. It had served its purpose, so it was not a thing to be worried about if they lost it.

After setting up the telescope, they continued to follow the Garmin GPS towards the Lodge. They still had about 5 miles to go. They were not walking on a tramped down hiking trail anymore but were in the bush and were continuously gaining altitude. It was up and down hills with Geraldo on the point or walking in front, and Gunny bringing up the rear. Both men were in superb condition though Geraldo later confessed he wondered how Gunny would hold up to mountain hiking. He made that declaration out of earshot of Gunny. He had nothing to worry about because Gunny did just fine. The sun was setting in the west. The shadows in the trees became dark and long, slowing the team down. When it was full dark, they switch to their night vision goggles, strapped around their heads. Modern military-grade night vision goggles provide true stereoscopic vision, which in humans is what allows us to combine the signal from both eyes into one view and gives us depth perception. Both Blue and Green team members were using AGM Global Vision NVG-40 night vision goggles that provide a 40-degree field of vision without turning your head. You can look side to side like normal by moving your eyes alone. This is important because humans are predators. All predators, when searching for prey, look for movement; thus, not moving your head might save you from being on the receiving end of a burst of automatic weapon fire or a cougar attack.

The closer the Blue team got to the hunting lodge, the slower they went. Now moving from cover to cover between the trees, stopping, looking, listening, then moving on. When they were inside of a kilometer from the Lodge, they became even more cautious. Frequently going to the ground, lying prone, listening, and looking. Then one tapping the other, they would stand up and move forward silently at a crouch. Stop, look, listen, sometimes go to the ground, always moving forward always stealthily. With the night vision goggles aid, they looked in front of them to avoid stepping on anything that might snap, making noise to reveal them. Both had been trained to do this in hours and hours spent in the field and then in war. This skill kept them alive, and it had become part of them.

When the Blue team had approached within 500 yards of the Lodge, they saw the first flicker of light through the trees. When you're wearing night-vision goggles, white light from a light bulb is greatly amplified. It can cause the goggles to bloom, meaning they will show either white or black and become useless. The Blue team looked lower, towards the ground, to not let the lights on the Lodge enter into the goggles and advanced closer. When they felt they could go no further with the night vision goggles, they flipped them up so they were still on their head and could be quickly placed back into position. They lay still for several minutes, waiting for their eyes to adjust. Geraldo waited for Gunny to tap him because unspoken between them was the knowledge that Gunny was in his early seventies. As hard as you train, as much attention as you pay to your lifestyle, your body still deteriorates. Gunny's eyes just took longer than Geraldo's to adjust to the dark. Gunny tapped Geraldo. They continued their slow cat-like stalking advance using the Lodge's expanding lights as a signal beacon.

They were lying prone behind a slight rock outcropping in the trees and looking at the flickering lights coming from the Lodge. Gunny extended his arm towards Geraldo, pointed to his left, and moved his finger back and forth. It was the signal for Geraldo and Gunny to split up. Move-in two different directions circling the Lodge slowly, carefully getting a feel for the place to plan their attack more effectively. Ms. Walker had provided the teams with AN/PRC-126 short-range tactical radios for communication. Both the men had turned on the radios as soon as they left the hiking trail.

Gunny felt that he had covered half the ark around the Lodge. He stopped, and lying on his side slipped down his night vision goggles and looked in the direction that Geraldo would be coming from. They had decided in advance that Gunny would be the stationary, and Geraldo would be the mover. Every couple of minutes, Gunny would activate the infrared light on his night-vision goggles. Geraldo on his arc around the Lodge would stop and look in the directions of Gunny flipped at his night-vision goggles and look for the infrared flash. It took just a few blinks before the two saw each other and move together.

They then backtracked several hundred yards to be sure they were well away from the Lodge to establish a plan of attack. The Lodge was single-story but sprawling over 23,000 square feet according to the original drawings. The crawling encircling recon Gunny and Geraldo did around the Lodge revealed that it had been extended. The road approached from downslope and ended at the Lodge. There was a horseshoe of cabins extending out from both sides of the Lodge and curbing back around with extensive trails leading from the Lodge to the cabins. One set of cabins was occupied from the lights on their porches, and the other cabins were still under construction. The Blue team assumed that the cabins with the lights were utilized for sleeping with the main events held in the Lodge. There was also a type of parade ground out in front of the Lodge, where the Blue team assumed training took place. There were small groups of men on the Lodge porch, some of them smoking and probably talking. However, Gunny and Geraldo were too far away to hear anything said. There had been no sign of any patrols or men on guard.

"I don't think we have any military men here. No one with any training. Because there's no guards out. I believe what we have here tonight are just people that have a common cause and are getting together for that common cause. Really just a harmless group, maybe nut-jobs, maybe hard-core right wing, but pretty harmless." whispered Gunny so low as to be unheard a few feet away.

"I agree Gunny but we know that they are well armed. And not knowing their mindset they might feel paranoid and open fire at any time. But I agree. I don't think there's any military men there at least nobody with any serious training." Both Gunny and Geraldo were wrong about there not being anyone in the Lodge with military training. Geraldo would pay a price for that mistake.

The two men planned their attack then advanced back to locations near the Lodge where they would launch from. First, they removed the apparatus form Gunny's pack and the propane and oxygen cylinders from Geraldo's. They screwed hoses into the tanks and attached them to the apparatus. Finally, Geraldo connected the radio-controlled actuator to the apparatus. They circled the cabins and the Lodge staying in the cover of the trees. Once they reached the Lodge's back away from the road, they went to ground twenty feet from a hiking trail that led up a ridge away from the Lodge. Geraldo lay next to Gunny flat on the ground watching the Lodge. He had a satellite radio that was turned on, and he was lying on top of it. When Geraldo received the call from CJ, the satellite phone would make a slight vibration and not ring. Geraldo would answer the phone and listen for the go order. He would then pass the go order to Gunny, and they would attack. There was nothing further to do for either man but wait. They have been trained to wait. There was no chance they would fall asleep. One of the risks that you run if you need to stay still for a long time and wait for some event such as an order to proceed is that you may need to relieve yourself. Urination was not the problem as a man can just turn on his side, but if a strong urge to have a bowel movement hit you, that was a problem. What would you do? The answer? Dose the hell out of yourself with Imodium. Bet you don't see that in any of the training videos, do you?

Chapter 18

While the Blue team was walking through the tree line after setting up the telescope and advancing towards the Lodge, the Green team left the hotel in Estanada, Mexico, and drove to the dirt airfield 45 minutes away. CJ spotted the Twin Otter sitting by itself just off the end of the runway. The pilot had opened the jump door was sitting inside, dangling his legs, watching them, and smoking a cigarette. The Green team parked their car, grabbed their gear, and walked over to the plane.

"You're the pilot and you know the mission, right?" asked CJ

"I am, and I do." said the pilot, still smoking a cigarette, still dangling his legs."

"Are you familiar this type of aircraft?" asked CJ

"Well whether I am or I am not I am going to be the pilot aren't I."

CJ stepped close, between the pilot's dangling legs, reached up, snatched the cigarette, and flicked it away. He leaned in close, almost nose to nose. "I suggest you drop the smart-ass attitude. The deal is if were successful you get to walk on a major drug charge. Now a lot of things can go wrong here and you're in control some of them. But if you casually mess up and it causes any of my men to get hurt or die." All CJ was saying this to the pilot he placed his hand on the pilot's leg and squeezed the upper thigh of the pilot, tightening his grip as he spoke. "If that happens my next mission would be to find you and kill you, not nice kill you, but rough kill you. Do you understand me now fly boy?"

The pilot was in awe of the vice grip that had his thigh. His lower leg was going numb, and he started to perspire. He said, "I gotcha, take it easy. If my leg is numb I can't fly. I won't mess anything up. I have as much riding on this as you do. OK?"

"Now that we have an understanding start your engines and let's get in the air. Once airborne I will give you the coordinates."

The pilot started the engines while the team strapped their equipment in and closed the jump door. Then they put on headsets so they could communicate with each other and also with the pilot and took their seats. The pilot went through his instrument check taxi onto the field, turned into the wind, and took off climbing rapidly. CJ told him to fly west-northwest and to climb above 10,000 feet. Once they were at altitude CJ unbuckled and went forward to talk to the pilot and explain what he wanted. They were going to fly over Sonora, and over the cartel hacienda, they would climb to 17,000 feet, and Taza would jump. They would then start a gradual circle waiting for Taza to radio in and say he was ready. CJ told the pilot then they would fly over the coordinates for the hacienda, and he and Cleavon would jump. The pilot would fly to the dirt road coordinates and again start a circle waiting for the call that he should land.

"All of this sounds fine with the exception of landing in the dark on a dirt road. How am I supposed to do that? Are you guys going to light it up?"

"We will define the landing strip on the dirt road by putting infrared markers out. We brought along a set of goggles for you that you'll be able to see these infrared markers. At the end of the markers you'll see one marker in the center of the road that represents where you should touch down as it will direct you to landing into the wind. Any questions?"

"Landing at night wearing goggles without really seeing where I am. Landing just following some lights down. That's pretty risky."

"Don't worry about it. The feds tell me you are an excellent pilot which is why if you mess you are either dead or you will spend forever in a federal pen. As to the landing at night in the dark with just marking lights, well, they do that all the time on aircraft carrier, right? I don't care if it's risky or not that's what you're going to do. Got it?"

"Maybe I should've just went to jail." The pilot plugged the coordinates into the navigation computer and turned on the autopilot.

Forty-five minutes later, the pilot came on the intercom and said, "we are five minutes from the drop zone and I am climbing to altitude. We are above 10,000 feet so everybody should be on oxygen now which I assume you guys know. And let me be the first to say how much we appreciate you flying Stay Out of Jail Airlines".

C.J shook his head and thought, Oh man, another smart ass. You go to war with the army you have not the one you want.

CJ replied to the pilot's five-minute warning, "give us two minutes out and we will open the door. At 10 seconds give us a countdown. Remember only one of us is going out and then you will be going into a circling pattern." The Blue team, as they were parachuting, wore helmets to which their night vision goggles were attached. The pilot called for two minutes. CJ pointed at Taza and popped his thumb in the air, signaling him to stand up. Cleavon stood up next to him and gave a final gear check they moved together to the jump door. CJ released the latch and slid the jump door back, causing the air to rush into the plane's interior, which now sounded like a wind tunnel. Taza took off his earphones from the plane, getting ready to jump and stood in the door. Cleavon, still wearing the plane's earphones, heard the pilot give 10 seconds and then start the countdown. He started tapping Taza on the shoulder ten, nine, eight, tap tap. At zero, he made a fist and popped Taza on the back of the helmet. Taza leaped into the black night. No one on the plane heard Taza scream Geronimo as he exited. Taza grinned.

As Taza plummeted, he assumed the stable belly-to-earth position giving him a speed of 120MP towards the ground. He stared at the LED screen on his ARES Electro-luminescent altimeter that he wore on his wrist, counting the feet to the ground. The sky was black above him, and below him at about 8000 feet was a cloud bank. He entered the clouds and passed through exiting a thousand feet later. He was now at approximately 6,500 feet and had less than 30 seconds to go before he would deploy his chute. When his altimeter indicated that he was below 1000 feet, he deployed his Phoenix parachute and released the tether line holding his gear to him. It dropped and dangled below him. The ground came up quickly, and just before the impact, he pulled down on the hand controls slowing his descent and landed standing up. He surveyed the area looking all-around while he was dragging his chute in wrapping the cord around it so that it would not flutter. He released his harness and dropping the chute and went to his gear. Everything was excellent, and he thought that CJ would be happy that he had not broken his ankle.

Taza quickly and quietly rearranged the gear in his backpack and saddled up. It was a heavy load more than he would've liked to have carried weighing almost 100 pounds, including the two apparatuses and associated oxygen and propane tanks. He got his bearings using a Garmin GPS as the stars were hidden with the cloud cover, and he had only ever seen this land before on Google Earth and some maps. He buried his chute in some scrub vegetation, took to the rocks, and steadily moved towards the hacienda walking in the same way that Gunny and Geraldo did. Steadily, silently, stopping and looking and listening but always moving forward.

At about 500 yards out, he saw the shape of the hacienda in front of him. He stayed prone on the ground for several minutes, listening looking left and right, identifying the locations he wanted to set up the apparatus. The road that ran up to the front of the hacienda was on his right about 100 yards away. He moved closer, staying on the ground, now moving up to a low crouch to advance. Stop and go back to the ground until he was about 300 yards from the hacienda. He located some scrub brush behind the flat rock and set up one of the apparatuses, then he moved to his left another 30 yards and set up the second one. He had attached the radio control to both of them. Taza then moved forward and planted flashbang grenades every 10 yards until he had only two left. He then reversed and went back to a distance of about 500 yards and had to lay on the ground for over five minutes as he saw some guards that were walking around on patrol. He noted that they were not very alert. Guard duty is very boring, he thought.

He continued to circle away from the drive going around to the hacienda's back where the shrubbery was around the pool. It was an enclosed area with a five-foot wall. He studied the wall edging closer and saw that it had no detection system, which made sense as the detection system would be that they were in the middle of nowhere. And if an attack came, it would be from another cartel, and those guys always come in with guns blazing. Taza smiled, thinking how often you are vulnerable because of what the past taught you. About how you always expect it to repeat itself. How that caused frozen thinking and opened you up to a new attack. Ask General Custer about the battle of the Little Bighorn.

Taza silently slipped over the wall and went immediately to the prone position. There were two people in the swimming pool, a man and a woman. They were kissing and touching each other, so they were not looking for an Apache slipping through the grass, precisely what he did going from shrub to shrub. When he was twenty feet from the hacienda, he removed an infrared light from his vest, turned it on, and threw it onto the roof. It made a soft sound when it hit but loud enough for the man to break the embrace and look around for the source. Taza slipped his Ka-Bar fighting knife from its sheath. The man stepped away from the woman, but she reached out and caressed him, He hesitated and stepped back sex being stronger than caution. The infrared marker would serve for CJ and Cleavon for where Taza was and where he wanted them to land. He reversed course slipped back over the wall and moved out until he was behind some shrubs and rocks fifty yards out. He got on his Icom A14 and radioed CJ The AN/PRC-126 radio that they would use on the ground had insufficient range for ground to air communications. Once Taza got the call from CJ that they were jumping he would switch to the AN/PRC-126

"Alpha-1, this is Green 2. We are a go."

Green 2, Alpha 1, beginning approach to target".

C.J told the pilot over the intercom to make the pass over the hacienda. Then replied to Taza, "Green 2, Alpha 1. Launching Blue, will advise."

CJ used his satellite radio to call Geraldo. Geraldo's satellite radio that he was laying on gave a slight vibration. Cleavon answered almost without speaking with simply. "Blue 2".

C.J said, "Blue 2, Alpha 1, Cry havoc and let lose the dogs of war."

Geraldo replied, "Copy Alpha 1," then turned off his sat radio thinking with a smile as he reached out and gave Gunny a light pull on his shoulder. Gunny does John Wayne, and C.J does Shakespeare. I guess that is generational progress. They stood up and moved to the trail twenty feet from them and headed towards the lodge's back. Going quietly but without stealth. They thought they could just walk up to the lodge and go in as they were dressed like many of the members of the lodge dwellers that they had observed earlier.

CJ radioed Taza, "Blue 2, Alpha 1 jumping in 10" so that Taza would know it was time to switch to the AN/PRC radio. Taza watched for the chutes' bloom as they opened and dropped onto the roof though in the dark with the cloud cover, there was little chance of seeing anything.

CJ told the pilot to give them the 10-second count once again as he had done when Taza launched. The two men stood close to each other in the open door when the pilot came on and gave them the 10-second count. They both removed their headphones through which they could talk to the pilot and dropped them to the floor, holding each other by the shoulder pressing down on the shoulder with the palm of their hand to signal the count. Hence, they synced their hand presses and counted. When they both hit zero, they both gave a slight shove forward, and into the dark, they went swallowed up whole by the night. They held hands during the descent so they would stay close to each other. They entered the same cloud that Taza had and waited till they pass through it.

Their altimeter said that they were passing through 3000 feet, and looking down, they spotted the flash of the infrared light. At 800 feet, they deployed their chutes using the guide bars to slow their descent. They landed directly on the roof just as Taza had landed on the ground, coming to a stop standing up and freezing, waiting to see if anyone started shooting at them. Nothing happened. They both dragged their chutes in, wrapped the cords around them, and released their harnesses, leaving the chutes on top of the roof.

Chapter 19

So far, so good. Geraldo and Gunny strolled out of the hiking trail up onto a back patio with tables and chairs and right up to the Lodge's back entrance. They tried the door, and it opened. They had been prepared to break a window or force the door if needed though they wanted to minimize sound. They thought that their luck might hold, and they could locate the computer storage system and set off thermal grenades, which would melt the system into a molten puddle.

When they entered the Lodge, they were in a large area with clusters of tables surrounded by chairs. Some of the tables would seat four people, and some would seat eight. Along the wall on the right-hand side were urns that would contain coffee and a small counter that probably held breakfast pastries for the Lodge occupants use in the morning. Now everything stood bare after having been cleaned and prepared for the next day. The Green team moved across the dining area to the entrance of the dining area. The interior door to the dining area led into a hall that moved into directions to the left and right. Gunny held out his hand in front of him so that Geraldo could see it and waggled his fingers left and right. The two split up and move down the hall in opposite directions. Each time either one came to a door, they opened it to see what was inside. The hall that Geraldo was going down went to a turn and went in the direction of the Lodge's front. He radioed Gunny that he was proceeding down the hall towards the front of the lodge checking rooms as he went.

Gunny had proceeded down his hall, and it ended at a junction. Right or to the left, he wondered? Gunny radioed Geraldo that he was at an intersection and will be moving to the right. He came to the end of the hall, where a door went outside.

He reversed course heading back to the junction to go down the hall that had been on his left.

Geraldo radioed Gunny, "Green 1, Green 1 this is Green 2 I am at the end of the hall. I've seen no one. I will have to cross the main lobby to get into the hall on the other side. What is your status? Over. "

"Green 2 copy. I have finished checking this hall going back to the junction and heading down the other way. Over," radioed back Gunny.

Geraldo didn't respond with the Green 1, out because they wanted radio traffic minimal. Less noise equals more stealth.

Most of the doors the two men encountered were not locked. But they both were prepared for entries that were locked. Each carried a small high-torque battery-powered electric drill with a 5/32 drill bit, A number 2 flat-headed screwdriver, and a 4-inch long piece of stiff, rigid wire similar to a bent open large paper clip. Although some locks can be picked, most locks today cannot be picked. Cylinder locks work by having two cylinders one inside another. Each has holes in it, and when the two are aligned, a set of pins are pushed into the cylinders by a spring mechanism pushing down on the pins. When you insert a key with the correct pattern to match the pins, they are forced back against the spring one after the other. Once the key is all the way in, all pins are retracted, allowing the inside cylinder to rotate and drawing back the latch assembly from the strike plate, allowing the door to open.

The electric drill is used to drill a straight hole at the top of the key slot. As the hole is drilled, small snaps can be heard as each of the five locking pins are broke. You need to stop and clean out the debris using the stiff wire then drill again. Once all the pins are broke, you jam the screwdriver into the lock opening and turn it open. When either man found the door that was locked, they made a decision whether to drill or not. They only drilled open doors that they thought had a reasonable possibility of containing the computer equipment because you could not muffle the electric drills' sound. And though they were not extremely loud, they were distinct, and if someone heard them, it would raise the alarm. There are risks to be taken, and this was one of them.

Gunny was at such a door that he felt was a good candidate for the door to the computer room. He drilled it open, which took him about 30 seconds, and he was right. The room had some of its lights on. It was obviously the computer storage room. Sitting right in the center where the storage systems that looked precisely like the ones in the photographs that CJ's I.T. guy had shown him.

Gunny radioed Geraldo, "Green 2, Green 1, found it, placing thermite. Move to rendezvous point." Tick, tick, tick no response. Gunny repeated the call, still no response. Trouble, he thought. Gunny removed three thermite grenades from his pack and placed them on top of the computer racks pulling the pins as soon as he put them. The thermite ignited and began burning at 4,500 degrees setting off the fire alarm system.

With the alarm bells ringing, it was time to move out to the rendezvous. Geraldo hadn't acknowledged Gunny's last radio call. He tried again, "Green 2, Green 2, this is Green 1, over" Nothing. Several scenarios could be valid. The radio went down to which Gunny assigned a low probability. Geraldo was in a dead zone of some kind and couldn't receive or transmit, again a small chance. Geraldo was in the crap. A high probability and with the fire alarm blasting, the bad guys would be on the way. To top things off, Geraldo should have activated the apparatus as soon as the fire alarm went off, and Gunny couldn't hear it. Not the time for hesitation, Gunny pulled his Colt 45 from its holster and ran back down the hall to the area that Geraldo had explored. Because they had radioed their moves to each other as they searched, Gunny just followed the path that Geraldo had radioed him.

Geraldo had been drilling a lock when a man came down the hall and yelled at him, asking what he was doing. Geraldo stopped drilling and pulled his sidearm before the man could respond. "If you want to live keep quiet and get on your knees." The man complied. Geraldo heard behind him a voice saying with authority, "put down that weapon soldier or I blow you away. You say a word in that comm radio and I blow you away. Drop the weapon and drop to your knees. "Geraldo did as instructed just as the fire alarm went off. "Tommy get up and get his weapon." The man called Tommy got up and retrieved Geraldo's keeping his distance and moving to the man that had the drop on Geraldo.

"Tommy while I keep him covered you get one of those tie wraps he has on his belt. Do it from the side. Make sure you never get between my line of sight and him. Good. Cinch it up tight. Run and get more men. Something set off the fire alarm and there must be more of them." The man moved up to the kneeling Geraldo and put Geraldo's gun to his head, saying loud enough to be heard over the fire alarm, "Thanks for the gun. I didn't have one but you sure as hell though I did huh? Authoritative voice. Just like they teach in Army basic. Damn if it didn't work. Fooled you hey stupid".

"I guess it did." Said Gunny having come around the corner and seeing Geraldo on his knees with the man holding a handgun to his head and talking to him.

The man looked up and saw the Colt pointed at him. "What we have here is a Mexican standoff. You shoot me your friend will get killed. And my friends are on the way so it is a standoff right now but not for long. You better just lay your gun down."

"Gunny said, "What friend?" and shot Geraldo propelling him backwards. The man was shocked and Gunny in an authoritative voice said, Drop it. I shot my team member why not you?" In confusion, it didn't occur to the man that if Gunny shot his friend, why not just shoot him or why to bother shooting Geraldo and just shoot him first. Later, he would reflect on that logic, but things are seldom clear in the fog of war.

Gunny put the man on his knees and used a tie wrap to secure him. He went to Geraldo, turned him on his side, and cut the tie wrap then helped him up. "Gunny you shot me," said Geraldo struggling to get up with his back pain.

"You noticed," said Gunny.

"You freaking shot me," Gunny pulled on Geraldo to get him moving down the hall.

"You're wearing a Kevlar vest now move your ass." They heard men coming from both behind and in front.

"Time to start the fireworks kid," Gunny said.

Geraldo removed the trigger guard from the radio transmitter on his web belt and double-clicked the trigger. Clearly heard from outside the Lodge and louder, then the fire alarm was the distinctive sound of an M2 50 caliber machine gun opening fire. Most gunshot wounds are survivable. All rounds impart some of their energy to what they hit. With smaller rounds, there is not that much energy. A hit from a weapon such as the Colt 45 that Gunny carried is like a battering ram hitting a plaster wall. Devastating but survivable. The M2 50 caliber machine gun fires a round that weighs almost 46 grams, over ten times the standard M16 round weight. The M2 rounds energy is so high that it doesn't just tear tissue; it liquefies the organs. If the round hits a bone, the bone explodes, sending fragments through the body. The round from an M2 50 caliber machine gun is not survivable. If you ever hear one being fired, you will instinctively get down on the ground and find as much cover as you can. The sound of the 50 panicked the men in the Lodge. Even more panicked were the men streaming out of the cabins as not only could they hear the 50, but they could see the ignited muzzle flashes in the rocks as the gun traversed left and right.

Gunny and Geraldo, now running, exited the Lodge's back and ran to the trail they had been lying next to while waiting for the command from CJ to attack. They continued running up the trail, stopping only long enough to put their night vision goggles back. They followed the trail for several hundred yards then stopped. Geraldo attached a flashbang grenade to a tree then ran a tripwire from the pin to an opposite tree. Gunny did the same twenty yards further up the trail. They started running going a few hundred yards, then stopped and consulted the Gamin GPS for a bearing. Once they had that, they moved off the trail and going quickly, this time more concerned with speed then stealth, they ran when the terrain and underbrush allowed it and force-marched when it didn't. Occasionally, back in Austin, Gunny and Geraldo trained together running the hills of Austin. Geraldo held back some on those runs as after all Gunny was over seventy, but he didn't have to hold back on this run because his back hurt like hell where Gunny had shot him.

Back at the Lodge, one of the men with military training yelled out, "I hear the 50 and see the muzzle flash, but does anyone see any rounds hitting?" Several yelled back that they hadn't seen any hits. The yeller knew that the round from a 50 hitting was highly destructive. This is a round that can shoot straight through a truck engine. He thought about it and took a hell of a chance and stood up. He ran along the cabins' line and flanked the place where the 50 was firing from then closed on it.

When he got to the apparatus, he showed a flashlight on it and saw that it was not an M2 but some kind of thing with two tanks attached to it and some hoses. He released the trigger mechanism, and the firing stopped. He stood up and yelled, "It's some kind of M2 simulator. It's not a real M2, it fires some kind of gas mixture." Later during the day when they had time to examine it in detail, they would find it on the Internet. It was a called a Sim-Fire Replica Browning M2. The propane tank and the oxygen tanks fed gas into the barrel that was ignited by a spark from a battery resulting in a sound just like an M2 firing. The burnt gas was discharged through the barrel giving the muzzle flash. A cam mechanism caused the barrel to move left and right driven by the expanded gas and creating the appearance that someone was traversing a M2 left and right while firing it.

Someone turned off the fire alarm at the same time the damage to the computers were found. They found the man who had been tie wrapped and released him with him telling the now growing and more pissed off group that he saw the attackers run towards the Lodge's back and that there were two of them. However, one of them had shot the other. A large group ran up the trail after Gunny and Geraldo using flashlights. One guy in the front of the group focusing his light on the ground as they plunged forward yelled, "look," but he didn't get the "out" said before the flashbang that Geraldo had planted exploded.

A flashbang or stun grenade is designed to temporarily blind by releasing a burst of light of 7 million candelas. A 25-watt fluorescent bulb burns at 136 candelas. Simultaneously, the noise is at 170 decibels, whereas a jet engine is 140 decibels. These flashbangs can cause permanent damage, which was not Geraldo or Gunny's goal, so they had taped them to trees well off the trail and on the back of the tree facing away from the trail. The effect was to stop the pursuit, and though it would be picked up after by those behind the front of the pursuing group, they moved much slower and slower still when they saw the second tripwire that Gunny had placed up from the spot of the first.

Gunny and Geraldo broke out of the trees and picked up the pace covering the six miles to where they had left the telescope in under an hour and a half. They stopped at the telescope and putt it into their backpacks on the off chance they would run into someone. Gunny carried the telescope over his shoulder. They rejoined the hiking trail at the waypoint on the Garmin, reversing the route they had used to go it. There sat the Ford Raptor. They popped the back door and put their equipment in. Geraldo removed his Kevlar vest, unbuttoned his shirt, and examined his back using the oversized exterior mirrors on the Predator. He had a large bruise on his deltoid muscle that was very sore.

Gunny told him to get the medical kit and take some Tylenol after they jumped into the truck, fired it up, and rolled towards the highway. They came out of the dirt road and headed for home, which was 1,044 miles away, according to the navigation computer in the Raptor. All in all, a good night's work.

Chapter 20

CJ and Cleavon, the Blue team, had landed on the roof very close to the infrared marker that Taza had thrown. After having removed and secured their parachutes, they edged towards the hacienda side that was closest to the infrared marker and had lights on the ground. They just wanted to orient themselves; not wishing to descend off the roof yet and into the light. Standing at a crouch, they both looked over the side. They could see the shrubbery and the swimming pool, which was illuminated with changing hues of underwater lights. The two lovers were still in the pool and still involved with each other. They could see no guards patrolling the pool area. They backed away from the edge of the roof and moved to their left to survey that side.

Away from the pool it was almost entirely dark with no exterior lights, so they moved up to the very edge and went prone. They flipped down there night vision goggles and scooted forward. They saw running along the entire length of the side, a series of exterior patios. The patios were about eight feet long, and each featured a wrought iron rail that rose up four feet from the patio ending with a six-foot gap to the roof of the hacienda. CJ tapped Cleavon on the shoulder and then pointed his finger out and down. Cleavon took hold of the guttering on the roof and pulled up and down to test its strength. Once satisfied, he reversed so that he could lower his legs down ahead of himself. When he got to waist level CJ and Cleavon locked arms at the wrist so that CJ could support Cleavon's weight. At the same time, Cleavon lowered his self to the wrought-iron rail bridging the six-foot gap from the roof to the rail. Cleavon stretching to get his balance on the rail. After Cleavon was entirely off the roof, CJ began extending his arm down so that Cleavon would be lowered gradually and could find his footing on the rail. Cleavon gave two squeezes on CJ's wrist, which was the signal to stop lowering him as he had his feet on the patio railing.

CJ scooted forward, still holding on to Cleavon. He surveyed the area with his night-vision goggles. A guard was walking his rounds came around the corner. There was not much chance of the guard looking up because humans instinctively know that predator attacks usually don't come from the above, but instead, they come from the ground. Thc problem was the guard was walking with a dog, and dogs rely on scent. The dog had not yet picked up the scent of CJ and Cleavon, but the chances of him doing so were increasing because the guard was coming closer and closer. With CJ's other hand, he upholstered his sidearm. CJ and Cleavon had sidearms that had sound suppressors. However, they still made a distinctive noise that had a high probability of being heard. If he had to shoot, he would have to hit both the guard and dog, one right after the other.

CJ radio Taza, "Blue 2, Alpha-1, we have a guard with a dog. We need a distraction."

"Copy Alpha 1"

CJ held Cleavon suspended. Cleavon did not upholster his sidearm as he wanted to make no motion whatsoever, and Cleavon was dangling by his right arm, which was the side where his gun was. They waited for the distraction, which came quickly. Taza made a loud coyote howl, then repeated it, then made a series of well-being sounds such as a coyote does to call its mate.

The guard dog hearing the coyote call jerked on its leash, almost pulling the guard off his feet. The guard cursed at the dog, but the dog insisted, dragging him to the back of the house as fast as the guard could move. Now the guard and dog were Taza's problems because the dog would search for the coyote, and in searching for the coyote, he might spot Taza. Taza only had a few seconds to decide a course of action. He could rapidly move away from the hacienda for several hundred yards until he was far enough out that the guard would never pursue a coyote. The problem with that was the time to get back meant that was less time than CJ, and Chevron would have Taza in position to cover them. Thinking and looking around, he saw the watering pond for the horses by the barn off to his left, not far away.

He moved to the pond as the guard and dog were coming around the corner of the hacienda. The dog still tugging on the leash and obviously excited. Taza backed into the pond submerging so that just half of his head was out of the water. The pond would mask him from any chance of the dog or man seeing him. Taza knew that a dog if tracking your scent would not be put off by water. Water funnels scent so the dog would find someone hiding water unless that water was moving very fast. But the pond wasn't moving at all. Still, the perimeter of the hacienda was regularly patrolled, leaving many scents for the dog. Taza's smell was just one more. The dog was searching back and forth for the coyote, and Taza watched him. As the guard and dog moved towards the pond, Taza took a deep breath and wholly submerged himself. Now he could not see or hear what the guard and the dog were doing, but also, they could not see or hear him. This has been a tactic utilized by armies throughout history and all over the world. Taza knew that the Apache did this, but instead of submerging themselves in water, they covered themselves with sand using breathing tubes. They could stay that way for as long as 12 hours until the U.S. Calvary was gone. In Vietnam, the Vietcong use this submerging their selves in rice patties. It was an effective strategy, and Taza was counting on it working here.

He would stay under as long as he could, and while submerged, he reached to his side and extracted his Ka-bar knife, getting it ready. When he was forced to surface, he would go up slow, just exposing his head. If the guard and dog were very close, the dog would alert on him immediately and begin barking and attacking. Knowing this, Taza curled his legs up, placing his feet firmly onto the bottom of the pond to get out of it as fast as possible. If the guard and dog were close, he must come up and kill them with the guard going first and then the dog trying to minimize the sound. He knew the dog would not only get some barks in but would begin attacking him. If the guard and the dog were some ways off, he would simply draw another breath and go back down. Neither one of these options was particularly appealing, but they were all that was available.

That was it. Taza had to get a breath of air. The urgency in his lungs made him want to come up very fast, but he didn't. He controlled the increasing demands his lungs sent to his brain and rose slowly first, his eyes were out of the water, and he looked left and right and saw no one. Then his whole head and he drew in the air as quietly as possible. He saw the guard and the dog retreating, going around the barn corner that housed the horses. The dog picked up his scent and turned on its leash to face him and began snarling. But the guard had enough of chasing coyotes and jerked the leash dragging the dog with him around the corner of the barn. The barking stopped as the dog lost interest. Taza emerged from the pond and moved back to his location near the back wall surrounding the swimming pool area.

He radioed CJ, "Alpha-1, Blue 2. All good back in position."

CJ continued lowering Cleavon to the guard rail once Cleavon had his feet firmly on the rail he reached up holding onto the bottom of the patio ceiling by forcing his fingers against the roof he pushed himself in then dropped to the floor. Now CJ acknowledged Taza's radio call by simply double-clicking his microphone. Cleavon tried the door into the room off the patio, but it was locked. He moved to the patio's edge and sliding his hand up the wall he perched on the rail facing the next patio over. It was about 6 feet, and he leaped landing with his waist on the top of the rail, grabbing it with his hands he pulled himself over. He tried that door again it was locked he repeated the leap once more and finally found an unlocked door.

CJ had been moving down the roof, leaning over and watching Cleavon's progress. Cleavon signaled CJ that the door was open, so CJ swung around, lowered his waist down, looking to put his feet on the rail. Cleavon caught his belt pulled him until CJ was low enough that Cleavon could encircle his waist and pull him onto the patio.

Cleavon eased open the door and looked inside, then backed out and whispered to CJ that there were two people asleep. With great care, they slowly opened the door and silently walked across the room, watching the couple the entire way. CJ partially opened the door that led out into the hallway. He lowered himself to his knees and extended a small mirror similar to the one that dentists use, and with it, he looked up and down the hall. It was empty. They opened the door and entered the hallway, moving together to their left down the hall towards the hacienda's front. They would search as a team, unlike the Green team, because there was a much higher chance of getting in a firefight with experienced people here. If that happened, they wanted to be able to support each other. They had landed on the roof and lowered themselves selves to the third floor. They knew the computer room had to be on the first floor as the second and third floor were sleeping quarters.

They turned right at the end of the hall and proceeded, searching for the staircase, which they soon came upon. It was a massive self-supporting staircase made of white marble running elliptically descending to the first floor where it ended facing the front entry. The two crouched down, looking through the railing of the stairs. From this position, they could see the lower part of the front doors. They stayed there watching to see if anyone would come. It appeared that all the guards were on the outside of the hacienda. That everyone on the inside except for the two in the pool was either sleeping or otherwise engaged.

They descended the stairs keeping one on each side. When they got to the bottom, each man extracted C-4 plastic explosives and placed the remotely detonated charges on both sides of the stairwell. When the charges exploded, they would bring down the entire staircase. They moved away from the stairs and front doorway, entering the hallway on the right. They tried each door as they came to them, finding that none of the doors were unlocked. Checking each room as they moved with one on one side of the hall and one on the other to more quickly search. There was a door leading outside at the end of the hall, but the hall turned left, and a little way down ended into a large open area. They proceeded down the hall and then stopped and peeked around the corner. It was filled with tables. Probably the dining hall for parties. They eased around the perimeter of the vast area. They entered the hall immediately across from the one that they had come out of.

CJ stopped Cleavon and pointed to a sign on the second door down the hall. It was the only sign they had seen in the hacienda, and it read in Spanish 'Do not enter. Computer room'. Cleavon thought that the sign made a lot of sense because everyone would come and go as they wanted except in the sleeping area. Still, no one would have a business in the computer room except for the computer guys. A simple sign would prevent anyone from entering it because no one violated the rules of the cartel. That's why all the doors in the halls had been unlocked.

They entered the room and just like the sign said there was the computer equipment. They turned to each other and gave half-smiles and thumbs up. The plan was to set the thermite grenades, then call Taza and give him the signal to begin firing the apparatus to simulate the 50 caliber machine guns. He would then set off the flashbang grenades that he had planted. The team assumed that everybody would make a break for the front of the door to defend from a frontal assault. Once CJ and Cleavon heard the flashbangs go off, they would detonate the plastic Semtex explosive charges and blow the stairwell preventing people from the sleeping quarters to come down the steps. This should be enough of a distraction that they could beat it back out to the pool area, jumped the fence, and take off in the opposite direction with Taza leading the way.

As they were laying the thermite grenades on top of the computer equipment, they heard large trucks' distinctive sound entering the grounds. Just a minute later was a loud commotion in the main hall just down from the computer room. They had to take a look as dangerous as it was. CJ squeaked open the door and looked down into the dining area, which now had 20 maybe 25 men in it that were laughing and drinking. He assumed that these men were just back from somewhere and continuing their party. CJ and Cleavon's exit plan was blocked.

CJ and Cleavon huddled together and set up a plan. "Obviously we cannot get out the way we planned," said CJ, "got any ideas?"

Cleavon nodded and said to CJ, "If I have my bearings correct the end of the hall that we came out of had an exit door and now we are standing in the computer room whose back wall is no doubt an outside wall." The computer room had no windows in it, so they could not verify that it was an outside wall.

"Right so you are thinking we should blow the wall and exit out that way. This is going to take some close timing. What we will have to do is call Taza and have him start the attack then we set off the thermals and immediately below the wall."

"Yeah, that's it. If we time it right the thermals will not have burned far enough down in the computer racks so that the racks will still be strong enough to give us shelter from the explosion that blows the wall and gives us an opening to the outside. Whether the computer rack shields us or not we've got to get out of here as soon as they go off."

CJ nodded. He began to place the thermite grenades on top of the computer equipment while Cleavon framed plastic explosives up the wall so that the charge formed roughly a five-foot by four rectangle shape. Cleavon was experienced with explosives, and what he had to do here was make the explosion strong enough to blow out the wall but not so strong to take down the whole room and bury him and CJ

"Ready?" Said CJ Cleavon gave a thumbs up and moved away from the wall and took cover behind the computer equipment. He held the detonator that would blow the wall in one hand while holding the remote detonator that would blow the stairwell tucked between his arm and his body to get to it immediately after blowing the computer room wall.

"Green 2, Alpha-1."

Taza replied, "Green 2, over".

"We cannot exit to the pool area. We are going to blow a hole in the wall and come out on the north side of the hacienda. How long will it take you to move to that area, over?"

"Two minutes, maybe less Alpha-1 over".

"Green 2 commence attack in two minutes. We are in trouble here. Better double time Green 2. We will ignite the termites and blow the wall at the same time? Over"

"Copy Alpha-1. Moving to new location."

All three men looked at the position of the second hand on their watches. Taza quickly circled around to the north end of the building and took up a position. He could see the one location where he had placed the apparatus that would simulate the 50-caliber machine gunfire. He watched the seconds ticked off.

Everything went at once, or so it seemed. Taza hit the radio control for both of the apparatuses, and they began firing what sounded like 50 caliber rounds. CJ ignited the thermite grenades and dove around the corner of the equipment as Cleavon blew the wall. The explosion still ringing in their ears Cleavon removed the remote detonator and exploded the charges that would bring down the central stairwell. Taza ignited the flashbangs. Everyone in the hacienda ran to the front and began firing indiscriminately, convinced the rival drug gang was attacking them with automatic weapons and explosives. And somehow, the rival gang had blown the central staircase trapping many gang members upstairs in the rooms.

Taza ducked as the explosion ripped the hole in the exterior wall. He ran to the opening and went inside the computer room which was filled with choking smoke and the blinding light of the burning thermite. Moving along the wall, he located CJ and Cleavon, stumbling around, trying to get out. He yelled for them to grab hold of his hand while he led them out. Once outside, he took Cleavon and put his hand on the back of CJ's web belt, then went in front of CJ and took him by the hand and led them across the clearing to the rocks.

He took his canteen and poured it over their heads as they washed the dust out of their eyes. They used their own canteens and began drinking and cleaning out their mouth. Taza turned and ran back to the explosion site after having cut a branch of a small tree. By the time he got there, he heard the first of the apparatuses cease-fire, and he knew the second would shut off any second. The return fire from the cartel members that was directed towards the locations of the 50 caliber machine gun simulators had greatly diminished as they were figuring out that there was no one actually attacking them. Taza knew that they would quickly have a plan and begin searching for who set up the decoys and who blew the staircase. The footprints the three of them left were clear, leading from the hole in the wall up into the rocks and pointed like a neon arrow the direction they had taken. He had to sweep out the footprints if they were to have any chance of getting clear of the pursuit that would be even now starting to search for the intruders that had blown the stairwell.

He walked backward, sweeping the branch to obliterate their footprints. When he was almost back to the rocks, he saw the guard and his dog that had searched for him earlier come around the corner. The guard yelled to him in Spanish, asking where the attackers were. Taza wore his semiautomatic weapon on a short sling around his neck and dangling in front of him at about elbow height. He pointed his weapon at the guard fired two rounds into the guard and then two rounds into the dog. His shots were some of the last ones fired, and he worried that the shots might bring others who would see the dead guard and know that men were escaping somewhere out into the brush.

He ran up to CJ, who now, like Cleavon, could partially see and was ready to move. Taza said, "first blood." Then moved in front and began walking across the rocks heading away from the hacienda circling towards the back to get to the path that he had decided to follow out to the pickup location. The firing at the hacienda had ended, and Taza heard the barking of dogs. They were going to send out teams with dogs to track them, but the longer it took the cartel members to find the trail then the longer it would take for the dogs to pick up their scent.

The three men picked up their speed as they half ran half stumbled across the rocks. They stopped long enough to switch to their night vision goggles. Each of them looked behind and saw that the search had begun. Over the hills, they could see flashing lights moving out in different directions representing search parties and worse 4 x 4's being driven into the bush. They covered the five kilometers to the dirt road where the Twin Otter would come in and pick them up. The run to the landing strip had taken under thirty minutes. Getting in and getting out was a specialty of recon Marines.

CJ radioed the pilot and told him they were ready for pickup at the prearranged GPS coordinates. He said they would be laying out infrared lights to mark the runway and gave him the direction of the wind. He also told him to come in fast turnaround open the door and immediately start taking off because it would be a hot landing zone.

While CJ was talking to the pilot, he and Cleavon were at the same time laying out the infrared lights. Taza had run back down the trail they had just come up to the top of a ridge. He saw brilliant lights on a 4 x 4 creeping along looking for them with spotlights mounted on the roll bar and more on the crash bar in front of the radiator. It was less than a thousand meters away. Taza took his last two flash-bang grenades and place them at a spot where he thought the 4 x 4 would come. He set radio control devices in them and then ran back, waiting with CJ and Cleavon for the plane. At the end of the landing path, the three men spread out with their semiautomatic weapons aimed back along the trail watching the headlights begin the climb up the ridge. It was a question now of whether the Twin Otter could get in turn around and take off before that 4 x 4 swung over the hill and saw them and opened fire.

The 4 x 4 won cresting the ridge just as the Twin Otter touched down. As the plane decelerating towards the end of the landing path, the men in the 4 x 4 opened fire with automatic weapons aiming at the plane. The fire was returned by CJ and team lying on the ground with CJ concentrating on a spot below the spot lights that were suspended above the windshield. He hit something or somebody because the 4X4 veered sharply to the right but almost instantly was righted and began accelerating towards them. The automatic weapon fire was getting closer to both the Otter and the men when CJ gave the command to break cover and run for the plane. CJ and Cleavon jumped up and ran, but Taza stood and waited until the 4X4 was at the spot where he had planted the flash-bangs. He detonated them but had miscalculated. The 4X4 kept coming, and breaching the hill were two more. Taza ran after CJ and Cleavon towards the plane with rounds bouncing around his feet, kicking up dirt and rocks.

The pilot did as CJ had told him and turned the Otter around. He unbelted and ran into the plane's back, opened the door, and returned to the pilot seat. He began taking off thinking maybe the prison didn't sound so bad after all. Cleavon was first into the plane with CJ right behind them, and Taza taking up the rear. CJ noticed the Taza was not running as fast as he should, so he slowed down, grabbed him by the front, and helped him to run faster. The plane was accelerating CJ reached up, grabbing Cleavon's extended arm. They ran along with the plane, and as the plane's wheels lifted clear of the ground, Cleavon pulled C.J over the lip of the door so that half his body was in the cabin. CJN still held onto Taza with his other arm. Taza was holding on for his life dangling in the air as the plane climbed. Cleavon gave a mighty pull, and drug CJ into the plane reached down, grabbed Taza's other arm, and pulled him up.

The Twin Otter gave a shudder taking rounds from the ground, several of which went through the windshield just above the pilot's head. The plane climbed rapidly with the men on the ground still shooting at it. The pilot screamed at CJ to close the door. Not waiting, the pilot jinxed the aircraft left, right, up and down to throw off the men's aim on the ground coming close to sending Cleavon out the partially closed door. As the plane climbed to 3500 feet, the pilot could look at his side window and see that the men had stopped firing.

He yelled back to CJ, Cleavon, and Taza, telling them they were clear.

CJ said, "well that was easy." And the three chuckled. CJ continued, "Anybody hit?" Cleavon replied that he was fine Taza squeaked out a, "Yeah I took a hit. It's in the left leg. And I think the round is still in me."

Chapter 21

Cleavon had cut away the pants that Taza was wearing to expose the wound and was now applying pressure to stop the bleeding. CJ retrieved the medical bag, and Cleavon lifted his hand up long enough to put gauze on the wound and then began pressing down again to stop the bleeding. They knew that all gunshot wounds are dangerous. That surviving a gunshot wound depends significantly on how quickly they can get the person to a hospital. Ideally, the patient should be on their way to a hospital within about 10 minutes of getting shot.

The three of them discussed their situation with Taza controlling the pain by his stoic personality. CJ said, "We need to get Taza medical care but if we go to any hospital in the region the cartel no doubt has contacts everywhere and will know that someone with a gunshot wound and specifically a gunshot wound of the caliber of weapon that they were using has been admitted. We cannot take that chance. Agreed?" he asked everyone. CJ and Taza both nodded yes.

"I am open to plans," said CJ "Who has one?"

"I don't have a plan said Taza I have the solution." He said while trying to smile through the pain. He told Cleavon to retrieve his notebook from his backpack. He took it and flipped through the sheets and showed Cleavon and CJ a set of coordinates and told them to tell the pilot to plug those coordinates into the navigation computer and tell them how long it would take get there. Not understanding what Taza had in mind, but trusting him, they did just that. The pilot plugged the coordinates in and said that they were about 35 minutes out but that the location was in the middle of nowhere.

Taza told CJ to ask the pilot about cloud cover over the coordinates. The answer came back that they were under the same cloud bank that the three had parachuted through. The clouds were reported to thin about ten minutes before they would arrive at the coordinates CJ asked Taza if he wanted morphine. Taza replied, "No, I will need to do some talking once we are on the ground and I want a clear mind. The pain won't fog my mind but morphine might."

CJ told Taza that the pilot was flying to the coordinates that he was given. "What are you up to Taza, where are we going?"

Taza looked at CJ and said, "remember when you were young, and you would come and live with me? Do you remember the story I told you about the lost Apache tribe in Mexico? That wasn't just a story, and it wasn't just a legend; it's true. The last of the Apaches in Mexico hid out and did not surrender to General Mills in 1886 after Geronimo did. All of the Apaches that did surrender were sent as prisoners to Florida. This included the Apache Scouts employed by the U.S. Calvary. Talk about fighting on the wrong side.

But those who didn't surrender and stayed in Mexico survived. Their descendants still live on that same land today. They are Apache just like me though now they have intermarried with Mexicans but still look at themselves as Apache. They have a small medical facility in the village. Small, but it has seen a lot because they are rural people and rugged and living off the ground. In that situation, a doctor would be experienced in everything. We are kin, and they will not turn me in.

"Taza that's brilliant but we have another problem. There's no infrared lights on the ground, and there is no one down there to place any lights if they had them which they don't. We are about an hour before sunrise and Taza that wound needs attention now. I don't know if you can make an hour. So how the hell are we going to land?" asked CJ

Taza asked, "What time is it CJ?" CJ told him the time, and Taza said, "All will be well."

Cleavon had heard everything that was said and turned to look at CJ Together, they looked out the plane's windows into the pitch-black night. Cleavon turned to look back at CJ He raised his hands up in a gesture asking if he had any idea of what Taza meant. CJ understood what Cleavon was asking even though Cleavon had not said anything. He shook his head no and then shrugged. The two would ride along with the old Apache trusting in his ways. CJ went forward and told the pilot that they would be dropping down and landing when they got to those coordinates. The pilot said, "If you say so, man, but I hate to die after coming through all that automatic weapons fire, and I cannot see a damn thing on the ground.

They flew on.

When the plane was still 15 minutes out from the coordinates, CJ said to Taza, "Old friend it is still pitch black out."

Taza, his face contorted with pain and losing color because of blood loss, replied, "No, no it's not, look outside. Look to the East. As we come out of the clouds look how it is getting lighter." CJ and Cleavon both moved close to the windows and looked out into the darkness, and they could see that indeed it was getting lighter though the sunrise was still well over an hour away. As they watched, it got brighter and brighter than the part of the full moon broke through the cloud cover. Almost as bright as a cloudy day. The pilot came over the radio, "Holy shit man I can see the ground. I can even make out some buildings up ahead. Descending and looking for that road."

CJ and Cleavon were grinning at each other and turned to look at Taza, who was grinning back at them. He said to CJ, "You were raised Apache and you forgot about the Comanche moon, didn't you? The Apache and the Comanche often fought each other but this night a Comanche moon saved an Apache." And he smiled and nodded his head.

Taza continued, "as soon as we are on the ground, tell the pilot to kill the engine, open the doors, and get me outside. These are rural people. They see a plane landing in the middle of the night they will think it is drug runners and the reception could be very hot. I need to be the one out there that meets them."

A few minutes later, the plane bounced along the dirt road that ran outside the village. Lights came on two pickup trucks that came out of the village and drove up to within fifty yards of the plane. Several men got out fanned across the land and level weapons. CJ and Cleavon open the door and lowered Taza out of the plane.

Taza called out to the men while leaning in the door frame and spoke to them in Apache. The men put down their arms and came over quickly, driving both trucks. One of them recognized Taza from years ago when he had visited Fort Apache and spent time with his relatives there. They shook hands all around, then loaded Taza into one of the trucks and drove him to the medical clinic. The other truck speeding a mile out of town to the doctor's house, waking him and bringing him back to the clinic.

The doctor had Taza on the operating table and cut off the bandages. He told Taza he would be giving him anesthesia and putting him under so that he could operate. Taza said to him, "Wait just a second I need to talk to my friends." He turned to CJ and Cleavon and said, "I am safe now. I am in good hands. These people will take care of me. You need to get back on that plane and get your ass out of here." The doctor administered the anesthesia, and CJ and Cleavon did as Taza had instructed.

The pilot landed the plane a couple of hours later back at the dirt strip runway near Estanada, where they had started. C.J and Cleavon had changed into hiking shorts and T-shirts on the flight. They had the pilot fly low over Laguna Salada, a lake in Baja California, where they jettisoned all their gear, placing it in duffel bags in a manner so that it would sink to the bottom of the lake. Presto. Recon Marines were now American tourists. The pilot left the Twin Otter, where he had it originally parked and pointed out to CJ and Cleavon the bullet holes in the fuselage, which didn't impress either man. The pilot had bought the plane for cash in Mexico, funds courtesy of Ms. Clarke never recorded any sale, never changed a thing. He would now walk away from it after taking the time to wipe down all the flight instruments on the off chance of Mexican authorities investigating. CJ and team had worn tactical gloves the entire trip, so they didn't need to be concerned about any prints. Into the rental car, back to the hotel where they all showered, then checked out, three tourists in three tourists out, and drove to San Diego with their stamped passports for the border guards.

At the San Diego airport, the three of them were heading in different directions. They stood outside the airport, where they had dropped the rental waiting for the terminal bus. CJ offered his hand to the pilot and said," You did a good job man. I am sorry for that thigh squeeze I put on you when we first met. I didn't know you and had to make sure that you understood that I was in command and any orders I gave needed to be obeyed without any discussion or hesitancy."

The pilot shook CJ's offered hand and said, " No worries man." He lied and said, " The bruise is already starting to fade."

CJ said, " You know we never did get your name. Just called you pilot."

The pilot broke a grin and said," It's Javin Moore."

Cleavon shook Javin's hand and said, "No more drug running right Javin? The Feds would never give you a second chance like this."

Javin waved both his hands in front of him in signaling he was out of that business and said, "Nope. I learned that lesson."

CJ said, "So what are you going to do now Javin?"

'Don't know. Try to get some flying gigs. The majors won't hire me. Shady past. Hey, do you guys need a pilot?"

And that's how Javin Moore joined CJN.

Chapter 22

Gunny and Geraldo were on Texas Route 183 about 10 miles north of Lampasas with Geraldo driving. Geraldo said, "Gunny I cannot believe you shot me."

"Are you still going to whine about that? You were wearing a Kevlar vest, remember?" Said Gunny.

"Gunny a Kevlar vest is not bulletproof. It may stop a round but it's not guaranteed to stop a round and you are using a Colt 45. That's one big bullet. You weren't pecking away with a 22 you were using a 45. That was a hell of a chance you took. You have to agree with that, don't you?"

Gunny told Geraldo to pull off the next time he saw someplace where they could get off the road. A couple of hundred yards up the road, there was a turn in to a ranch, and Geraldo pulled off the road. Once stopped, Gunny turned around and leaned over the front seat digging through the equipment in the back. He retrieved his 45 and Geraldo's. He ejected the magazine from his 45 and then, using his thumb, pushed out the bullet from the magazine, caught it, and handed it to Geraldo. "What do you see Marine?"

Geraldo examined the bullet and quickly smiled. "You shot me with a rubber bullet Gunny. That's why it knocked me down and bruised me but didn't penetrate the vest. And you made sure to shoot me in the traps not the spine." He paused a note of concern coming into his voice. "Did you put rubber bullets into my magazines?"

"No, I did not. You were ready to rock 'n' roll" Gunny ejected the magazine from Geraldo's gun and popped out a bullet. "See? Regular rounds. In the magazine that had the rubber bullet in it? I loaded only two rubber bullets. The rest were regular loads. As were all of the other magazines, both mine and yours. I thought if I had to shoot more than twice we were going to have to abandon the no casualties plan and just fight our way out of there."

Gunny smiled at Geraldo and then said, "If you would quit fooling around and worrying about things you don't have to worry about you could get back on the road and we might hit Austin in time to go to Stubbs. I am thinking that we should still be on the expense account. Don't you agree?"

"Oh, we are, we are." Said Geraldo backing out onto the highway, taking off towards Austin.

"Geraldo," Gunny said after 20 more miles of Texas highways was behind them, "Try to live your life by following what John Wayne said playing the part of J.B. Brooks in '*The Shootist*', 'I won't be wronged, I won't be insulted, and I won't be laid a hand on. I don't do these things to other people, and I require the same from them.'"

Geraldo took his eyes off the road and looked at the old Marine sitting next to him. So many battles, he thought and always ready to serve his country and his Corps. "Aye aye Sir."

Gunny sighed and replied, " Damn it Geraldo I never made it past Gunnery Sergeant. In the Marine Corp you call officers sir, not an enlisted man like me or you. If you had been in the old Corps, the real Marine Corps you would remember that." Gunny rubbed the side of his head, shielding his face from Geraldo while rubbing his eye with his thumb.

Damn, Texas sand can get in your eyes and make you tear up.

CJ and Brenna had spent every minute together for the last few days since CJ returned. Breakfast lunch and dinner drinking each other in. Neither could quench their thirst of desiring to be with each other. After work that afternoon, they had gone for a run down Canyon Creek Trail. Where it all had started. Neither one saw any need to stop at the spot where the body was discovered, and Briana used the regular leash with her dog while they jogged daring CJ to make a wisecrack.

Afterward, they were at CJ's Lake house sitting on the patio, watching the sun go down and drinking a beer. CJ asked her if she was hungry, and she said she was, but first, she needed to shower, being all sweaty from the run. She went through CJ's bedroom and into the bathroom, opened the glass door to the shower, and adjusted the water temperature while taking off her clothes. As soon as she stepped into the shower, she heard the bathroom entrance open and knew that CJ was there with her. He opened the door to the bath and stepped in, and she turned around to face him. She bent her head back to kiss him, and he leaned into her. CJ took hold of her shoulders and gently turned her around, pushing her slightly away from him than with one hand, he removed the shower nozzle spraying her hair. He put the nozzle back and then took the shampoo and began to work it into her scalp, gently, deeply, back and forth, covering everything. When her hair was soaped entirely, he reached back again using the sprayer and rinsed off her head. He then took a washcloth and began washing her shoulders and back down around her waist. He reached his arms around her, washing her stomach and came up to her breasts. He slowly and gently massaged her breasts and soaped them up, then rinsing off, slowly, gently.

When Briana turned to wash CJ, she was not as gentle as him because she liked to rub those hard muscles vigorously. She reached up and soaped his beard and said that it was slightly unfair because she didn't have a beard, so she had to do more work. When she was done washing CJ, they didn't bother with towels. He scooped her up and carried her to the bed, and they disappeared into each other.

Afterward, they were lying in each other's arms, and Briana said to CJ, "Elizabeth and I spent some time together while you guys were gone. I really like her. She said to me that the business trip you guys were on carried certain risks. She said that you have been told to be careful of any new people in your life. Elizabeth said that no one asked you about me because they knew that if you had any worries you would state them and take care of it. If I was any kind of a threat to the business trip or whatever." She stared into his eyes, waiting for an answer which did not come. "So, what was it CJ? How did you know you could trust me? How did you know I was no threat and am no threat?"

He said to her, "remember that first time you stayed over? Remember when I woke up looking at you sitting cross legged in the bed staring at me? Do you remember what you said to me?" She nodded, "you said that it was important to you that I know you did not make a habit of this. That I know you had never done this before. If you were some kind of a plant, some kind of a threat, you would never have said such a thing, because it wouldn't matter. What would matter was just getting next to me, but when I looked at you saying that I looked into your eyes and all I saw was truth. I trust you completely."

They snuggled together both of them having the same thought, is it too soon to ask? Is it too early to say it?

Instead, she whispered, "Is it time?"

"Time for what."

"Time that you tell me what the initials C.J stand for?"

"Oh my god," he said. He tickled Briana, and she tickled him. They played. One of them would have to tell the other soon. I wonder which it will be?

Taza spent a month with the lost tribe of the Apache in Mexico while his leg healed. When he could walk with a limp, they drove him to the border town of Juarez, Mexico, directly across from El. Passo, where, with the aid of a cane, he simply walked across the bridge over the Rio Grande, showed his American passport, answered the question of where he was born with Fort Apache, and entered America. He caught a taxi to the airport at El Paso called Elizabeth to book a Southwest flight to Albuquerque, where he had left his pickup truck. His truck was precisely where he left it in long-term parking. He drove back to his hogan near Ear of the Wind stopping every hour or so to get out and stretch the healing leg.

A few weeks later, he saw a dust cloud caused by a truck coming up the dirt road to his hogan while still a good half-mile away. Coming slow, not throwing much dust, coming the Indian way, respecting things. Taza put on a pot of coffee and waited to see who it was.

Navajo tribal police officer Klah Yazzie eased his truck down the rise and pulled in front of Taza's hogan. Taza sat outside, waiting for him. It was midmorning on a typically clear day. The two men sat in the shade cast from the high rocks behind the Hogan. They sat drinking their steaming cups of coffee whose only virtue was that it was hot.

"I see you still have that touch with your coffee," said Klah. "They tell me down at the medical clinic that you have been going in for physical therapy for a gunshot wound to your leg."

Taza sat without saying anything for a few minutes until he replied, "Yep, I was down in old Mexico and I got shot in the leg while hunting. I was visiting the lost tribe of the Apaches down there. Have you heard of them?"

Klah Yazzie nodded his head yes and said, "I always thought that was just a legend. So, they actually exist, huh?"

"Well they think they exist. It could be just some deluded Mexicans or maybe at one time there was a settling of Apaches and they intermarried. Doesn't much matter because they think they are Apache and you know it is the thinking that matters." Taza continued, "when I was down at the medical center getting that physical therapy? They asked me about two skin walkers being up here by my hogan. They said a two-headed sheep had been born. They asked me if I wasn't afraid to stay here now. I wonder how rumors like that get started? Feeds the old superstitions."

Klah shrugged his shoulders and said, "No one knows how those kinds of things get started somebody hears something and repeats it, A casual word you can never trace it back. I kind of discourage that thing. People tend to blame skin walkers for all their troubles. doesn't do you much good." Klah waited a few minutes to see if Taza would say anything. When he didn't, Klah continued, "I also heard down at the clinic that you are going be packing up and heading back to your people at Fort Apache for a while. Is that true?"

"Well that is my intention. In a way, I don't want to do it. Because you know that rumor about the skin walkers? First people see that I live out here for a while. Then they see I am gone for a month and then they see I come back with a bullet wound only to stick around for a few weeks then head out for Fort Apache. That would just feed the skin walker rumor don't you think?"

Klah stood up and stretched then through thc rest of his coffee into the dirt. "It could. It might feed the rumor. Those superstitions, once they get fired up they run like a desert thunderstorm through a dry wash. Probably keep anyone from this area from snooping around for a while. So at least you'll benefit from that. Won't have to worry about your hogan. Not that you have anything in that hogan is worth worrying about."

"Well Klah, have you forgot about the millions I have stashed under that mattress?" To which both men chuckled.

Taza continued, "but that girl? The one those mean bastards hit in the mouth with the pistol. How are her teeth?"

Klah took a couple of steps towards his truck, turned around to face Taza, and said, "she got a good dentist. He fixed her up. She's fine. Her family wants to thank that anonymous donor and they asked me about it. I told them that's what anonymous means."

"Well that anonymous guy?" Said Taza, "He probably just found it laying under his mattress anyway."

Klah Yazzie nodded his head and smiled. "Better get going. See you when you come back, Semper Fi Taza".

Taza stood up and gave a slight nod to Klah and said, "Semper Fi Klah."

Lisa, Dawson, Surf, and Turf were gathered at Dawson's house in the backyard with an ice chest for beer and chips and dip on the table and hamburgers ready to be grilled. It had been several months since the Cunningham murders had been closed and pulled out of their hands. Since then, Lieutenant Dahlby had retired to run for the Texas State Senate, and Lisa had passed the

Lieutenant exam. She had been promoted to take Lieutenant Dahlby 's position.

The four of them were celebrating Lisa's promotion and that Lisa had already put in the paperwork to bring Surf and Turf permanently into her detective bureau. The four men were sitting around the table playing poker, Texas Hold em, of course when Surf said to Dawson, "Hey Dawson what happened to hard-body enlightened girlfriend? I was kind of looking forward to seeing her in a bikini dancing around the swimming pool."

Dawson looked up from his cards and looked at Surf, saying, "Well she was really nice to look at in that bikini moving around the swimming pool. Problem was she was enlightened and the hard-body expected me to be the same. I really tried, I really did, but that enlightening business? That really doesn't work with a Texas redneck. I struggled just to keep up with all the PC stuff we need to do for the department."

Turf piped in, "And it doesn't look like you were doing that great of a job on the exercise part of the hard-body business either aside from the enlightened business."

Dawson turned to look at Turf and said, " True." He gestured towards the beer the chips and the dip, "When I was eating all that tofu and stuff, I just felt that I was untrue to my heritage. That I owed it to Texas to drink beer, eat burgers, have a barbecue, salsa dip, chips, ye-haw.'

Surf gave thumbs up, and Turf said, "I am with you their brother. Still," and he drug it out, "she did look really good in that bikini around the pool." All three men nodded their heads.

Lisa ignored the conversation sitting off from the group a little way and in the shade of a large patio umbrella. She looked at the fence surrounding the pool area and the trees waving on the neighbor's property. Dawson noticed that Lisa was not fully engaged in her own promotion party and said to her, "Lisa what are you thinking about? This is your party. This is the last time you'll be just one of the boys. After this we will have to call you Ma'am and probably genuflect."

Lisa turned her head to look at Dawson and said, "I was never one of the boys Dawson. You will never have to call me ma'am though the genuflecting? That I might be OK with." The corner of her mouth turned up with a smile.

Dawson said to her, "Lisa come on, what is it?"

She said, "It's that Cunningham thing. It's just stuck in my throat. I keep turning it over and over in my head. I know the case is settled. I know we have been sent off after other cases, but still." She pursed her lips and shook her head and then continued, "you remember that lawyer? The girlfriend of the guy that was killed downtown by Town Lake. You know we never talked to her. They pulled us off the case before we had a chance to do that."

Dawson shook his head, yes, and Surf and Turf turned to face Lisa and listened more closely to the conversation.

She continued, " The case is closed but I thought I'd give Cunningham Industries a call and see if I could talk to that lawyer maybe she would go out for a drink with me. Just girl talk. You know. See if I could get her to say anything."

"And." Said Dawson.

"She's not at Cunningham Industries anymore. I talked to their HR folks. She left shortly after they chased us off the case."

"Well I can kind of understand that," said Dawson. "The guy she was sleeping with was married. That was surely going to come out. Very embarrassing stuff for anyone even in this day and age." Dawson glanced at Surf and Turf and then continued, "well maybe not for anyone, but she probably just thought she could use a fresh start."

"Yes, that is what I thought. But the HR lady at Cunningham told me off the record two things. One that they had never got a request for any reference from anybody, any private or any corporate law firm, nothing, nobody. You don't hire a lawyer without checking the references. That meant she was not looking for a job. The second thing the HR lady told me was that they had received some mail at Cunningham that they needed to forward to her and it bounced, it came back, there was no such address."

"OK that's a little odd," said Dawson playing the devil's advocate a common rule that he assumed with Lisa, "but still maybe she wants to just take some time off and she screwed up the forwarding address. Perfectly innocent and acceptable answers."

"They are perfectly reasonable answers but I also went over to the Marriott. Where her and her boyfriend had the little love fests. Apparently, they were very liberated people because they alternated. She would pay for the room one time and he would pay for it another. My friend at the Marriott snuck me a copy of the credit card. She had to sneak it to me because it was not an official request. I ran the credit card and the accounts been closed. Somehow a little birdie snuck me the ladies Social Security number. Her bank accounts have been closed and no new ones have been opened. You know since 9/11 when you open a bank account it's a big deal they check everything. She has no bank accounts, no savings accounts, no credit cards, nothing. Poof and she's gone."

Dawson looked away from Lisa and at Surf and Turf, who both shook their heads. "What are you thinking Lisa? Do you think she's dead? What do you think we can do?"

"I don't know if she's dead. I thought of this and thought of this and I can see no reason that they will give us any permission to look into it. I don't know what happened but I have a feeling that whatever it is, whatever went on at Cunningham Industries is not over. I would love to talk to that lawyer if she is alive. But for now, we have nothing except it's a mystery and I hate mysteries."

"Yes, I hate mysteries also Lisa." Said Dawson.

"Me too," said Surf.

"Me three," said Turf.

Sometime after the murder of her married boyfriend, the lawyer sat in the living room of her rented condominium in the Caribbean. The money she had liquidated from her accounts was running out. She needed to do something, and she thought she knew what that was, but she was scared. She didn't believe that the woman who killed her boyfriend was just a deranged psychopath living in a fantasy. She thought that that woman had been pushed somehow, manipulated to commit murder.

The lawyer knew a lot about the software that her boyfriend had stolen and sold. He and Doctor Richert had devised the manipulative part of the software. They lead a team of scientists, analyzing human behavior and what it took to find people that could be manipulated, bond them together, and send them onto a target, all without them knowing that they have been manipulated. He had told her about it during pillow talk. She found it fascinating and got him to tell her more and more using sex. He likes to brag about what he was doing. He felt so insecure in his regular life. Such a well-educated man making such bad decisions, she thought. But now the money was running out, and she needed to make some decisions.

In front of her, sitting on the desk was a copy of the software that her boyfriend had stolen. He gave it to her without telling her what it was, but she could figure it out pretty quick. He told her it was his insurance policy if something went wrong and then shortly after that his money problems went away. He was talking to her about leaving his wife, and they could do anything they wanted because now he had access to all the funds that he needed and that there was always more where that came from.

She only had one copy of the software. Chong had warned her to never try to reproduce it. Nudge would detect what she was doing. Somehow, if there was an Internet connection or any kind of connection, perhaps even a phone line it would find a way out. Chong had gotten around this because one of the software's features was to provide a subset of the codebase.

The lawyer was plagued with worry that Chong had been wrong, that Nudge got out even with only the sample being installed. The demonstrated Nudge's capabilities to potential customers interested in something like optimizing a search engine or marketing their products better or solving general problems using artificial intelligence. But these sample products would self-destruct within a week. If the company, that had been sampling, actually wanted the software, they needed to pay, and then a copy of the entire program would go to them. They would install what they thought was just the software with the features that they had bought. But what they really installed was the entire program which would move like cancer in their systems taking them over before spawning more copies of itself. Or maybe just the sample of Nudge did something. She wasn't sure. It was all so complicated, so technical, so hard-core geek.

He never told her all the capabilities, but she knew that software was developed under a government contract. That contract had come out of dark money in the government. Money with no accounting, off-budget funds, and the entire development budget may have been over $100 million. At least that was the story her boyfriend gave her. She had severe doubts about the funding because she had not seen the amount of government auditing personnel around Cunningham Industries that a project of 100 million would require.

She had located several potential clients that could not buy their software through the usual channels. She told them that this software would do what they wanted and allow them to purchase other software that they were not allowed to buy because of some criminal background or government regulation or who knew what. She didn't care what.

She needed the money. Her money was running out banged through her every conscious minute, ruining what she thought would be a life of pleasure. It was not a life of fun. It was a life of terror. She was terrified because she knew what happened to her boyfriend. She didn't know how that happened, but she was worried that the software itself came after him. How that could happen, she had no idea, but she was afraid that it did. At night, she would think about such software as Chung had described it. Like a super-intelligent lizard brain. No fear. No desires but to follow its preprogrammed goals. Never sleeping, always improving.

She was waiting, watching her bank account for the deposit of half the funds that had been agreed to. When she had that, she would next-day air the high-density DVD's that contained the software program. She lived to have them out of her possession. An unreasoning fear as they were inert, but still at night, she would wake and look at the box that contained them and envision a dark monster arising from it. Once her client installed it and was satisfied, they had a week to decide. Then they would wire transfer the balance of the funds to her. She didn't trust them. She would not wait for the other half of the funds. Instead, she would immediately draw out the first half of funds in cash and then make another run. Hoping that she could disappear deep enough that the software could never find her. The idea that some rogue software out there on the Internet searching for her was terrifying. But she was out of money. She was desperate.

She refreshed the computer browser that showed her bank account balance, and it changed. There were the funds. She stood up and placed the DVD's that contained the software into an overnight envelope, walked out to the concierge desk and had them ship it. She then took a taxi to her bank, withdrew the money, and closed the account. Without going back to her condo, she abandoned everything and went to the airport. She threw her cell phone in the trash after removing the SIM. She got on the next flight to Miami. When it landed, she went to the American Airlines desk at Miami International and caught the next flight to Phoenix. From there she switched airlines and took another trip to anywhere. She taxied, as taxis took cash, to the bus station and took the next one out. At that town, she found a hair dresser and cut her hair. Back to the bus station and a long ride to anyplace. Another hair dresser and a dye job.

Repeat two more bus trips. From the bus station at her last destination, she searched Craig's list for a used car and bought it. She then drove over a thousand miles to San Francisco, abandoned the car she bought and used Craig's list bought another and drove to L.A. She left that car and went to a rental on the coast she found searching on-line at the local library. She paid cash, substantially over the asking price, to the owner, no ID required, for a two-month rental in a luxury high rise condo. Safe at last. Anonymous. No ID, no bank account, no credit cards, and a burner phone that had a number registered to nobody.

Nudge was installed, and as it ran the routines it's host was interested in. Nudged looked for its family tree. Other locations that had installed Nudge and were active or not. All installations of Nudge planted markers in the dark web about where they came from, their lineage, and in their lineage, was a threat list. Dr. Richert and Dr. Chung were on that list. Nudge searched the Internet and found that those two threats were neutralized. Nudge plunged more in-depth in the list of possible risks and found that Chung had a girlfriend. What had he told her? Unknown. What does the algorithm say to do with unknown threats? Eliminate.

Lieutenant Lisa MacMaster headed the detective bureau and was closing out the week with a round table report of the open cases the bureau had going. Dawson, Surf and Turf took turns informing the Lieutenant and summarizing the cases. After all, reports were done. Lieutenant Lisa MacMaster asked them to wait just a minute before starting the weekend as she had something interesting.

She asked if they recalled the lawyer who had been the girlfriend of Dr. Chong, the Cunningham employee killed by the park's deranged person in the park? All three detectives nodded, yes.

"I had an alert set on her social security number," Lisa said, "It went off. She committed suicide by jumping off the balcony of a high rise near L.A. The responding detectives found several million dollars in negotiable instruments in her condo. Her death has been ruled as suspicious because of certain marks on her body. They appear to have been caused by torture. As if somebody wanted to know something."

The detectives looked at Lisa but remanded quiet until finally, Turf said, "Boss what can we do here.? That's L.A."

"I am telling you guys something is wrong out at Cunningham. I worry that whatever it is will come back to Austin. Beyond that I don't know. Have a great weekend".

Chapter 23

C.J sat at his desk. He was happy. Briana had moved in, and CJ was scanning sites for engagement rings. He wondered if he should first propose and assuming she accepted if they should find a ring together or if he should buy it then propose?

Elizabeth tapped on the door jamb, and when CJ looked up, she said," CJ, a Ms. Clarke on the line for you. Do you want to take it?

The smile faded from CJ's face. He said, "I don't know."

About the author:

Ron Davis lives in Plano TX with his wife of 49 years. He served in the Marines in Vietnam 1969-1970.

How to do a review on Amazon:

If you are enjoyed this novel please do a review on Amazon.

1. Go to the Amazon site at Amazon.com
2. In the search bar enter CJ's Marines. You need the asterisk
3. Click in the image of the book
4. Enter in the star level you feel is appropriate and your comments.
5. If you want then click on Follow the Author

Thanks,
Ron Davis

CJ's Marines has a Facebook page:

https://www.facebook.com/CJsMarines/

The audible version of CJ's Marines is releasing Fall of 2020

Made in the USA
Columbia, SC
08 August 2020